Danu's Children

S. M. SAVOY

Published by
Ace Lyon Books
September
2020

Published by
Ace Lyon Books
Acelyonbooks.com
First Edition
Cover Design by S. M Savoy
Danu's Children
ISBN 978-1-947122-38-3
eBook ISBN 978-1-947122-39-0

BOOKS BY S. M. SAVOY

*

Valor
A Warrior's Fury
A Sun Priest's Magic
Beyond Valor
A Rogue's Passion

RELATED SERIES

Return of the Fae
Enter the Frey

COMING SOON

Realms Protector

*

Essence of the Storm

*

COMING SOON
Dusted

TABLE OF CONTENTS

Let There Be War

Jen jumped to her feet, her sword appearing in her hand without her will. By the brightness of colors and clarity of sound she knew her eyes glowed. The crowd behind her exclaimed and spoke loudly amongst themselves.

Jon gave her a grim smile. Soot smeared his clothes and face, mixing with blood and bits better left unidentified that matted his hair and caked his armor. Danu gusted about the Fae in dense blue clouds lit with flickers of static, bringing with her their feelings of anger, fear and sorrow.

The air smelled charred and rank with drying blood and the scent of fear. To either side of her, her fellow knights began to rise from their knees. Over a hundred captives lay bound and gagged on the stone floor behind Jen. Shaman silencing totems, spaced to blanket the captives, gave off a red glow. The shamans were keeping the captives silenced to prevent them from accepting a summons and escaping.

Over a thousand people had jammed into the main room of the castle. Jen imagined she could still hear the crying of those who remained with their dead, preparing them for burial.

"Look around you, Jen," Jon said. "Our people need us. We can't go rushing off!"

"The children need us too. Jia, Mary…" Jen trailed off as Ling began to sob. She couldn't utter her son's name, to do so would shatter her control and she'd begin to cry or worse. She took a deep shuddering breath and tried to speak in a calmer voice. "I cannot wait, Jon."

Jon pinched the bridge of his nose.

"Ethan and I will go," Jen continued. "I can take Sota and fly over Childebert's entire territory. Sota will be able to spot his daughter."

Jon stepped from the dais to embrace Sota and Ling. "And if you find her?" he asked.

"I'll take her back!"

Jon released Ling to shake his head. "Jen,

the children might be inside the castle itself or a church full of people."

"So? If they have our children, they fucking deserve what they get! We've been warning them for months! And look what they did!" She gestured to the crying citizens and blood-splattered walls. "They had no qualms about killing the children of their friends! How many did they kill by poison and fire? It isn't just our children who were taken! Our citizens have missing children too!"

"And how the hell will we find them?" Jon threw his hands in the air and began to pace before his throne.

"By being quick. Stay here and do what needs doing but let us begin the search. I'm not an idiot, Jon. If I think there are more than we can handle, I'll return for help."

"We both know Danu won't let you." Jon halted his aggravated pacing and spun to face her with his hands on his hips. "Take a full group. I'm sorry, Ling, but you and your husband should stay here. Not only do you have two other children to care for, but I'm afraid your need will compel Jen to attack when she shouldn't. Warren, will you go?"

"Of course," Warren said and grasped Sota's shoulder. "I can see the children. Jen and I will find them."

"Matt, I'd like you to go too. You and Ethan." He snapped his mouth closed and nodded hard, his gaze traveling the now quiet citizens. "Return to your homes and comfort your families. We'll do everything possible to restore the lost to you."

A man shouted, "Oh, aye, you'll wave your hands and our families will remain dead!"

Loud talk erupted, and more men hollered about the injustice of the Fae only resurrecting their own.

Arden stepped forward and rose her hands and the crowd quieted.

"As much as the Fae wish otherwise, they can only heal and resurrected Danu's children. Lord Moorland has offered as many healing potions as I need. The Fae are doing everything possible to restore your kin. Kin killed by humans. You have family bound before you. I can't imagine the horror of that— a sister or brother who attempted to murder you…"

Her gaze hardened and she glared at the captive men and women before her. Her hands shook as she gestured. "And you, how could you justify these murders? Leo, you were caught with poison! The same poison that killed your brother's entire family! A poison you made while pretending to be my student! You took an oath to do no harm!"

Jon put an arm around her, and her shaking stilled. She choked on a sob and clutched Jon with both hands. "How can we trust them again? Our knowledge can too easily be used to cause harm."

Jon kissed her brow before saying, "Unlike us, oaths don't bind them. Hate and fear turned them into monsters. They think they'll die as martyrs to the church," he said the last derisively, glaring at the captives. "Even the church can't justify the murder of innocents by poison. They'll turn their backs on you. God doesn't accept the unrepentant into Heaven."

He released Arden to stride forward and grab the senior priest present. He dropped him far enough away from a totem to allow him to speak and yanked the gag from his mouth.

The priest coward as far from Jon as he could.

Jon retreated to the steps of his throne and said, "What can you say in your defense?"

The priest shook his head, trying to dislodge the gag that hung from his ear. "We have nothing to repent of. *You* are an abomination and it's our duty to destroy you and all those who support you!"

His laugh rose the hair on Jen's arm, and she turned away from the globule of spit that landed before Jon's feet.

"You and your followers will never be safe! Eventually, we'll learn your secrets and destroy you! And then those who followed you will burn!" he shrieked.

"He's crazy, Jon," Arden said in a shaky voice.

"Crazy, and as vicious as a rabid dog," Jon agreed and turned to Father Dom. "See what your church is preaching? Murder, lies, betrayal…"

The crowd began muttering, some yelling accusations at the captives and priests and some yelling complaints to Jon. Jon placed his hands on his hips and glared and they quieted to low murmurs of discontent.

Father Dom clenched his hands beneath his chin in a prayerful pose. "Not the church. Discontents. Fanatics. I swear on my soul this isn't church policy. I'll travel to Rome myself and speak with the Holy See. We can learn to live in peace together."

"Live in peace with these devil worshipers? Harlots and sodomites?" The trussed priest laughed loudly and spit on the floor again. "You swallow their lies and fawn at their heels and meanwhile they snicker behind their hands as they tell our daughters they may fornicate as they will and teach our wives they need to obey no one, not even God! You use your vile knowledge to prevent the conception of God's children and then scream when your demon spawn is slain! You'll never fool the church! We see what—"

Jon waved at Warren and Warren slapped the gag back over the priest's face. The priest continued to rant, his curses muffled by the gag.

Jon closed his eyes and rubbed his temples as if his head hurt. "Take the prisoners to the stadium. They'll each get a chance to speak and face their accusers."

Galahad stepped forward and motioned with his spear. Fifty men wearing black armbands pushed through the crowd and began yanking the prisoners to their feet. Voices raised in threats and entreaty followed the men and women being dragged from the room.

Jen waited impatiently, mentally planning where she'd go first. Her husband glowered beside her. Ethan grabbed Kirk's arm.

"Will you look after my daughter until we get back? Can you keep her in a room only Fae may enter?

"And Agnes," Jen added.

Ethan glared at her, then nodded tightly. His shoulders sagged, and he appeared sad when he said, "And Agnes. It isn't her fault her brother is a murderer. She's always been kind to the children and good to us."

Sam turned to hug Jen and said, "I'll take good care of Diana." Her blue eyes filled with tears as she gazed after the prisoners.

Jen bit back a sob. "I'm the worst mother, constantly leaving my children behind…." She pressed the heels of her hands against her eyes. "What if I can't find him? I might never see my son again." Vomit burned her throat. Alex's absence, the fear she felt for his safety, threatened to overwhelm her. She wanted to chase after those prisoners and kill them all, and she would if she thought it'd help, but she knew it wouldn't. Mondred wasn't stupid. He wouldn't have left anyone behind who knew where he'd planned to take the children— and if she began killing them, she wouldn't be able to stop.

Yes, Danu whispered, and Jen pushed her back, an internal effort that left her hands shaking.

No, she thought as hard as she could, resisting the urge to summon her sword.

Sam kissed her cheek. "You'll find him, Jen. They wouldn't have taken him if they meant to harm him. Kirk and I will see to the kids. All the kids. Cass and Lou are planning to train more guard wolves. No one will get through the windows or walls again. I'm going to be catching rats to test our food and drink. Next time, it will be much harder for them."

Jen wished she could reassure Sam, but she knew as well as Sam did there *would* be a next time. Her dream of a peaceful future was irreparably shattered. She dropped her hands and tried to project surety. Sam bit her lip and rubbed Jen's shoulder.

"We'll get them back, and the bastards will pay, Jen," Kirk said. He stood behind his wife wearing full demon armor. Only a blue glow from his eyes was visible. A lesser demon crouched on the floor behind him. Shiny black with glowing yellow eyes, it flicked its forked tail and fluttered diaphanous bat wings. It was only a foot tall and possessed limited capabilities. The imp followed Sam as she went to Ling and hugged her. Kirk rarely summoned any demons. Even the small cute ones like this that took hardly any magic to control, but Jen appreciated why he'd done it. This small imp could place a doorway and notify him if the target it was set to guard was injured. As long as Sam stayed in the zone, help was mere seconds away from her.

"She's terrified," Kirk whispered.

"I know."

"We *will* get them back." Kirk grabbed her shoulder and gave it a hard squeeze.

Jen said nothing. Her glance caught on Britina and Princess Chrodesinde who stood together beside the main doors surrounded by Chrodesinde's knights. A pallor overlaid Britina who clasped her hands beneath her chin, her eyes beseeching Jen, and Jen was reminded of their conversation weeks earlier.

"I still care about the humans!" Jen said, infusing will into her voice so it would carry over the crowd. The sincerity of her thoughts seemed to settle Danu. Or maybe it was the sad affection Jen felt for Britina, but whatever the reason, Danu retreated. The blue mist that had been swirling around Jen dissipated and the room regained its normal color. Sound and motion returned to a normal human range and Jen knew her eyes had reverted to human brown. The need to summon her sword eased, and her shoulders relaxed minutely.

The crowd settled down, most turning to stare at her.

"Thank you, my lady," Britina said into the silence. "Will you escort us home?"

"Will it be safe for you there?" Jen gestured at the men and women still being carried out. "Will you be treated as criminals? You've already lost so much."

Britina pressed her hands to her mouth and closed her eyes.

Chrodesinde took her maid's hand. The billowing sleeves of her gown fluttered, revealing her nervousness.

She said, "I must return and speak with my father. Britina has yet to inform her husband of their daughter's death. We'll bring Ada home with us for burial."

"Yes, of course. I'll see you safely wherever you wish to go. I'm so sorry…" Jen trailed off as Britina sobbed behind her hands.

Tears of sympathy filled Jen's eyes. Ada had been such a sweet girl. The loss must be beyond devastating. She'd had Diana for mere days and just the thought of losing her made Jen feel sick.

Danu surged, Jen could practically hear her whisper, *'Kill them all.'* The urge to summon her sword grew almost overwhelming.

Jen rubbed her head and closed her eyes, trying to make Danu understand, but all Danu felt was fear and want. Danu was afraid and wanted her children. And Jen was afraid and wanted them too— it was hard to argue.

Jen lowered her hands when she realized

she was mumbling, *'I will not kill them,'* to herself.

"Are you okay?" Kirk asked as Jon spoke.

"Tell your father you're under my protection!" Jon's voice rang over the crowd without magic behind it, only his force of will. "We consider him our enemy— but could be persuaded to mercy for your sake and the swift return of our children."

Jen didn't answer, and Kirk didn't ask again. Chrodesinde curtsied deeply. Her knights appeared angry and worried, their gazes lingering on Sir Ewan and Bruno, their countrymen and former companions who were trussed with the rest of the prisoners.

"Lady Frey will escort you home at dawn tomorrow."

Chrodesinde bowed again and gathered her skirts. Her guard followed her through the crowd to the main stairs.

"If the council would please join me, we'll discuss our plans. Jen, I forbid you to leave until dawn, am I clear?"

His magic shivered across Jen's skin.

"Yes, your majesty." She bowed her head and stomped to the door behind the throne.

Jon continued, "Cass, I need you with me, but Ling and Sota, if you'd go on patrol? Your boys will be safe with us."

Ethan grabbed Ling's arm as she passed him. "Summon me if you find anyone else."

She nodded woodenly and continued to the main door. The door leading to the small conference room behind the throne closed with a soft snick behind Jen, cutting off sound from the main hall. Four wolves with glowing blue eyes picked up their heads and laid them back down when she entered.

She nodded her greetings to the five women who watched over the Fae children. Flynn, Matt's firebird, was perched on a limb above the door and greeted Matt with a soft coo and rustle of blood-red wings as he entered behind Jen.

Jen headed directly to her daughter. Baskets containing children covered the table used for meetings. More baskets were pushed up against the walls, leaving only a narrow aisle to reach their seats. Each basket held an infant, some mere days old. None were older than five months. She knew which one held her daughter without being able to see her or being told. Diana slept soundly with a tiny thumb in her mouth. Most of the babies slept.

A flick of Jen's fingers casted Sanctuary beneath her daughter. A golden glow permeated the rock floor and lit the room with a soft radiance. She flicked her fingers again, healing the sleeping children. Tony entered and began to cast. Small yellow sparks careened about the room. The one crying child quieted, calmed by Tony's Soothe spell.

She kissed her daughter's brow and eased aside to make way for Sota to see his boys. The room became crowded as the Fae peeked in on their sleeping children.

"She's sound asleep," Jen said when she rejoined Ethan.

The main room had emptied except for the Fae. Jen frowned at the soot-covered table and blood splattered chairs but took her seat at the round table. Ethan sat beside her and took her hand.

"You must be exhausted," he whispered.

"I'm fine. Angry, but fine. I really want to go."

Ethan sighed in exasperation. Jen shrugged guiltily. She'd been pushing him for days. They'd flown day and night to reach Camelot as fast as possible, only taking breaks to let their magic regenerate and had been here less than a day when Dillion was killed. Since then, they'd traveled to three different kingdoms and defeated thousands of attackers, and she hadn't slept yet.

Ethan said, "Soon. It's better to plan, Jen. Fatigue will lead to bad choices. We don't know what else the church might do. Let's hear the reports and see how Jon plans to protect us."

The main door opened, and Jen turned to peer over her shoulder.

"I've asked Galahad to join us," Jon said, waving Galahad to a seat.

Galahad took a seat beside Dillion who sat with his foster parents at a small table behind the round table.

"Your highness, before you declare war on the church, let me go and speak with them," Father Dom pleaded. He remained standing to the right of the throne, wringing his hands and looking worried.

"We *are* at war with the church."

"Jon— won't you at least—"

Jon cut Arden off with a wave of his hand and a hard frown.

"We aren't savages. I'm not going to rush to France and burn down their churches and kill their citizens. Father, you may go and speak to whomever you please, but we're *not* asking for the church's permission to live. Whether the church likes it or not, we're here to stay, and we have our own mission. Danu didn't bring us here on a whim. We'll protect the Earth with all the power at our disposal. If that means annihilating the humans, so be it."

"Jon!" Arden said, horrified.

Jon continued to glare at Father Dom. "I still think we can live peacefully together, but only if both parties remain civilized. I have no idea how deep the rot has spread in your church, but there can be no doubt there *is* rot. The attack against us could be understood, but the attack against our citizens— that was beyond evil. Those killed were good Catholics whose only crime was working with us, and yet, what they worked on was for the betterment of all mankind. How can it be wrong to learn how to safely prepare and store foods or make good clothing or have light and books? Only a twisted mind, a mind full of hate, could construe that as evil. So now it becomes my job to protect my people from this hate. The question is how best to do that?"

"Send the father to speak on our behalf," Arden pleaded. "Wait for their response before acting."

"No! we must act!" Jen said, and half rose to glare at Arden.

Arden gave Jen an exasperated glance. "I didn't mean don't search for the children but attacking."

Jen settled back into her seat.

"Before we attack, we must know who our

enemies are." Jon squeezed Arden's shoulder, then stood to lay his hand on Jen's cheek. "Childebert is our enemy. More so now that we've declared his son a murderer. Prince Mondred will pay for his murders with his life. He thinks to hide from us, and maybe he can for a while, but we'll find him. But first, we must see to the safety of our citizens."

"An impossible task if their families and friends will turn on them," Arden said dully. She leaned forward, resting her elbows on the table to cradle her head in her hands. "This is my fault. I taught them how to make the ether and the drugs they used as poison."

"Don't be stupid," Sam said." You taught them to help. They gave their oaths to do no harm and treat all equally and broke them. It isn't your fault they corrupted healing to harm."

"I should've kept better track of my supplies."

Ethan snorted. "I have to second Sam here, don't be an idiot. This wasn't small amounts. They were manufacturing the drugs and explosives themselves. Believe me, you'd have noticed the missing amounts they used to blow up Kirk's tower or the docks. The ether used on us in Constantinople didn't come from here. They made it there. We all knew our knowledge could be used against us. This is hardly your fault, Arden."

Arden lifted her head. Tears had tracked across her face leaving lines through the soot on her cheeks. "But I taught them."

Jon wiped a trickling tear with his thumb. "It doesn't matter. We all taught them. We didn't teach them enough! Somehow, they missed the important lessons. We don't have time to beat ourselves up over this. We need to plan and strengthen our defenses."

"Maybe we should retreat. We could go to America or Iceland, somewhere where we could build slowly," Rob said.

Cass shook his head. "It's too late for that. If we retreat, the church will entrench. When we return, or they find us again, they'll hate us even more."

Jon nodded his agreement and said, "And besides, if we retreat, what happens to the Earth? No— we must stay and change how man thinks. Not just about us, but about the world and their place on it. Man must become responsible for their actions, all of them. They must stop acting in another's name and claim responsibility. Each man and woman must think for themselves. Life is sacred— all life— and man must learn to respect that."

"*Ha!* We were just beginning to learn that,

and it took thousands of years. In the here and now men see nothing wrong with taking anything they want by force," Warren said.

"And women are barely considered people," Sam added. She grimaced at Father Dom. "Sorry, but even you, who I think is very enlightened for your time, treat women as if we're lesser."

Father Dom wrinkled his brow. "How do I do that?"

"In ways too numerous to count. Why can't a priest marry? Why must a woman obey a man? Why is birth control wrong? Can you answer any of those without saying it's God's will? You'll pick and choose your arguments to benefit man. Science can be used, but not to benefit a woman. Laws can be written, but they don't apply to us." Sam's voice softened, and she took Kirk's hand. "Vows that join people together for life are one-sided in a man's favor. Your church argues that a father has a right to give his girl child away and that woman has no say but must submit her body to be used as a man wills. How can that possibly be right or fair? And you preach these things. Until you preach true equality, your church is a problem."

Cass absently tapped a pencil on the scorched surface of the round table as he spoke. "In the future, the church sees this and changes its stance, which leads to a weakening of faith worldwide. The church splits and splits again. Sects develop that allow for divorce or the clergy to marry or the use of birth control. The harsher churches cease to exist except as small cults that spring up occasionally and die back down with the end result being large groups of people don't believe in God at all.

"In our time, the Catholic Church has mellowed drastically from what it was. The church preaches love and acceptance now, not war. God has become a God of love, not vengeance, and the people respond. Most people in our time despise the religions that espouse violence against anyone."

"We're getting off topic," Jon said.

"No, this is the topic," Cass insisted. "What good does it do in the long run if the church accepts us but continues to preach hate and inequality? We're being naïve allowing freedom of religion. I mean, we should allow it, but we should also be preaching our version. We should give the people a healthy religion."

Jon nodded thoughtfully. "I see your point. A strong alternative to the Catholic church."

Cass beamed at him. "Exactly."

"You can't just make religion suit yourself," Father Dom said indignantly. "The Bible is God's word and His words are law."

"And interpreted by man and bent and twisted to support politics and opinions." Jon sniffed in derision and turned away. "Cass, begin at once on the King Arthur version of the Bible."

Jen loosed a sharp bark of laughter as Father Dom exclaimed indignantly.

"I'll need access to the originals," Cass said thoughtfully. "Father, consider that warlocks, wizards, priests and mages can read any writing. How will it hurt to let us translate the holy texts?"

"Twisting God's word to suit yourself is a sacrilege."

Cass said, "I agree, and I'm willing to take an oath that I won't but will instead give a true and accurate transcription."

"Work out the details later, Cass," Jon said. "For now, we'll settle for the First Church of England. Father, you're welcome to preach there, but first all sermons must be approved by Cass, or whoever he picks to oversee this. I really think our citizens will be comforted by this. Let's begin building a cathedral at once. A stone cathedral to rival any in Rome." Jon turned to Kirk. "Will you help with this?"

"Yeah. I'm not religious, but I see these people are and need a good church, not one that preaches hate. I'll speak to Henry and Nina about finances and we can shift things around to get this done fast."

"It isn't as simple as that, Jon," Cass said. He slapped a loose-leaf notebook closed and reached for another. "The church is built in Rome because of the tombs beneath it. The martyred remains of the apostles themselves are there." Cass rubbed his face hard and pushed the new notebook to Jon. "This isn't our Catholic church. These men use the church as a way to worldly power. They're gaming the system."

Jon pursed his lips as Father Dom exclaimed, "That is untrue! They are godly men!"

Jon waved him to silence and motioned Cass to continue.

Cass tapped the cover of the notebook Jon held and said, "Archbishops rule their lands with the same power of kings. They have guards and servants, mistresses and even wives. They sire children and wage war."

Father Dom's lips tightened, and he sat back in his seat but said nothing.

"The clergy under them have sworn obedience and their word is law. To disagree is a sin, one punishable by death. The church is just beginning to feel its power…" Cass trailed off, looking thoughtful. "Maybe that's why we're here? This is the cusp of the church's tyranny."

"We aren't tyrants," Father Dom said.

"You will be." Cass slid a folder to the father. "I've correlated the Fae's recollections of this time period into these reports. That folder documents the church's rise and abuse of power. Soon the church will grab even more power for itself, and you'll suppress science and women and even the kings themselves will bow to you. You'll fight amongst yourselves and wage war on every other religion. In the future, we call it the Dark Ages." Cass waved a hand in dismissal. "It doesn't matter. My point is, the church is in Italy because that is where the powerful bishops reside, and that is where the tombs are. We can't move it."

"So, what do we do?" Jon asked.

"We build a spectacular church here and take over Vatican City as the new Swiss Guard."

Jon rubbed his chin. "I see."

"They won't fall quietly into line," Cass

warned. "These are powerful men. Ruthless men. Italy is made up of what they call Papal States, and all have standing armies."

"We can be ruthless too." Warren half stood, leaning on his hands braced on the table. "Look how they tremble when Jen enters the room. They respect her, Jon. We tried sweetness and light and look what happened!"

"And we become tyrants, forcing the world to our will!"

"So, fucking, what! Let's be tyrants. We'll force them to behave. Slap them down hard. They're a bunch of thieves and rapists. What's so bad about making them obey fair laws? If they could, they'd march on us and force us to their will and make us slaves. I say we give them a taste of their own medicine!"

Cass rose and pushed Warren back into his seat. "I agree. Rome is already falling. War will rage across Europe for a thousand years, and we can stop that. Forbid the clergy to have any armsmen at all. Make Vatican City be neutral. Separate church and state as it is in our time."

"You'd destroy the church?" Father Dom asked in horror.

"Not at all. We'll support it. In fact, I think Jon should ensure that every city has a strong priesthood. The church will have no need of guards if we're the guards."

Father Dom nodded slowly. "But we'll be powerless."

Jon quirked an eyebrow. "And what power do you need to save men's souls? Vatican City can become a retreat, a place of learning where any may come without fear of persecution. The clergy will renounce their earthly possessions and work for all mankind, not their own small corner. They'll be neutral."

"Or we could save ourselves the trouble and just level it," Warren muttered.

Cass gave Warren an exasperated, laughing glance. "It'd help if there were more of us. We could keep a permanent contingent there."

"I agree." Jon closed his eyes and took a deep breath, then surprised Jen by falling to his knees and taking Arden's hand.

By her shocked expression it surprised Arden too.

Jon said, "I'd hoped to do this privately with romance and flowers, but the realm needs stability. I love you, Arden. Your kindness and wisdom are exactly what my people need in their queen. But my Fae need a queen like themselves. As much as I wish you to be my wife, how can I ask when you can't truly understand us? I'm worried Kuan will take you without your will because he feels my need."

Arden stared down at him with wide eyes.

"I'm asking you to become my wife, but more than that, I'm begging you to become a Greater Fae. You were meant to be a healer, a priest like Tony. I wish you could have more time, but our realm needs you. I need you." Jon's voice caught, and he squeezed his eyes closed and kissed her hand.

Arden's dark hair swung forward to hide her expression as she slowly crouched and rested her face against Jon's.

A sense of expectation, a tenseness grew until the small hairs on Jen's arm stood straight up. She expected Danu to appear in a storm of lightning and swirling blue magic, but it was just Jon and Arden.

"I love you too," Arden said.

She sounded so sad and scared tears came to Jen's eyes. Jon would be heartbroken.

"Yes, I will ma—"

Jen had no time to feel relief.

"No! Sorry!" Kuan screamed as lightning bloomed and flashed past Jen's face.

It rolled Jon and Arden over, then flashed back, slamming into Kuan again with a sizzling crash.

"Get back!" Warren yelled needlessly.

The Lesser Fae were already scrambling for the back of the room.

Jen leapt to Kuan's side, jumping over the stone round table in a single bound. "It's okay. Let it go. She agreed. Let Danu have her," she said, ruthlessly suppressing the guilt she felt. Arden might have meant to say yes to marriage but no to magic, and Jen needed her to have magic too.

Kuan sobbed and sagged, falling to his hands and knees. The lightning jumped from him to Arden. Long tangled skeins pulsed brightly and entwined, crawling over and around she and Jon.

Jen began casting heals. Tony and Cami joined her. Their stronger heals lit Kuan Arden and Jon until they glowed as if translucent. For five minutes, the lightning surged in scintillating arcs over them. When it disappeared, all three collapsed.

"Bring them to Jon's room," Jen said and bent to pick up Kuan. "I'll get him. Ramiro, do whatever needs to be done to ensure the welfare of our children. Order the Fae as you see fit to make our children safe, then do whatever you think best for the citizens. Jon will be out of commission for a while. While she's ill, we'll need to run things for him.

"Galahad, set your men on patrol and begin recruitment for the Emperor's Guard. Pick men who are willing to learn, follow, and enforce our laws."

"The emperor?" Kirk asked, rising an eyebrow.

"Yes. Tomorrow I'm going to France. Jon will be king there too before too long. He's already High King over Wessex and Mercia. We'll crown him Emperor after he and Arden wed.

"Jesus, Jen…" Ethan trailed off, then laughed. "You heard her. Bring the emperor to his room."

Brandon snickered and lifted Jon. "He's going to be so pissed."

A glint of humor in her eye, Jen smirked at Brandon. "Your problem. I'm going to be gone."

Brandon snickered again.

"Jon can worry about politics and policy. I just want the kids back."

The laughter died and the Fae exchanged guilty glances.

Jen never forgot, not for a second. Danu screamed inside her soul for her to find the children and make them safe. Brandon and Vicky didn't seem to feel the push like she did. She wondered if it was because they didn't have any children yet, or maybe Kuan thought she should be the one to go. She shrugged irritably. It didn't matter. She agreed with Danu. The children needed rescuing.

What We Don't Have

Ethan tugged her away from the table, ignoring her protests.

"You need sleep."

"I need to learn where the most likely hiding spots will be," she disagreed, yanking her arm from her husband's grasp.

Galahad glanced at them but continued his lecture on who lived where in France and how the different families were allied. He stood beside Father Dom on the musician's platform beside the stairs and used a wooden pointer on an illusion Rob had placed on the wall. The picture gained detail as Galahad spoke.

Rob was an artist and his illusions were

always crisp and clear, three-dimensional images. If Jen peered closely, she could make out familiar faces in the people on the Paris streets.

The farms and villas that appeared on the map as Galahad spoke lacked that detail, but numbers floated above them if Galahad or Father Dom told Rob how many lived there. They were amazing well informed. Although, when Jen considered it, she supposed it made sense. Politics was the major entertainment for these people. Who was marrying whom or attacking whom comprised most of their conversations.

"No. That family lost their holdings in the battle of *De Lyon* and joined Totila in the north," Father Dom said. "Archbishop Maximus has replaced Archbishop Thynin when he died childless."

The father and Galahad conferred quietly for a minute and Jen yawned

"Jen, I'm not kidding. Go lay down for a few hours." Ethan shook her lightly and spoke louder with real anger in his voice. "You need to rest to regenerate your magic. We can't afford for you to be weak. Not to fight the Franks, but Danu. You know she'll be angry and it'll take effort to hold her back. What the hell will we do if you collapse? Go rest. I'll stay and listen!"

"Go rest, Jen," Warren said. "You and I will be scouring the countryside while Matt and Ethan see what they can find out in town."

"A full group," Jon said crossly from the top of the stairs.

Everyone turned to the stairs as he leapt to the bottom floor and landed lightly, coming to rest exactly behind Jen.

"That means a healer," he continued and thumped into an empty seat at the table. "Man, my head. Kuan is waiting with Arden. Cami is with them." He squeezed his eyes closed and rubbed his head again. "Arden's still out. She's going to be pissed… I should've known better than to entice Danu like that."

Jen shrugged, forcing back her guilt. "*Meh*, she'll get over it. And I'm not bringing a healer. We won't need one, and it puts them at risk."

"What part of a full fucking group didn't you understand?"

"Whoa!" Warren surged to his feet and made a calming motion with both hands. "Can't you guys compromise? How about we bring Maria? She can heal if we need it and fly to stay with us. Jen is right though, we won't need healing. This is a reconnaissance mission, not an attack. It'll slow us down if we have to keep summoning a healer to us. Even Lou will slow us if we have to stay on the ground with him."

Jon glared and said, "Don't kid yourself. If you find the children, Jen will attack."

Warren smirked. "And we'll kill the bastards who took them."

"Don't get all cocky," Brandon said as he rose to clasp Warren's shoulder.

Jen eyed Brandon's pristine armor enviously. It glittered, the flickering oil lamps catching on the black gem-like feathers of his helm and shoulders. A protection paladin like herself, his armor never dirtied or broke. Each time he summoned it, it would appear as fresh and new as the first. *But his looked like armor while hers resembled a stripper's outfit,* she thought crossly, annoyed with herself for choosing it even though it had only been a game.

"They had traps prepared and some worked," Brandon continued. "You can bet your life they're done trying to capture us. The traps they'll have waiting will be meant to kill you, and there *will* be traps. This was a planned assault. They didn't decide on the spur of the moment to steal the children— they planned it. We can thank our lucky stars they rushed the job in Constantinople and we got away to warn them here. If they hadn't rushed it, they might have captured us. So, wherever the kids are will be defended. Go in there thinking you're immortal and you'll be killed."

"I'll be careful," Jen said and gave Brandon a quick hug. She knew as well as he the next attempt would start with their deaths. Now that they knew no bonds would hold a paladin, they wouldn't make the same mistake twice.

She said, "Warren is right though, a healer will just slow us down. You, Vicky, Kuan and Cami can keep searching our coast, but stay in groups of two. I'm betting they already crossed the channel though while we were busy fighting."

"We still don't have a full count of the missing," Rob said. "Ramiro wants us to go door-to-door and inspect every house. So far ten of the women who kept their children have been reported dead and the children missing. He thinks, and I agree, those women were targeted first, and the ones not reported missing haven't been found yet because their entire families were killed, and their neighbors have been too busy to check on them."

"Jesus. How will we keep them safe?" Jen asked.

"We fucking can't! No one can!" Jon

slammed his hand down so hard the table wobbled. "How can we protect against their own loved ones? Sure, we can build walls and lock doors, and that won't help at all if your own father knocks and kills you when you open the door."

"The new church will help," Cass said.

"Maybe, in time, but our citizens need security right now."

Jen crouched beside Jon and took his hand. "We can't offer what we don't have. What we can do is keep a closer eye on fanatics in the future."

"Spy," Jon said disgustedly.

"Yes. It wouldn't be my first choice either, but if the choice is spy or let this happen again, I vote spy."

"Our citizens will be more on their guard too," Cass said reassuringly. "You can bet we'll all be more careful and suspicious. We'd all seen glares and dark glances and ignored them. Now, we'll report them, and Ethan can watch and see if it's more than that."

"Jon, no matter what we do, our citizens will be unhappy and some will leave," Ethan said.

"I know, and we can worry about that later. We should've suspected the refugees from Limenware were up to no good when they returned, but I thought they'd realized we meant to help them…" He rubbed his head with both hands, then straightened. "Fine, take Maria if she's willing."

Maria nodded her assent.

Jon continued, "Deliver Princess Chrodesinde and inform the king of his son's treachery. Leave Ethan and Matt while you, Warren, and Maria search. Report every eight hours. We still have so much to do here… You should be able to scour France for our children; rangers can pick them out from strangers. It's the citizen's children I'm worried about. How will we find them?"

"I actually have an idea for that," Sam said. If Kirk will supply summon stones to whatever family remains for the children, maybe if they're summoned, they could answer? I see how Diana reaches for Jen and Ethan. The babies must miss their moms, and if they hear them calling, they might be able to accept a summons—"

"Most of the moms are dead," Jon interrupted angrily. He rubbed his face hard again, obviously trying to reign in his temper. He gave Sam a small apologetic grimace when he dropped his hands. "It's a good idea though. I'll get Ramiro on that. It'll take a day or so to organize. If we can find one stolen child maybe our rangers could track the rest."

"Offer a huge reward," Cass said. "Not for the children, but for information on who took them and where. Make it clear we won't accept any child unless there's also a culprit, otherwise we'll get a hundred more babies."

"I'll consider it and talk it over with Arden when she wakes. Jen, go get some sleep. You can leave at dawn."

Jen inclined her head and gave her husband a rueful half-smile. He snorted and pushed her toward the stairs. "Sleep! We'll cuddle both our kids when we get back."

She nodded and plodded up the stairs and into the first guest room she saw with an open door. Suddenly exhausted, she fell into bed without bothering to undress and closed her eyes. Ethan woke her by shaking her shoulder. Dim gray light announced the coming dawn and she felt as if she'd just laid down.

"Chrodesinde and her ladies and guards are already aboard. We can leave whenever you're ready."

"Let's go then," Jen said and rose wearing her protection armor

The Search is On

Gallant's hooves echoed along the quiet Parisian street. Men and women peeked furtively at them from windows and doorways as they passed. Their arrival at the docks had left men scurrying away. Something was up. Jen suspected word of the attack on Camelot had already reached here. Her suspicions were confirmed when they reached the castle.

Armed men lined the outer walls and filled the courtyard.

"If they attack, protect the princess and her ladies, and stay low," Jen said to the knights surrounding Princess Chrodesinde, then louder and adding will to her voice, magic making it ring clearly to the most distant soldiers, "We've come to escort the princess to her father!"

No one approached as they advanced. The streets remained eerily quiet. The men in the courtyard parted to let them pass. Jen didn't like this one bit. The thought of leaving Chrodesinde here defenseless rose her hackles, but only hers. Danu didn't care at all.

"Are you sure you wish to stay?" Jen whispered when they reached the door.

"He's my father." Chrodesinde stepped forward to open the door but her hand trembled and her face was pale.

Jen didn't say it but she was thinking of the fathers mothers and brothers who'd killed their families in Camelot for consorting with Fae. She picked up her pace and passed Chrodesinde, entering first. The main hall was empty except for the king, his bishop, Sir Dante, and a man Jen didn't know. The group she escorted dropped to their knees. The Fae remained standing.

King Childebert waved one hand. "Daughter, rise and be welcome. We heard rumors and worried for your safety. I'm glad to see you well. And your brother?"

"Has been declared a fugitive for the murder of the king's ward Dillion Shepard, Lady Ada and Sir Galahad's squire, Fredrick."

Chrodesinde's voice caught and Britina sobbed.

The ladies murmured condolences and patted her back all giving weary glances to their king. Chrodesinde's knights grasped their spears uneasily, their eyes scanning the bowmen on the balcony. Jen felt a small measure of relief at this sign of loyalty from Chrodesinde's knights.

She said, "We have come for our children. Return them and mercy can be yours. Harm them, or Chrodesinde and her ladies, and we'll have no mercy for anyone here!"

The silence that had followed Chrodesinde's words deepened.

Childebert inclined his head the barest degree and said, "Your children aren't here."

Jen leapt forward, traveling the fifteen feet that separated them in a second and landing directly before the king. A ripple of movement on the balconies warned the archers had pulled back their strings. The king held up his hand.

"I have none of your children," he repeated in a firm voice.

"You were involved with the attack on us— your men, your money, your son's plan. Do you think we'll trust your word? We have letters Mondred penned. Letters to you and

Bishops Rufus and Maximus. Letters that tell how to hold and how to kill us." Her voice rose. "Letters that speak of taking our children to breed your own Fae!"

Ethan placed a hand on her arm. She took a deep breath and tried to speak calmly.

"Return them. Admit your treachery to your people. Treat Chrodesinde and her ladies with respect, and we can forgive. Continue to hide them, harm Chrodesinde, and you'll have war!"

Jen spun to stalk out. She was tempted to fight her way to the basements to let Warren search for the children, but she thought it unlikely any would be on the premises. Childebert was doing his utmost to distance himself from his son's actions. The half-burned letters that Rob had salvaged from the fire in Mondred's room used vague language and promised money for unspecified expenses. Childebert had also warned his son against angering the Fae. He wouldn't keep the children here.

"Jen, Lady Frey!" Dante called after her. He followed down the aisle. "We'd heard ships bearing the church's banner had sailed on Camelot but nothing of the prince… Please, I swear to you on my honor, no children have been brought to the castle."

Jen halted and spun to face him. "We caught Callahan covered with Dillion's blood, carrying his head. His fucking head, Dante! They meant to kill him forever. Ewan and Bruno were caught laying explosives inside the new orphanage. Their movements over the last week are still being checked. My children were stolen with the prince's help! We've been poisoned by knowledge Mondred supplied, but worse, our citizens have been murdered with supplies paid for by Mondred and his fucking father. We can't resurrect them. They'll stay dead! So, don't tell me there are no children here! I know he has them! Maybe not here, but he does have them! And I'll find them! And when I do, I'll kill everyone involved— despite their rank!"

She brushed his hand from her arm and continued outside where she kissed Ethan and summoned Gallant.

"I want to beat the truth from him, but I doubt he knows where they were taken."

"He won't know," Warren agreed grimly. "I'm tempted to beat him anyway."

"Harming the king won't help us," Maria said.

"I know that!" Jen shouted. She took a deep breath and offered Maria an apologetic smile. "I know," she repeated in a calmer voice. "I read the fucking letters too. I know Childebert is keeping his hands clean. But he did encourage his son."

"We'll find Alex," Ethan said.

"Call me if you find any," she said.

"You too." The lines around his eyes deepened as he examined them. "Try to hold her back, Warren."

Maria laid a hand on her husband's arm and took Jen's hand. "If they attack, I'll summon you, Ethan, and I'll hang back in case Jen enters a trap."

"We'll be careful," Jen said and urged Gallant into the air.

The men gathered in the courtyard exclaimed. She almost wished they'd attack, but they did nothing. Ethan disappeared. A split-second later Matt did too. They planned to return to the castle to spy and search. Maria jumped into the air and transformed to her eagle shape. Wind whistled through her wings, buffeting Jen's face as Maria sailed above them until she became a black speck in the sky. Jen headed Gallant back to the docks to begin her sweep for the children.

➤———————————

Exhaustion finally stopped Jen's search. She brought Gallant to the ground in a deserted stretch of woods bordering a narrow river.

"You and Maria rest. I'll set wards and prepare food," Warren said as he slipped from Gallant's back and stretched.

Marie grasped his arm and tugged him to the grass beside her. "You need rest too. I'll sleep better with you near me. Please," she whispered and clutched him tightly.

His eyes darkened, and he ran a hand over her bald head. "Yes. I'll always be there when you need me. Always!"

Guilt and anger laced his voice. Jen rolled to face the other way to give them privacy. Maria's fear tightened Jen's shoulders and her guilt threatened to choke her. Marie had suffered because she'd told Warren to guard Ethan. She tried to tell herself Maria's pain wasn't her fault, but she knew better. She fell asleep and had continuous nightmares of her family and friends burning.

Cold sunlight against her eyelids woke her. When she opened her bleary eyes, Warren sat beside a small fire preparing verbena tea. Fragrant clouds enveloped his stubbled cheeks. His hair had begun to grow back since his transformation to Greater Fae but it barely reached his neck. It'd take him years to regrow his long ponytail. He still looked like he could be in a rock band though with his tight leather pants and unbuttoned shirt.

She gratefully took the cup he handed her and sipped as he spoke.

"The borders of these mini kingdoms change so frequently I'm not convinced we're still in France at all. I propose we fly north for two hours and begin crisscrossing. Even if they followed the Seine and had fresh horses waiting, they can't be much further than that."

"Don't assume they don't have fresh men and horses spaced to get them from the zone as fast as they can. They might even use summon stones," Maria said as she took the tea he offered.

Jen eyed Maria unhappily. "We're assuming everything. If I stole them, I wouldn't come to France at all. I'd head to Africa or America, somewhere far where you wouldn't think to look, and by the time you did search, I'd have them safely underground."

"But they don't know how rangers see. They assume we track by prints. How could they know to hide them below ground?" Warren asked in a tone she was sure he meant to be reassuring but came off as nervous to her.

"They can't, I guess. I'm just saying what I'd do." Jen slurped the rest of her tea and handed the cup to Warren to stash it in his pack. He placed a paper wrapped sandwich in her hands and rose to kick out the fire.

"We know Bishop Maximus was involved, so it makes sense to scour this region," he said.

"I agree. It's just, I really thought we'd see them right away in or near Paris. Every day that passes they get further away. And the world is huge. We could never search it all."

Maria said, "Word will spread of the reward. With so many children stolen, someone involved is bound to get greedy. We just have to be patient."

Jen snorted and rose to summon Gallant. She and Maria soared into the air. Warren clutched her around the waist and searched with his eyes closed, looking for a flicker of green in his minds-eye that would warn of a friend nearby. She and Maria scoured the ground from the air, searching for any sign men had passed. The occasional smoke they saw was always innocent crofters, shocked when the Fae appeared and questioned them.

Jen thought most answered truthfully, too surprise by their presence to consider lying. They were greeted with awe and sometimes outright amazement. Those who lived alone on the hills hadn't heard of them yet. They'd encountered two entire towns that hadn't had news from the capital in over a year. They left them shocked, staring after them as they leapt into the sky to continue their search.

———➤———

"Let's go back to Divona and force the priests there to tell us where the children are."

They'd stopped at sunset to rest and even though Jen was tired, she couldn't bear the thought of trying to sleep. She tossed her empty cup to Warren and kicked at the fire. Sparks scattered and smoldered. She impatiently stomped on the small flames, not really caring if she burned this forest to the ground.

"Jon will be angry—"

"Fuck that! I'm angry! I need those children safe! I need it!" Jen summoned Gallant, mounted, and offered Warren her hand.

He exchanged uneasy glances with his wife but mounted behind her. Danu pushed so hard Jen would've left them behind. She felt bad about her angry impatience, but Danu needed those children. She couldn't take another night of sleepless tossing and turning. It had been four days of searching with never a hint.

She'd flown less the forty minutes when Warren excitedly grabbed her arm.

"Stop!"

Danu surrounded them in a wild storm. He'd found them.

Jen stared into her husband's blazing, blue eyes. "These aren't Fae children, but I believe them to be the children of our citizens. Can you remain calm enough to spy?" she asked the second he appeared.

"If you can, I can."

Jen grimaced wryly and released her glowing blue sword, letting it return to mist.

"Maria, stay with Jen," Warren said and kissed his wife's brow. "We'll go back and investigate."

"Thirty-three children. What else could this be?" Maria said angrily. "If they've harmed them…"

Ethan touched his fingertips to Maria's face as he spoke. "Some might be innocent. The women with them will have been ordered and might have no idea where the children are from. No sense arguing about it. We'll go see." Ethan kissed Jen and darted away already invisible.

"How will we get them all home," Maria asked when the men disappeared.

"Same way we got here. I'll fly them back and return with Brandon and Vicky."

The idea of transporting the kids one at a time didn't thrill her. If they'd found thirty-two that meant twenty-one human children were still missing. Or murdered. The thought angered her, but Danu didn't care. Danu wanted her to continue searching for the missing Fae children.

"I have a better idea," Maria said and whispered Joash's full name. The fire bird appeared above her head seconds later

He cooed softly and settled to her shoulder where he rustled his golden wings as she wrote on a paper she pulled from her pouch.

"Ramiro," she said as she handed the bird the paper. The bird cocked its head then nodded and soared into the sky, trailing sparks until it disappeared.

"Ramiro?" Jen quirked an eyebrow at Maria.

"I've asked him to ready the *HMS Enterprise*. Brandon and Vicky can tow it. It should be warmer and safer for the children."

"I didn't realize we had any airships

finished. When we've found our children, and secured our borders, we should work on radios and transport."

"It isn't quite finished, but it floats. We should keep our science secret though. Look how they abuse the knowledge we give them. These people are so violent."

Jen threw an arm around Maria's shoulders. "We'll work it out. I sort of hope this slows our expansion. I'm totally cool with Camelot being just us."

"Me too, and that worries me. When we first arrived, I really wanted to help, but now I don't care. They're so cruel to each other… the things they were willing to do to us to steal our magic… Well, it changed how I think of them."

"Not all of them. No one blames you for hating the church, but don't hate all of them. You were worried about Chrodesinde and Britina. Ada and Fredrick…" Jen had to clear her throat before she could continue. "Their deaths hurt. We still care. Maybe we were trying to care too much? I think we feel it more because we're women and seeing the women of this era is shocking. But I think we mind their state more than they do."

"Because they can't imagine life any other way. And that horrifies me. It'll literally take hundreds of years before women begin to believe in their self-worth and that's the church's fault."

"Our church will preach equality."

Maria relaxed, her shoulders easing, and the lines in her face lightening. "Cass had a great idea with that. I wish he'd had it sooner."

"We've been here barely a year…"

"I almost can't remember a time before this. Until Warren, I wished to go back, but now I wouldn't trade him for anything, not even cell phones and fast food."

Jen laughed and sat cross-legged on the ground.

"The connections Danu give are amazing," Jen agreed. "I'd give up my magic but would never willing give up the closeness I feel for the Fae."

Maria lay back in the grass beside Jen. "When Warren kisses me, standing in our magic, and I feel his love and lust… I feel sorry for the humans. We have so much they'll never have."

"That's why we should keep trying to help them. It would be so easy to isolate ourselves and just enjoy being together, but humans without magic would grow to hate us."

Maria snorted softly. "They already hate us."

"Not all. We have human friends and supporters."

"True," Maria said thoughtfully.

They were quiet until Ethan returned.

He said, "I'm sure the kids are from Camelot. The guy in charge, Jarmis, is in a hurry to deliver them and go."

Jen jumped to her feet and summoned her sword. "Deliver them and go where?"

"The Abbey of *Le Laire* in Switzerland. Although I don't think it *is* Switzerland in the here and now. It's a papal state headed by Archbishop Arnulf, basically a king in his own right, albeit of a small kingdom. From what we overheard, Arnulf is originally from Metz and a relative of Archbishop Maximus. He's a German who follows Roman law and a nominal subject of Childebert. The men we found have already delivered fifteen children to a church outside Divona. Jarmis and another guy argued about taking the children all the way to the abbey. Jarmis thinks it's a waste of time when they're just going to be handed out to their surrogate families on arrival and recross the border. Maximus has arranged for the babies to get homes within his parish. He thinks he can hide them in plain sight. I already summoned Cass and Sam to backtrack the ones given away. We have about fifteen hours of travel before they reach the abbey. I'm worried if we attack them now that word will reach the others and they'll kill them before letting us take them back."

Jen asked, "Do the families that took them know they're stolen?"

"I don't know. The women with them are aware something is afoot, and they're scared. Women have been disappearing from Paris, and they're afraid they'll be next. They're scared to death of these men."

"And the men?"

"All know the mission is important and secret. They spoke like they believe all the kids with them could become Fae in time. I don't know if that means they don't know they're holding our citizens children and think them ours, or they think all the kids from Camelot can be Fae. Some of the kids are older, almost walking. They're keeping them drugged. From what I overheard some have died of it."

"Jesus, Ethan."

Ethan's angry gaze flickered to deep loss for a moment. He was terrified for Alex too. Jen wished she could offer comfort but had no words to ease this loss. He rubbed his face hard, and when he dropped his hands, he appeared angry again.

"Let them reach their next campground.

They'll have to stop to feed and clean them. When they do, we'll attack. We can't wait until the reach *Le Laire*, too many might die, but we can keep them from escaping and warning anyone."

"How many men?"

"Nineteen men and seven women."

"Fine. I'll go in first and offer surrender. We'll each pick our targets in advance. Anyone who isn't face down on the ground is fair game. Single target spells, no AOE, or fire."

"I'll tell Matt and Warren and lead you to them."

Lady Anise

Jen waited impatiently for the last wagon to stop. Traffic remained nonexistent on this stretch of road, which was partially overgrown with weeds and littered with rocks. Deep ruts lined the muddy path. Tired horses hung their heads and snorted at the scent of grain as a man slit a burlap sack and emptied the contents into a wooden bucket.

"See to your charges," Jarmis said and dismounted his horse. Burly, with a long unkempt beard and expensive chain mail, he swaggered and gestured imperiously.

He reached to a pack tied to the back of a trailing horse as the women hurried forward, clutching shawls over their bowed heads.

To Jen, the evening air felt comfortable,

neither cold nor hot bothered her. To the shivering women with their mud-covered-feet, the night must be cold, and they tired from following behind the wagons, driven at spear point down the road.

A baby's soft cry made her eyes flare. She recognized the protective sensation and enhanced senses and knew if she drew her sword it'd glow blue without her will. Ethan signed to her from across the rough encampment. She drew her sword and leapt, landing twenty-five feet away before you could blink, casting Sanctuary on the first wagon as her feet hit the ground.

"Get face down on the ground or die!"

Jarmis shrieked and grabbed for his sword. Ethan appeared behind him and slit his throat before the blade left the scabbard. He disappeared, reappearing immediately behind the man to Jarmis' left and killed him while Jarmis still fell. A glowing green arrow streaked past Jen's face and knocked a fleeing man to the ground where he writhed, screaming in pain. Ethan flickered and appeared behind a man holding the horse's reins.

"Attack!" Jen screamed her attack cry, increasing her party's speed. Arrows crashed into her shield and fell to the dirt, her magic pulling all attacks to her. Men screamed as they were forced to turn and face her, leaving them vulnerable to Ethan.

Ethan struck so fast he blurred. The men he fought yelled and cursed but Ethan ducked their blows as if they stood still. He'd killed three more and leapt to the next in under seven seconds.

Jen leapt again, landing before a man who fumbled with a pouch on his belt. She struck him dead in one blow and watched in horror as a glass vial of oil slipped from his hand and shattered. *They planned to burn these children.*

A woman screamed shrilly, jerking Jen's head around. She hung from the arm of a man at the back of the second wagon. Flames raced up her arm and caught in her hair as she screeched.

"Stop, they be babes! Dear God, stop!" An arrow thunked into the man, pinning him to the wagon as the woman frantically batted at the spreading flames with her shawl. The fire flickered and expanded, then contracted to a pulsing red ball before it disappeared with a whoosh of air. Matt had grabbed it. The woman had saved the babies, but now lay writhing on the ground, clutching her blackened arm and sobbing through burnt lips.

Jen recast Sanctuary beneath her and leapt, crossing the fifteen-foot gap between the wagons and landing on the driving board of the second wagon. The horse stood rock still caught in Warren's magic. The women cried and cowered on the ground with their hands over their heads. The woman in her Sanctuary sat, cradling her burned arm. Jen winced and turned away to see Maria leap in cat form and claw at the face of a man who withdrew a glass vial from his pouch.

Jen half crouched and threw her shield. It knocked down three men and returned to her. The three lay dazed on the ground. Before they could rise, arrows thudded into their backs, pinning them to the mud.

The women began to scream.

"Quiet!" Jen snapped, and the screams died down to wails and sobs muffled by their hands. Jen casted Deadly Ground on two men trying to flee, and Warren killed them both as they strained to escape the glowing red patch of earth beneath them. She looked for another target, but none remained.

In under a minute, the Fae had killed every man standing, leaving only the women and two men cowering on the ground alive.

"Maria, make a fire and see to the women. Warren, check the perimeter. Make sure no one saw. Be quiet!" Jen said again more forcefully as the women began to cry again. She knelt beside the burned woman and gently drew her hand from her face.

Blood coated her cheek and black flakes of skin glistened with pus. White of bone and yellowed muscle shone through the cracked, black fissures on her arm. Jen canceled her Sanctuary. The woman screamed shrilly again and collapsed. Small flickers of light danced from Jen's fingertips, landing and fading to nothing. A baseball size sphere of greenish-white light casted by Maria hit the woman's chest and disintegrated without the glow that showed a successful cast.

Ethan grabbed her hands. "It won't work. Sanctuary is the best you can do."

Jen recast Sanctuary and took the woman's hand as she fumbled one handed at the bandolier across her chest that held healing potions. "I have a potion that can heal you. I swear on my soul I'm no demon and the potion won't damn you. Please, I beg you, please accept it."

The woman closed her eyes and appeared to pray. When she opened them, she nodded. Relieved she'd accept her help, Jen poured the healing potion into the woman's mouth.

Blackened skin sloughed away, and new

pink flesh formed before their eyes. Before Jen could stand, the woman was whole again. Light patches of skin remained beneath the drying blood on her face and arms, but they'd soon tan to match the rest of her.

Ethan left Jen to haul one of the cowering men up by his collar. "Have you dosed their milk?"

"Aye. They poured a foul-smelling liquid into it and warned us no to drink it," the woman said before the man could answer.

The man dangling from Ethan's grasp glared at her but nodded agreement.

"Maria, boil some water. Matt dispel the bottles," Ethan said as he dropped the man and fumbled for his pouch. The green healing potion he withdrew sparkled in the starlight. A flick of his thumb opened the flask and he leaned over the side of the wagon to examine the children.

"Give one to each. We don't need them, and Kirk will make us more when we go home," Warren said as he poured a flask into a baby's mouth. "They're cold and wet," he continued as he picked up a crying child and jiggled it against his shoulder.

"We have supplies," the woman said and nodded to a pack tied to a trailing horse.

"What's your name?" Jen asked.

"Anise, my lady. Are you a demon?" She rose a trembling hand to her now healed face, grimacing at the blood that coated her fingers.

"No. I'm a Fae. They're the demons." Jen kicked a corpse at her feet, then bent to retrieve a glass globe filled with oil from the man's belt. She hefted it thoughtfully in her hand. "Will you help us with the children? They're just children, not Fae."

"Yes, my lady." Anise scrambled to her feet and took the pack Ethan handed her with a bob of her head and a mumbled, "Thank ye."

The other women rose, murmuring in nervous whispers, and began changing the babies.

"I'm sorry we can't have a bigger fire for you, but we wish to remain unseen until the other children are rescued." Jen handed the oil to Ethan who glared and began checking all the corpses. He piled the oil filled globes away from the fire.

"I've heard your kind can't tell a lie," Anise said.

Jen glanced up from the baby she held. "We can. We can't break an oath made to Danu."

"Will you give me your oath you'll leave us women unharmed if I tell what I knows?"

"I will," Jen said eagerly and took Anise's hand. She squeezed her hand a moment before backing away, placing the baby she carried gently into the wagon, and raising her right hand. She reached eagerly to the magic she carried inside her that was Danu. "I swear on my honor as a Fae to deliver Anise to a place of her choosing unharmed and rewarded for information she has about the children."

A bolt of lightning struck Jen, knocking her to her knees. The women exclaimed and ran. The lightning lingered for only a moment. When it passed, Jen rose and again offered her hand. "My oath can't be broken. Please, do you know where our children are?"

"Bishop Rufus brought us from Tail End Tavern and bade us care for these children. There be others there."

One of the captives yelled, "You're a fool, woman! They lie and are sure to kill you! Will you trade your immortal soul for treasure?"

Ethan hit the man, knocking him to the ground unconscious. The other captive prostrated himself.

"I swear I won't harm you!" Jen said urgently.

Anise licked her lips and nodded. Her expression hardened when it lingered on the man cowering at Ethan's feet. "I already be damned. God has no love for one such as I. I knows it. When the bishop come, I thought maybe he speak true, that God could forgive my life of sin. I be grateful for a chance to live in peace and pray." Her angry gaze traveled the women with their bowed heads as they cared for the babies.

"We be that grateful for the chance," she said again and kicked a corpse at her feet. "But we shoulda knowd it be a lie. No Abbey would accept the likes of us." She straightened her shoulders and turned to Jen. "The bishop took babes with him. I only got a short glimpse, but they be wrapped differently than the others. One be wrapped in a green cloth with light green trim. Two be wrapped in dark blue and another in dark red. More be wrapped in pink and blue clothes, but I couldn't count them. They lay stacked together in a wooden box. I think ten at least. Two of my friends be told to go with them. I heard Bishop Rufus say, *'Take the younger girls as they be least likely to be ill on the ship,'* but I know not where they be headed."

"Will you show us where this happened?" Jen asked.

"Yes."

"And then?" Ethan asked.

He grasped the sword from Jen's hand and

dropped it to his feet where it turned to mist and disappeared. Jen absently nodded her thanks. She hadn't even realized she'd summoned it.

"We left with these wee ones here and fifteen more. Yesterday afternoon we met with a man who took the fifteen. I know not the man's name. He spoke with Jarmis of seeing to their placement, but I know not where."

"And these?" Jen gestured to the children who'd begun to cry and fuss. The sound relieved her, proof that the healing potions were working.

"These are intended for the Abbey of *Le Laire*. We're to deliver them by midday tomorrow. They told us we were to be their guardians with clean clothes and warm beds, but I fear they lied. I overheard Jarmis speaking to him" – she gestured with her chin to the man cowering on the ground— "he promised Ethel as a treat. Said he could use us as he wished as long as the mess was tidied up."

Ethel exclaimed in dismay, pulling her shawl tightly about her shoulders. "And you said naught?"

"What was I to say?" Anise curled her lip and kicked at the corpse again. "I planned to whisper a warning tonight in the dark, but what was I to do? Should I have run like Bernit and be struck down?"

"These men have killed?" Ethan asked in a dangerous voice.

"Aye, Bernit had a man and didn't wish to leave him. Our first night out she ran. They killed her with less feeling then if she be a hurt horse."

"Who be these children, Lady?" Ethel asked in a quavering voice.

"The church has attacked Camelot and stolen our children. These are our citizens children."

"Commoners?"

"Yes. Born of regular folk and baptized into the church."

The women exchanged confused glances. "And you come to seek them?"

"Yes, and every man who had a hand in their taking will pay."

The two men on the ground blanched and tried to push away. Jen ignored them.

Anise said, "We'd heard Camelot was wondrous but inhabited by demons who steal your soul and enslave you for all eternity."

"We aren't demons and are against slavery in all its forms. In Camelot, men and women have equal rights. You can make your own decisions and live alone if you choose."

Ethel curled her lip. "*Ha*, you'd be robbed and murdered in your sleep by the first man you bedded."

"No. The law protects women exactly the same as a man. You can work at any job you choose. It isn't like here where only one way remains to make a living if you have no man."

"Camelot is dangerous though," Maria warned. "The church sent assassins and likely will again. We're doing our best to protect from them, but we can't guarantee your safety when the church convinces neighbors and friends to murder."

"You could keep your old job. There's no law against it," Matt said and winked at Anise.

She flushed and lowered her head, her burnt hair falling forward to hide her face.

"Sorry, I meant no disrespect," Matt said, clearly uncomfortable he'd upset her.

Jen rolled her eyes and tugged Anise to the fire. "Got any shrunken cloth in that bag of yours?" she asked over her shoulder. "These women are cold and wet too."

"Let's see," Matt said thoughtfully and began rummaging in his pack.

In preparation for finding their children they'd brought shrunken bottles and warm clothes. Matt carried a pack like Jen's crafted by Dillion. Made of black leather with silver trim, an iron cross bisected by a lightning bolt that was their guild symbol shimmered, giving off a faint glow on the back. The pack was the size of a normal bookbag, but Matt could carry over a hundred pounds in his. Jen's pack was the same size, but she could carry almost a thousand pounds.

Matt still carried more than her though. His ability to shrink any item and dispel it as needed let him carry a huge store of supplies. Jen carried mostly food in her pack with only a few shrunken items. Anything inside the pack entered stasis. Milk stayed fresh and cooked food remained the exact temperature it was when placed inside. Finding things could be tricky though, it paid to be organized.

It took Matt a minute of removing and replacing tiny pouches of various colors until he smiled and waved one in triumph.

"How you be doing that?" Anise asked in awe as Matt removed a tiny square of wood and canvas and flicked it into the air. Flynn grabbed it and set it on the ground ten feet behind them. White motes drifted from the bird's wings and settled to the ground, and before you could blink a fully made building had formed. The building was made of canvas nailed to a wooden frame. It reminded Jen of the buildings used during World War Two that she'd seen in movies, although Matt's canvas building was much fancier. His tent was light blue with orange trim on the windows that rolled open and tied close, and it had a real door and a wooden floor with built in bunks and tables. Hers was made from the cheap canvas-like fabric they'd just begun to make in bulk and held no furnishings. She carried four small ones meant for two people and two larger ones meant for ten, shrunken in her pack.

"We make these cheaply on purpose," Matt explained as he removed another and set it behind the first. "I can shrink them and take mine with me, so mine are nicer than Jen's, but everyone has one in their pack."

"But how does it fit in there?"

"Magic. I shrink them. This pack is magic too and made by a mage." Matt held out the pack so they could examine it. "It always glows like that and anything that fits inside the opening could be placed in a mage pack. Only the recipient of the pack can open or use it. I don't need to worry about thieves. Interior pockets form as items are added. The more you add, the smaller the items grow, but they retained their mass. The weight," he clarified when the women looked puzzled. "Items a wizard shrink lose both mass and size. Once you dispel them, unless a wizard is with you, you have to leave them behind if they won't fit into the opening of the pack. We make these tents to be taken apart too. I could put the parts inside one at a time, but they really aren't that expensive to just leave behind if you're in a hurry."

Jen giggled at the women's amazed expressions at this. They seemed more astonished over the idea of leaving the tent behind then of it shrinking to fit inside a magic pack.

The women continued to ask questions as Maria and Warren prepared a meal. Eager faces lit by firelight gazed at Matt with interest, exclaiming in wonder as he transformed postage-size scraps of fabric to billowing yards with a flick of his fingers as he dispelled and handed out what to them were riches.

Joash appeared over Jen's head and settled to her shoulder where he began rubbing his face against her cheek. Golden sparks trailing from his wings flickered and disintegrated. He clutched a thick packet of paper and Jon's bangle.

"Jon is in France," Jen said worriedly as she scrambled to her feet.

She'd sat with her back to a wagon wheel.

Four babies slept beside her, snuggled in the folds of her cloak. She bent to feel their cheeks as Ethan called for Jon. All felt warm. Only one fussed when she touched him. She rubbed his back until he settled, falling back asleep with a small thumb stuck in his mouth. The sight made her long for Alex. She wanted to hold her son, smell the scent of his skin, and watch his eyes close in peaceful sleep.

"We'll be home soon, Jen." Ethan said, his longing gaze on the small boy too.

Jen made no reply. She'd never stop searching.

Jon arrived and knelt on one knee to examine the babies. "Your daughter is fine," he said.

"Why are you in France?" Jen asked.

She eyed him uneasily. He'd shaved his head into a short crew cut and jagged black claw marks had been painted on his face as if a bear had scratched him diagonally from brow to chin. His blue eyes blazed, seeming more otherworldly in his painted face.

"Chrodesinde called for help. I went personally to retrieve her. She and Dante are headed to Camelot. Brandon and Cami are on their way here with an airship. Vicky is busy bringing Father Dom to Italy. Any word on our children?" He straightened to peer into the wagon.

"Yes. Bishop Rufus has them. Anise has agreed to show us where they were."

A commotion by the fire drew Jen's attention. The women argued in whispers with the bound men. All quieted when Jon approached.

"Are you a Fae too?" Anise asked boldly.

"I am," Jon said.

Jen laughed and pretended to cough to cover it, earning an eye roll from Jon.

Anise's gaze flicked to Jen and her shoulders straightened. "I believe the lady will protect me, even from you."

"I will, but you don't need protection from Jon," Jen said reassuringly and stepped between them.

"He's a demon," the man at her feet said. "Can't you feel it?"

Anise glared at the man. "Demon or no, it isn't right to steal children from their mothers. You be a murderer. I saw that with me own eyes. We knows you're up to no good. You always be a bad one. As soon as I saw ye all chummy with Jarmis I knowed we be in for trouble, but trouble or no, these children be innocent and baptized. The lady says she'll return them, and I believes her. I see how kind they be to them. Even if I believed your lies, I will no help such as you."

"Well said." Jon lifted her hand to kiss it. "You are a lady of great insight." He brushed the burnt wisps of hair from her face and removed his cloak to place it around her shoulders.

Jen had to stifle another laugh at Anise's expression. She looked both terrified and proud of herself.

"Anise be no lady," the man on the ground said derisively, then snapped his mouth closed and turned his face away. He made an abortive attempt to rise, then tried to rub his arms.

Jen grinned and nudged him with her foot. "If the king says she's a lady, then she is. Don't make him any angrier or you'll be crying in a minute."

Jon said, "Lady Anise, will you accompany the children to Camelot? They have need of a kind guardian. A home is being prepared for them. Some are orphans and will require care for the rest of their lives. I offer you the Barony of High Street two miles from Camelot itself, which consists of a manor house and twenty acres suitable for gardens, and a yearly stipend to assure the children's care."

Anise frowned at Jon while the other

women gasped.

"Why me?" she asked suspiciously. Her narrow-eyed gaze flicked from Jon to Jen and narrowed further on the man on the ground. "He be right. I be no lady. I be no hero like the Fae there say"— She gestured to Matt— "I tried to save the babes to earn my way to Heaven. If I'm to die, maybe saving an innocent will save me soul."

"I decree who is and isn't a lady in my kingdom. Kneel!" Jon said in a voice that rang with command.

Anise's face flushed and she dropped slowly to her knees in the mud of the road.

Jon drew his sword and lightly touch both of her shoulders. "Arise, Baroness of High Street, our faithful servant. You have much to learn, but your heart is large and courage great. Be welcome in Camelot."

Anise rose shakily to her feet and stared at Jon with her mouth agape and her eyes wide. "You be the king of the Fae?"

"Yep." Ethan slapped Jon on the back.

"You'll have funds enough to hire nursemaids and rooms to house them in." Jon glanced meaningfully at the women gathered around Anise.

"Warren calls," Maria said unexpectedly, interrupting them. She disappeared a moment later.

"He went to begin tracking," Ethan said before Jen could ask. She hadn't even realized he'd left.

"Go," Jon said and kissed her cheek." I'll see the children safely home."

"And Anise. I promised her my protection."

"She shall have mine."

Jen touched the pulse in his neck with her fingertips, then summoned Gallant. All the women exclaimed again. She offered Ethan her hand and urged Gallant into the air.

War Paint

A brilliant flash of green caught Jen's eye.

"I hope that isn't Ling or Sota," Jen said worriedly.

Green sparks drifted to the treetops and disappeared. Whoever had casted had canceled the spell before it could light the ground. A mental command changed Gallant's direction. As she drew closer, she saw Maria flying in lazy circles. Jen followed her to the ground. At the last second Maria transformed, landing on her human feet.

"We would've summoned you, but Sam needed time to get us ready."

Jen reached forward and tipped Maria's chin. A design of vines encircled her head and trailed across her left cheek, completely covering one eye. Thorns outlined the other eye. Maria's eyes flared blue and she gave Jen a hard smile.

"Sam's idea and a good one. War paint. We can't control Danu showing in our eyes when we're emotional, but the paint will warn we'll attack and hopefully humans will be more at ease with our flaring eyes." The blue faded from Maria's eyes as she spoke.

Jen joined Sam beside a small fire and watched with interest as she finished the last strokes on Warren's face.

"All done. Give me two minutes, Jen." She handed Ethan a small jar of white paint and dipped her brush into the black paint she held. Ethan used his fingers to trace a wavy line beneath his left eye and his fingertip to make a line of dots below his right.

Sam began painting Jen's face as Warren spoke. "I ran through the town here and marked every house that had children. All children are greenish-yellow in my minds-eye. We'll have to break in and question each family."

Warren said, "Maria, we'll bring any children we find here to you. I'm worried they'll kill them if word leaks out that we've come for them, so be quiet and leave the people tied and gagged behind you."

He handed Jen a map of the village and traced his finger along the line of houses sketched on it. "These here Sam and I will check. Ethan can get the bigger house and the three smaller ones near it. You start on the outskirts and work your way in. Almost every house contains at least one child. We'll have to check each." Warren placed both hands on Jen's shoulders and lightly shook her. "Jen, if Danu will force you to harm the people, let us go. We can't afford to make noise."

"I'm in control," Jen said and rose to her feet.

Sam made no protest although she clearly hadn't finished her design. The arrows on Sam's cheeks were dry and a bit cracked as if she'd applied it a day ago. Jen wanted to ask how things were going at home, but it'd have to wait. The children called to her.

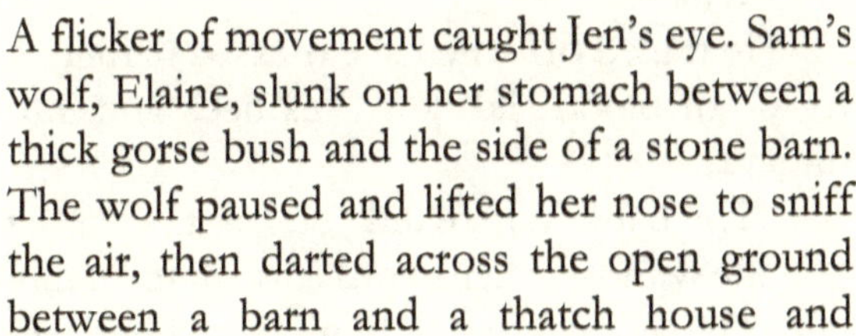

A flicker of movement caught Jen's eye. Sam's wolf, Elaine, slunk on her stomach between a thick gorse bush and the side of a stone barn. The wolf paused and lifted her nose to sniff the air, then darted across the open ground between a barn and a thatch house and jumped inside an open window.

The inhabitants didn't make a sound. Jen glanced around, and seeing no one, ran on the verge of the muddy road to her target home three doors down from the house Elaine had entered. This house too was made of thatch with wooden shutters blocking the window. Jen eased the shutters open, letting out a gust of fetid air.

Snores and snorts greeted her entrance. The entire family slept together on a single pallet against the far wall. A fire flickered in the fireplace, lighting the room with a wavering glow. For this day and age this was considered a nice home. It had a stone floor and a thatch ceiling high enough you didn't need to stoop. It also possessed furniture; four stools, a wooden chair with well-worn arms, a table, a wooden chest, and a built-in counter beside the fireplace.

Jen drew her sword and pressed the tip against the sleeping man's throat.

"Wha—"

He trailed off when she pressed harder. A trickle of blood slid down his neck and into his shirt.

"The baby. Where did you get it?"

She withdrew her sword enough to let him talk. The woman beside him opened her eyes and grabbed his arm hard.

"I'll know if you lie," Jen said and let her sword flare blue. She was lying. She had no way of knowing if they spoke truth or not, but they seemed to believe her. She could only feel truth from a lie if enough magic were present and emotion ran high, and she could sense evil if she wished. There was no evil in this village, which relieved her.

The woman whimpered and the three older children beside her stirred. Jen's gaze flicked to the sleeping baby, and the sword in her hand pulsed.

"Bishop Maximus…. Please— spare my wife and children." The man clasped his hands and his lips moved as though he prayed.

"And where did he tell you the child was from?"

"He told us there's sickness in the city and offered us gold to raise this child as if it were our own till he came to retrieve it."

"What were you told to do if someone asked about them?"

"Nothing. Who'd ask other than their parents?"

Jen lowered her sword and stepped back. Every man she'd questioned had said the same.

The man sat slowly, his gaze darting to the

pitchfork in the corner beside the door.

"Many were brought. We thought them the children of nobles and rich merchants," he continued.

"He lied. They're the children of Camelot stolen by violence." Jen threw two strips of cloth to the man. "Tie your wife and do it tightly. I believe you and have no wish to harm you, but I can't take the chance you'll alert others. I'll leave you in peace, tied, but alive."

The man nodded and tied his unresisting wife. Tears trickled down the woman's cheeks. Jen felt bad for scaring her. Bishop Maximus had a lot to answer for.

"Who else received our children?"

The man gave her names and told where they lived. She gave him no indication they'd already recovered children from the places he named. Sweat trickled down his brow and he glanced continually to the children sleeping beside his wife.

"We have guards set outside. If you try to signal, you'll be silenced. When the sun rises, your children can release you."

The man relaxed slightly, nodded again, and offered his hands so she might tie him. She gathered the baby, climbed through the window, and shut the shutters behind her. The small village remained quiet. The babe in her arms cooed and fussed but didn't cry. She sprinted away.

Maria glanced up from the child she held and gestured with her chin to a mossy indentation in the ground beside her. The black design Sam had drawn on her face and over her head gave her an even fiercer expression when she scowled. Jen lifted her fingertips to Maria's cheek then dropped her hand not wanting to smudge Sam's artwork.

Maria smiled slightly and lifted a hand to her head.

"I'm freaking them out even without glowing eyes or sword. How many are still missing?" Jen asked as she leaned over the indentations and examined the children, most of whom slept.

"Six still to find," Maria said.

"He told the same story."

Maria burped the baby she held while she spoke. "Yeah, I believe them. They didn't know the children were stolen. I wonder what they would've done when rumors reached here?"

Jen placed the child she carried into an empty mossy depression and covered it with a light blanket. "Killed them maybe? Or perhaps someone would come to us? We'll never know. Stay alert and summon me if anyone comes."

Maria nodded agreement as Jen summoned Gallant. A foot off the ground, she galloped back with only the slight whistle of wind to betray her presence. The village remained quiet. Sam climbed from the window Elaine had entered and jogged over.

"Not one of ours. Elaine will stay. I tied him and the wife, but he was angry enough to do something rash. Called the men who took the kids greedy bastards. I think he was angry because he didn't get one. I hate these men. His kids and wife are terrified of him."

"Even where we came from some men still treated women like possessions. It'll take time, Sam."

"I know, but I wanted to smack him."

Jen snickered and threw an arm around her shoulder. "Let's get the rest. Send up a flare and gather everyone. None of the foster parents have orders to hurt the kids and the rest are out of town. It shouldn't matter if we wake them."

Sam lifted her bow and pulled back the string. A glowing green arrow soared into the sky where it exploded silently in a blindingly bright flash of greenish-white. Motes of green trailed to the ground where they sank and infused the ground with light until Jen stood in daylight brightness.

Elaine jumped through the window. Immediately, the man inside began thrashing about.

Sam flicked her fingers and Elaine spun and jumped back through the window.

"That guy… he needs a beat down."

Jen snickered.

Warren ran up, holding a toddler to his chest. The child stared about him with wide eyes but didn't cry. *Rangers calming aura made them the perfect nursemaids*, Jen thought wistfully, wishing she possessed a calming aura as Warren handed the child he held to Sam.

"Where did you get this one?" Jen asked.

"Last house on this street."

"If Ethan retrieved one, the last five will be outside of town. I got directions—"

"Me too. They all spilled the beans." Warren grinned at her.

The black batwings bracketing his eyes likely gave him a menacing air to the natives although they reminded her of Kiss stage makeup.

Ethan arrived empty handed. Jen's heart sank. He kissed Jen's cheek and lifted the light blanket from the child to examine him a moment before kissing Sam. The baby burbled nonsense words, and Ethan smiled.

Warren bumped fists with him and gestured west.

"The rest are further out," Warren said.

Ethan rested his hand on the child's back and turned an angry face to Jen. "Another one dead, Jen. The child never woke. There must be an accounting for this. Whether they intended their deaths or not, they killed those children."

"Bishop Maximus is responsible, not the families here," Sam said.

"Don't forget Bishop fucking Rufus and the goddamn prince!" Warren snapped.

Jen turned to examine the street where men peeked furtively from shuttered windows. "Go retrieve the rest. I'll join you in a few minutes." She hugged her husband hard. "No one involved will get away with it."

He turned himself invisible and sprinted west.

Jen infused her voice with will and bellowed as Warren and Sam jogged away, "The Fae have declared Bishop Maximus, Bishop Rufus, and Prince Mondred fugitives from justice! Any found harboring them will be considered our enemy! Your king will be deposed! His daughter Princess Chrodesinde will ascend the throne! She is our ally and won't tolerate the theft of children, regardless of class, nationality or station, in her realm! All those involved will be found! Your only hope for mercy is to turn yourself in and tell what you know!"

Jen's magically amplified voice bounced between the walls of the squat homes. Shutters banged opened and closed the length of the street. She waited five minutes and repeated her warning. A thought summoned Gallant, and she cantered down the street, holding aloft her glowing sword.

Dawn was breaking when Jen arrived in front of Jon, clutching two screaming children.

He winced and held out his arms. She handed him a child as Anise offered a bottle of warm water.

"Three more dead, Jon. Ethan is retrieving the bodies for burial in Camelot."

The baby in Jon's arms shuddered, making Jen wince in sympathy. The dead angered Jon, which empowered his aura. He was scaring the child he held.

Jon patted the child he carried. "Lady Anise, will you take the children, please? Jen, take Sam and head south. I'm not exactly sure where we are. You'll need to find the airship and lead it back here."

"Are you sure it's safe?" Jen handed the child she carried to Anise who bobbed her head as she accepted the baby.

"Well, tests show it floats. It isn't complete yet. Without the druids or paladins to pull it we wouldn't get far. Motors are still in development. The two, small, foot-operated propellers can't do much propulsion wise. They're meant to steer it. But as long as no flames get near it…"

Jen grimaced. "Can't we just summon back? Isn't this our zone now?"

"Not until I kill that lying bastard Childebert. He ran like a coward. Headed to his brother, I think. I'll worry about him later. Let him plot his little heart out. We need to get these children safe and find the rest of them. There's plenty of time to find and stop our enemies. You can bet they're thinking twice right now about attacking us!" Jon finished viciously.

The baby Jon carried began to cry. Red of face it scrunched its eyes and pushed away. Jen hastily took the child and cooed, "There, there, you're safe, little one." She motioned Jon away and continued to speak comforting words until the baby calmed. Sam appeared and settled the children she carried in the wagon before taking the hiccupping child from Jen.

The baby relaxed, tear smeared lashes sliding closed on a dirty face. Jen joined Jon at the edge of the muddy road where he stood alone over two hundred yards away surrounded in a blue cloud.

"My rage is freaking the kids out."

She placed a comforting hand on his shoulder. "We're all angry, Jon. I'm going to take Anise back to Paris and follow her leads. You say there isn't any hurry, but I can't wait for this."

"I know. That isn't what I meant. I meant there's no hurry for our vengeance. But there will be vengeance!"

"Good! Jon, I feel your conflicting emotions. None of this is your fault. We all think you're doing a great job."

"*Ha!*"

"No, seriously. Our life experience hasn't prepared us for this level of violence, this harshness these people live with and accept as if it were normal. We literally can't picture acting in the ways they do, but we're learning. I think we need vengeance, more to show them we aren't weak than to punish the perpetrators. Nothing we do can bring back the dead, but we can make the world think twice about trying something like this again. Show them no mercy. I want you to be angry. I need you to be angry! Your anger will be our shield. Let the world feel it and cower in fear. The world understands fear and might of arms. Show them we're mighty, and once they're afraid, we'll teach them kindness."

"Maybe you should be queen."

"Hell, no! Kuan is right. This is your destiny as it's mine to protect the weak. The children call to me. Danu pushes. They're her children and she's afraid for them. I want to save these kids, but she doesn't care about them. They mean nothing to her. I'm unable to balance her needs with those of the normal people in our realm. If it were up to me, I'd abandon Camelot and our allies and encourage the Fae to rampage about the world until we find them."

"Don't think I don't want to, but we can't, and not because it would be wrong, but because those people rely on my protection."

"We are as our natures make us. More than humanly possible as Danu shapes us to her will."

Jon drew her into an embrace, tucking her head beneath his chin. The steady beat of his heart against her cheek filled her with peace. She hadn't lied or exaggerated. She needed him to be angry. His anger soothed her wild need. *No, not hers, Danu's,* she thought ruefully and hugged Jon tighter. His anger felt like safety to Danu, and she was suddenly exhausted, wishing to lay at his feet and sleep.

He kissed the top of her head. Danu transmitted her feelings to him as clearly as his to her.

"You should rest," he murmured.

Jen said nothing. Her son was with fanatics who thought nothing of burning children alive. How could she rest?

They remained in an embrace until Ethan and Sam joined them. Ethan laid his glowing hand against her cheek. She smiled ruefully and kissed him before summoning Gallant and offering Sam her hand. A human man would be jealous to see his wife hold another so closely but to a Fae close contact was necessary to pacify and comfort Danu. Ethan's brief touch had revealed his worry and love without a hint of jealousy.

HMS Enterprise

Broad sweeps of Gallant's wings gusted cool air over Jen. The heat of Sam's body against her back warmed her, more from her presence than her body heat, and it occurred to Jen she hadn't made much time for her best friend lately.

"Sorry, Sam. I'm so busy that I've been neglecting you."

"I'm not a child! I didn't mean it that way," she added quickly. "I meant, I understand completely. We're good, Jen." She snickered. "And Kirk keeps me busy."

"You guys are happy?"

"More than happy, which sometimes makes me feel bad and I have to remind myself I didn't choose any of this and there's nothing wrong with making the best of things."

"No there isn't. I feel that too sometimes, like I stole Ethan from his wife."

"You didn't."

They flew quietly for a few minutes before Sam said, "I know we've spoken of the kids before, but I hope you know in your heart that I love them as if you'd borne them."

"That makes me so damn mad! How dare Miguel steal them from me! I'm sure Danu meant me to have them, and instead they were born years too early and have all this crap hanging over their heads. I wanted to wait until we were firmly settled here before having children."

"I think you'll have to wait hundreds of years for that."

Jen snorted in derision.

"No, seriously. Arden thinks we'll live a lot longer than a human, just another thing for them to hate us for."

The idea shocked Jen. It also made her uneasy. If she were a human she might be jealous of magic, but longer life might push her jealousy to hatred. "Makes sense I guess, what with perfect health from heals, but humans could use health potions."

"Arden says potions don't do the same thing. She's been studying the differing types of heals, and casted heals regenerate every cell to perfect condition while healing potions only regenerate damaged cells. She thinks it will provide a greater life span if used daily but nowhere near as long as a Fae will live. And really, at the cost of a potion, almost no one could afford to take one a day."

Jen banished her worry of differing lifespans to the back of her mind. It'd be years before anyone noticed and warlock potions would help. Kirk wouldn't always be the only warlock and the price would lower. "We're so lucky Kirk was along and willing to help us. Without him, we couldn't pay for anything for a long time."

"Arden is pissed he charges for health potions, but it isn't like he's trying to be greedy. He was willing to help the plagued for free."

Jen patted the hand on her waist. "No one doubts his generosity."

"He is generous. And kind. More than I saw until we married. He's working with Rob, building orphanages, and he wants to build me a palace with high walls surrounded by deep woods."

Sam laughed and spread her arms. "My life is so surreal." When she sobered, she rested her forehead against Jen's back. "I'm afraid I'll lose myself in Danu. Things that used to horrify me don't bother me, and it worries me. I killed people, Jen. Shouldn't I feel bad about that?"

"They were trying to kill you… and maybe you will feel bad once this all calms down. Not that I think you should." She paused thoughtfully. "Danu's reaction to the deaths of her enemies is different from mine. She feels no remorse. I do, but I also see the necessity. Believe me, I hate the killing, but I hate the thought of my family hurt more. It isn't wrong to protect yourself and those you love. Steve's kids will need to be watched closely, but the rest of us will be able to balance our human nature with Danu."

"Those poor kids. All these poor kids. A nation of orphans."

"And we'll show the world how to care for those less fortunate. We'll be a nation that cherishes life too. Give our church fifty years and our citizens will begin to see the merits of equality."

"That was a brilliant idea Cass had."

He has a lot of them. I knew him for years and never knew he was such a serious student."

"Back in the future, we spoke of travel, but briefly. Basically, he reassured me that planes were safe. Even sent me a copy of his dissertation on air travel."

Both women laughed a moment.

"I wonder if he'd have continued playing once he received his doctorate or if being a history professor would've drawn him away from the game?" Sam mused.

"He'd have continued," Jen said firmly. "I wonder how much Danu influenced him in the future."

"Like Kuan?"

"I guess not," Jen said after a moment's reflection. "Kuan is uniquely connected to Danu. I guess Cass was just our good luck like Arden, Henry, Nina, and all the people with skills we need. I just feel useless in that respect. What good is a computer degree here?"

"Better than being a trained dancer."

Jen snorted with laughter as Sam continued, "We'll have electricity soon. Arden already has it in her lab. Maybe you can fix the broken computers. There must be tons of useful things on them."

"Who has time… two kids, a husband, and a job that takes me all over."

Sam tightened her grasp and spoke hesitantly. "I sort of feel bad for not adopting, but none of the kids call to me. I mean, I like them and all, but…"

"Don't worry about it. No one expects you too. Someday, you and Kirk will be ready and have kids."

Joash appeared above Jen. Bright gold underwings flashed in the night sky. Jen halted Gallant and held out her arm so Joash could rest while she read the note he carried. "They're over Paris. Brandon wants to know if he summons us will you be able to find your way back to Jon?"

"Yes. Never getting lost is one of the cooler things of being a ranger. The sky is a map I can read at a glance. If I've been there once, every tree and rock I pass becomes a signpost telling me exactly how far away my goal is."

Jen handed Joash the note she jotted, and the bird disappeared.

"What would we do without them? We need a better means of communications."

"I'm just grateful we have them. Brandon calls," Sam said a moment before she disappeared.

Jen accepted her summons a second later and appeared before Brandon in a rocky field. "Holy crap!" she said when she glanced up.

The *HMS Enterprise* glided above her head about three hundred yards above the trees. A dark whale of a ship, it coasted silently through the black night.

"If you grab the left line, we can help Cami and Kuan pull it," Brandon said.

"Are you sure it's safe?"

"Cass assures us it is as long as we have no sparks. He based the design off a Zeppelin used for tours. It can carry about twenty thousand pounds. Well, more now, that's the estimate for when it's finished. Right now, it has no engines, hence muscle power. Landing will be tricky, but we can load and offload while it's in the air. The kids will be fine. We brought supplies. Their families are worried and grateful. This is a good chance to show them technology can help them, and it scared the hell out of the people of Paris when we floated over," Brandon finished in satisfaction.

Jen summoned Gallant again and offered Sam a hand to mount. The massive airship impressed and awed Jen and she'd seen blimps and large aircraft before. She could only imagine the Parisian's panic when this behemoth floated overhead.

Sam grabbed a taunt line and shimmied up it. Jen resisted the urge to call a warning but sighed in relief when Sam reached the hull and scrambled aboard. It only took her a few minutes to find the rope and don the dangling harness.

The ship slid smoothly through the air. It felt good to stretch her muscles. Wind resistance felt like peddling uphill. She was just beginning to tire when she spotted Sam's green flare to her left.

Jon must have summoned her back, Jen thought as she headed Gallant to the spot of light in the woods. She shrugged from the harness and joined Brandon, letting the airship continue on its momentum.

"I'll help ferry the passengers aboard, but I'm not going back to Camelot. We have a lead I'm going to follow."

Brandon said, "Get some rest, Jen. You look exhausted. "

"Can't, the kids need me; I feel it."

"They need you well. Let me go track these leads."

"I need to do this, Bran. Danu insists. I'll rest later."

"Well, compromise then. Help us load up, and catch a nap as we return. You can disembark at the coast."

Jen nodded agreement and galloped Gallant through the air to the waiting children.

The massive airship coasted to a stop above them, casting a shadow that seemed to blot the stars from the sky.

"We're riding in that?"

Dread laced Anise's voice.

Jen peered upward at the ship. The wide bottom of the wooden hull blocked the view above it, leaving just the ends of the two hundred and fifty-foot-long balloon peeking out. Grown into the wood, an uplifted eagle head graced the prow with wings backswept along the sides and bottom.

After much trial and error working with Cass, Kuan had specially grown the wood and plants used in the fabric that covered the semi-rigid balloon to be lightweight and stronger than nature intended.

"They are. We're only going as far as Paris." Jen turned to Brandon. "Will you come back and get Anise? I'll leave her on the coast where Maria met us the first time we visited Paris."

"Sure."

Jen turned to the cowering women who stared upward with terrified expressions.

"It's just a ship. We make a gas that floats. It's science, not magic, and no more dangerous than a sea voyage. The flight to Camelot should only take a few hours. You can ask Cass for a tour, and he can explain how it works."

The women didn't appear at all reassured by her words. Maria soared overhead, clutching a basket in her talons. The women exclaimed and milled in a nervous bunch. The exclamations grew louder when Kuan and Cami spiraled to a landing, both grasping baskets, and transformed to humans.

"We brought sacks for carrying the kids," Kuan said and handed her a sling like contraption. He adjusted it to his satisfaction and stepped back. "Three at a time. Be careful of the one on your back." He smiled at the women but made no attempt to engage in conversation.

Jen handed Ethan a baby sling, mounted Gallant again and carefully placed a child Warren handed her into the sling she wore. When she had three children settled, he offered a basket containing two toddlers and climbed on behind her holding a one-year-old against his chest. The child gazed about with wide eyes but didn't cry. Jen again blessed the ranger's passive ability to calm those near them.

Gallant hovered alongside the ship so Sam could take the children from them. It didn't take long to bring them all aboard.

On her return trip, Jen offered her hand to Anise who gripped it and let herself be pulled to Gallant's back.

"This feels like a dream, not a true thing," she said in awe as Gallant soared into the sky.

"I feel that way too sometimes," Jen assured her.

Jon waited at the stern of the ship and lifted Anise aboard. Jen returned for the others who cried and clutched her hard but boarded. Jen let Gallant return to mist, dropping her and Ethan. They both grabbed the sides as they fell and swung aboard.

"Cass needs to put a ramp or something off the back for us," Jen complained as she straightened. She stamped her feet. "Feels nice and solid. I'll help pull this back to the coast, then Anise can show us where she was taken."

"No. You sleep the two hours it'll take to get there. Maria can help pull it," Jon said.

"We all need rest, sweetheart," Ethan added in a cajoling voice.

"Go below. That's an order," Jon said.

Jon's command settled Danu as he'd known it would. Jen smiled ruefully at him and headed to the steep stairs. The main cabin consisted of bare walls and flooring now covered with pallets and baskets holding the retrieved children and crates of supplies. The women still stared about in awe. Only Anise gazed from one of the wide windows lining the side of the ship.

"Jen," Cass said and clasped her hand. "We put pallets inside the two back cabins. We didn't have time to furnish the interior. Go rest. We can see to the kids."

Babies fussed, bringing the women from their awed staring. Sam and Maria began filling and handing out bottles.

"Maria needs to rest too."

"And she will," Warren said as he sat cross-legged at his wife's feet to feed a crying child. "She can find an uninhabited forest, assume her tree shape and sleep while we track. We can summon her and Ethan to us."

Jen glanced at the rows of fussing children.

"They got this," Ethan said and pulled her by the hand to the narrow corridor at the rear of the ship. Two cabins at the prow and aft separated the stairs to the engine compartment and bridge from the main room.

"The bathrooms don't work yet, sorry!" Cass called after them.

"When this is finished, I want to go on a sightseeing trip," Ethan said as he gazed out the dark, cabin window.

Jen flopped on the pallet and closed her

eyes.

"*Mm*, sounds good," she mumbled and fell asleep before he answered.

A baby's wail pulled her from a sound sleep. Bright sunlight lanced her eyes. She groaned and rolled to her side, wishing there was a cover to pull over her head.

"You've got to see this," Ethan said.

His odd tone of voice got her attention. She rose and stretched, muscles and joints flexing and popping, before joining him at the window.

"We should talk Kuan into growing small balconies," Jen said as she leaned against the glass to see out. Paris lay below her spread out in all its squalid glory, but what had captured Ethan's attention was an army of men gathering outside the city.

"Childebert is going to try to fight us. What an idiot," Jen said.

Ethan snickered. "I estimate about three thousand, but it's been less than a week. I'm sure he can raise more men than that."

Jen shrugged and turned to examine the room. "I'm starving."

"Look, they're gathering on rooftops."

Ethan gestured out the window. "God, we must be terrifying. Imagine if this happened to us. Powerful people from the future arrive and tell us where doing everything wrong, that how we think is wrong…"

"How they think is wrong!" Jen called over her shoulder. She had no desire to see the awe and fear on their faces.

"Close your eyes," Jen said to Anise.

Anise tightened her hold on Jen's waist but kept her eyes open.

Jen shrugged and jumped, expecting the woman she carried to shriek, but Anise remained quiet. The impact with the ground barely jarred Jen. Her shield absorbed the damage, making it feel like she'd jumped mere feet, not three hundred yards. She placed Anise on her feet and summoned Gallant.

"Is all you need to do is show me where Bishop Rufus met you."

"It be on the docks, my lady."

"Just Jen. I hope we become friends."

Anise smiled and Jen realized she was younger than she'd first thought. Worry had prematurely aged her. She was likely not much older than Jen was.

"Let me take her, Jen," Ethan said.

Jen shook her head. "She'll be safe with Warren and I. Warren can backtrack the men who kidnapped Anise while I continue down the coast. I'm tempted to head straight for Italy but maybe they plan to sail north to Germany."

"Promise you won't leave France without us."

"I won't. I'll summon you in a few hours, but you could go home. Warren and I can search."

"I'm tempted, but when you find them, you'll need me. And we *will* find them, Jen."

"The world is so big. I'm afraid Danu will keep me from home forever." Jen's voice hitched, and her breath caught on the lump in her throat.

She missed Diana and wanted to see her to assure herself she was well, but Alex needed her. It felt as if her soul was being torn in two. She tried to tell herself Diana was fine and wouldn't miss them but she knew she lied to herself. Diana was a Fae and needed her mother. She needed to be held close as much as Jen needed to hold her close. Tears sprang to her eyes.

Ethan wiped a trickling tear with his fingertips. "Then home will come with you.

We'll work something out. Gallant can fly much faster than a boat can sail. Brandon will be searching with a ranger too."

She kissed her husband hard and urged Gallant aloft. Anise pressed against her back and grasped her waist tightly even though Warren sat behind her.

"Thank you, Anise," Warren said. "This must be terrifying. Not just flying but dealing with us. I swear to you, we aren't demons."

Jen felt her shrug.

"I already be damned."

"God loves you. Your courage and goodness shine. I'm honored to meet you and hope we become friends," Warren said.

"I agree. How could God turn his back on a woman who'd risk her life for the children of strangers?" Jen clasped Anise's cold hand in hers. "In Camelot, you'll be our treasured friend."

Anise remained silent until they reached the dock. "There, where that small ship now lies."

"The one with the blue stripe on the sail?"

"Aye."

"This is close enough, Jen." Warren let himself fall into the water beneath them.

Anise exclaimed in dismay.

"He's fine," Jen said as she turned Gallant

and urged him higher. "He can breathe underwater and no one will see him on land. Brandon will bring you to Camelot, I swear it. The airship flies slowly so it might be nighttime before he arrives, but he will return. I wish I could see you safely home, but my husband or Maria will guard you until Brandon comes."

"Did Bishop Rufus steal your child?"

"Yes. Mine and Danu's. They're all Danu's children; Fae like me. Danu lives inside the Fae and she wants her children back."

"The blue glow?"

"Yes. When a Fae gets emotional, Danu manifests."

"Your king is very upset then."

Jen snorted. "His wife is ill, his realm attacked, his charges stolen; I'd say upset is an understatement."

"When he executed those men, they groveled before him and my fear of him left me."

Jen bit back a laugh. She hadn't even realized he'd executed the two men who'd surrendered. "That's his magic. One of the spells a warrior has is called Fearful Presence. The angrier they are, the more frightened their enemies become. Weak enemies will cower before him unable to move or they'll run away screaming. Fae don't really feel the effect unless his anger is directed at us. His citizens feel it like you did, either with an urge to flee as if a storm is about to break, or a release of tension and a deeper trust. He was protecting you, so I'm not surprised you felt trust. The feeling fades as his anger does.

Jen clasped Anise's hand in hers. "Anise, be careful in Camelot. The Fae will never harm you, but men and women who hate us might. Allow no one into your home you don't trust. Our warlocks will lock your doors so none may enter without permission, but if you let them in, they can harm you. Sam will train a wolf for you, and we can hire guards, but guards can be bribed."

"Life is dangerous, but one can't hide from it. I'd heard of your kind but hadn't considered meeting one. Now that I have, I no think you be demons, but I be an ignorant woman."

"You can learn to read and write. Anything we know, we'll teach you."

"The priests say that be the temptation that proves your demonic origins, but I never understood how knowledge proves you be demons. The priests teach to read and write too."

"The minds of men are indeed a mystery."

Anise laughed and was still laughing when Jen landed lightly beside Ethan.

Ethan lifted her from Gallant's back and kissed Jen's cheek.

"God speed," Anise said and lifted a hand in farewell.

Never Give Up

Miles of dense forest spread out beneath Jen to the horizon. She'd lost track of where they were days ago. Trees blocked the view of the river she'd been following, and Jen growled. Ethan placed a hand on her shoulder. His presence didn't comfort her.

"Jen, go lower. There's no point in flying blindly," he said.

Gallant's wings stirred the air, kicking up a cool breeze that soothed Jen's hot cheeks. She'd been angry and scared so long now it felt like a permanent condition.

"Please, Jen."

A thought nudged Gallant downward. The horse spiraled down in an impossibly tight loop. He didn't need his wings to fly.

Magic kept him aloft and propelled him where Jen willed.

She dismissed Gallant with a thought and she and Ethan plummeted to earth, crashing through the tree limbs. The destruction, mild though it was, eased Jen. She wanted to slash and scream. Every day that Alex remained in the hands of cruel captors added to her stress. Her eyes shone blue continually now and she was unable to dispel her protection armor. When she dropped her sword, it reappeared the instant her hands emptied.

Ethan's fear and worry exasperated hers. She avoided touching him as much as she could, afraid she'd lose control and kill the next group of people they ran into whether they were guilty or not.

"Fuck!" Jen snarled, gesturing with her sword, slashing at the tree limbs. "I thought I was right over it. Go west. I'll go east. We're bound to run into the river again."

"Jen… we need to go back."

"I'm not—"

He kissed her hard, surprising her.

"No, we'll never give up, but we need more summon stones and let's face it, we're lost. It's stupid to search this way. Without a ranger, we could pass right over them."

"I can't give up. Even if I wanted to."

"No. I know, and I don't want too. But we can do this smarter. Let's go back and stock up and then head straight to Maximus's hometown. We'll question everyone and find out who he might trust, where he might go."

Jen slumped and sat in the brush, leaning against a tree. Ethan crouched before her. "You need to rest. I know you don't want to. Hell, I don't want to. It kills me thinking we might be too late. He's so small…" Ethan trailed off and rubbed his face hard. "I wish I could summon Gallant, but I can't. So, we're going home, and you can sleep while I restock our bags. Diana needs us too, and we need her."

"One day," Jen said and extended her hand.

Ethan pulled her to her feet.

"One day. Twenty-four hours from when we arrive."

Jen began jogging, forcing herself through the dense shrubbery. It felt good to stretch and use her muscles, but the slow pace was aggravating. Ethan followed, letting her lead until they reached a clearing large enough for Gallant to manifest. It took Jen five seconds to summon him, and her frown grew. Ethan said nothing. He knew as well as she that she was dangerously depleted. Flying used magic and she'd been resting the bare minimum to regenerate her magic for days now and had no reserves.

She headed Gallant straight east, urging him high enough for a panoramic view. They raced across the sky so far above the thick woods it just appeared green.

"Do you need to rest?" Ethan asked twenty minutes later. He squirmed behind her a moment before handing her a sandwich wrapped in paper.

"Yes. I'll sleep a few hours. Don't let me sleep too long. I wish we had potions like in the game."

Ethan hugged her and kissed her neck. Jen let the paper flutter away in the wind and Ethan handed her a bottle of water. "Dillion's conjured water is better than nothing."

Jen used both hands to sip from the cut-crystal decanter. Dillion's water refreshed in a way real water didn't. It did help restore magic, but unlike in the game where you could sit and drink two bottles to refresh yourself completely, you could only force yourself to drink so much in real life. She managed half the bottle before handing it back to Ethan. He placed it back into his pack and settled against her back again.

"Stop at the first clearing we see," he said.

She nodded agreement, already guiding Gallant lower. *Drinking a lot of water also had other drawbacks,* she thought irritably as her bladder began to complain.

"There," Ethan said, pointing over her shoulder.

Without her will, Gallant turned and descended. Ethan could control him, but Gallant would disappear if she slept. They'd tried to have her sleep astride him but as soon as she fell asleep, he returned to mist. It took her will to make him corporeal. Ethan could even ride him alone and out of the zone, but Jen hated to do that, afraid she'd fall asleep or forget and call Gallant, leaving her husband trapped in a different zone.

The clearing Ethan had spotted was an overgrown campsite beside a dirt track that others had used. By the height of the weeds, it'd been a while since anyone had come along.

Jen stepped behind a tree to do her business, then laid on the ground and was asleep in seconds. Ethan would guard her.

Sunset tinted the sky a rosy pink when Ethan woke her. She used the tree again before summoning Gallant. As Gallant soared into the darkening sky, a glitter of light caught her eye and she instinctively headed toward it.

"We can't stop and investigate everything

we pass or we'll never get there. That's exactly what we're doing wrong," Ethan said.

Gallant halted, surging forward and stopping again as Jen fought Danu as hard as she could. Without her will, Gallant wheeled and charged east. Ethan urged her horse faster until they flew along at her top speed. Jen cried as the light faded behind them.

"I'm so sorry," Ethan said.

"Don't touch me," Jen gasped as he laid his hand on her cheek. "It makes it harder to feel your pain too."

"I'm sorry," he said again, this time grimly. He withdrew his hand and by his movement Jen knew he was opening his pack. She accepted the water he handed her and sipped as Gallant flew. They raced home as fast as Gallant could go. She landed when she tired and napped for thirty minutes, peed, and remounted. This time it was easier to fly past the small house in the distance, but Danu still pushed her to go and urged her to violence.

"They're innocent people," she said.

Danu didn't care. She wanted her children.

"They're innocent!" she screamed.

"Jen… How can I help?"

"Get me our children!" Jen snapped and immediately felt bad. He was worried too. Alex was as much his son as he was hers. "I'm sorry. I'm not mad at you, but I want them so much. It's so hard holding her back when I want them too. Our son could be dead already. We might never know. And if he's alive, what will they do to him?" She began to cry again, her tears cold on her face.

For the first time since they'd married she felt alone. Ethan hugged her tightly and she sobbed and turned to face him. Danu surrounded her in a wild storm. He kept his magic from her, but she knew he was heartsick as well.

"We'll find him, Jen."

"And the humans will try again."

"*Shh*, don't think like that." He ran his hands through her hair and rubbed her back as he spoke. "Some are bad, but not all. If you start hating them too, you won't be able to stop Danu. And you know that wouldn't be right. Remember, we were once human too. We have human friends, good people who deserve our help."

"I wish Dillion had bought that locate spell."

"Me too, but we do have Kirk's minion. We can give our kids jewelry and his minion can find it."

"They'll just take it off when they take them."

"Kirk could enchant it but if they do take it, we could use it to locate the thief," Ethan said with vicious satisfaction. "Only the Fae know the full abilities of a warlock. We'll get them pets the rangers can train and enchant their clothing. Our friends will help us."

Jen sniffed hard and pulled away to wipe her face. "I wish we could be normal. I picture us having dinner with my parents and going to watch our kids play little league. We'd have been so happy…" Tears choked her, and she squeezed her eyes closed.

"We *will* be normal. We have a huge family that loves us, and the kids will have friends and play-dates." Ethan's voice cracked, and he kissed her cheek. Neither said another word until Gallant settled to a landing twenty minutes later.

"Get salty foods when you restock," Jen said as she sipped Dillion's conjured water.

Remounted and flying again after another half hour catnap, she yawned and stretched. Weights pressed on her eyelids and her muscles ached. Each time they stopped she fell asleep instantly and woke harder. Ethan guided Gallant now while she rested against his back.

"Jen! Wake up!"

Wind whistled passed Jen's face as rough

hands shook her. It took her a second to realize Ethan had grabbed her and they fell.

"I'm awake," she said, and his grip relaxed.

"We're far up. I was trying to place us by the landscape. You okay?"

"Yeah, sorry."

"We're almost home. Sleep a few hours. Who knows what we'll find there and you should be rested enough to fight if we need to."

They fell over cultivated fields. Starlight and a half-moon illuminated the sparsely populated countryside. She gritted her teeth and closed her eyes. Danu pushed, wanting Jen to search. She summoned Gallant and yanked her husband to his back.

"I'll make us camp. Head to that pond there." He pointed to their right, and she turned Gallant to follow his pointing finger. "You're lucky I hadn't fallen asleep too. If you hadn't woken…" he trailed off, but his tone was grim and worried.

She longed to feel him be happy or content. Deep and dark, his depression smothered her. She missed the physical closeness of sleeping cuddled together too.

"Can we be a normal couple and just sleep together?" she asked as Gallant hovered a foot from the ground. She slid off and stretched until her back popped.

"I miss you too," he said and unfurled a thick sleeping bag he'd taken from his pack. He began removing his clothes. Jen sighed gratefully when his bare skin touched hers and curled tightly against him. She fell asleep and slept deeply without dreams. Sunlight on her face woke her. The smell of bacon frying pulled her from the warm cocoon of her blanket.

"Eat first and we'll go," he said as he handed her a bacon and egg sandwich on freshly toasted bread. He handed her a hot cup of verbena tea and began putting items back into his bag.

"Joash already checked in. No one has any news. More teams have been sent out to search."

"Where are we?"

The coast was about fifteen miles away, but I'm not certain where on the coast we are. We'll need to go as straight as we can and time it. If we get lost over the ocean…"

He trailed off and busied himself stuffing the bedroll back into his pack, cursing quietly as the fabric fought him. Jen rose to help him squash it into the opening of the pack, then sat back on her heels as he reached in to adjust the now smaller heap of fabric.

"I'll go high." She shaded her eyes to stare into the sky. Only a few white clouds scudded the vast expanse of blue.

Ethan said, "I'll be counting but don't let yourself get too tired. It's better to come back to this shore and try again then miss the coast of England and find ourselves lost over the ocean."

"We need compasses and maps."

"I sent a note with Joash. They'll be copying the atlas for us, but it will just be a rough guide. Getting lost is a real possibility. Getting lost too far from shore will be a death sentence."

"I'll be careful."

Danu's Demands

Jen was just about to turn Gallant back when Ethan pointed.

"There," he said excitedly, and Gallant turned before she could make him. She strained her eyes and finally noticed a darker smudge along the wide expanse of blue behind them that had caught Ethan's eye. As soon as she noticed it, it took on startling detail and she knew she looked at a rocky shore even though she couldn't really see it.

"Sometimes magic is so cool," Ethan said.

"It's always cool. We're just getting used to it. Can you imagine seeing Gallant or a firebird if you'd never seen one before? I mean, we never really saw them, but we knew what they were. They weren't mysterious just amazing."

"I get what you mean. We see Warren become a dragon and it amazes us, but we know what he can do. We know it isn't real. Not real—true, maybe. I'm not sure how to explain the difference. He's always Warren no matter what shape he has."

"When we first realized where we were, I thought the magic would be the big hurdle, but I realize that's the smallest one. Our viewpoints, the way we live, the way we think— that's a bigger hurdle."

"The church realizes that *is* the danger from us. They don't want to believe we aren't demons because then they'd have to consider we aren't lying about anything."

"Well, they're fucking wrong if they think that's the only danger."

Ethan slid closer to rest his chin on her shoulder. "I like to believe most are decent men."

Jen snorted.

"For their time, I mean."

"Reading of how women were treated and seeing it are two different things. I always sort of blamed them for being weak and not standing up for their rights, but they truly believe they have none."

"We'll teach them."

Jen shrugged. "I'm tired of that battle already and we've been here barely a year. I wish we'd hidden. I know it's my fault. That stupid fight in Paris, but I really thought if we told them how strong we were that they'd leave us alone."

"It wasn't your fault. I'm not saying it was Matt or Brandon's fault either, but they were the ones who told King Childebert that we had magic. And they were right to do so. It was only fair to warn them. It isn't your fault they're a bunch of lying, murderous assholes."

"Look." Jen pointed and changed Gallant's direction.

Two small boats sailed beneath them and they could now see the port of a village that hugged the coastline.

Ethan said, "We're farther north than I thought. I think that's Ebrauc. Head south and we can call for a summon when we hit Mercia."

Jen urged Gallant southeast, instinctively following the first river she saw. They'd spent the last few days following the twists and curves of a river that flowed Northwest from the Seine, hoping to spot the boat with Alex onboard and stopping to question every person they passed.

The sword in Jen's hand pulsed and Danu surged hard. Gallant screamed and pawed the air.

"What?" Ethan called as the horse spun and galloped across the sky, heading down at sharp slant.

"No idea," Jen said, but she didn't try to halt her downward momentum.

She was certain something dangerous lurked. Ethan knew it too. He clutched Jen tighter, his fingers tapping in See-the-Future pattern against her chest. She grasped his arm to keep him steady while he channeled the spell.

"One man. I see him throwing a glass ball into a fire and it explodes violently when it breaks. Try to talk to him before killing him," Ethan said and then called Joash.

Joash appeared and screamed defiance as he circled their heads.

"I'm not certain whose land this is. It might take a while for help to reach us. I don't even know where to tell them to head except north."

"For one man?"

"Your sword thinks this is urgent."

Jen grimaced and flexed her fingers. The sword glowed so brightly it made her eyes water. She slammed it into the sheath on her back.

To her relief, it stayed although it still glowed, glinting off the water beneath them. The river below them was wide with a strong current. Thick trees bordered both edges. A small island lay in the center, the current making small waves against a rocky shore.

Joash disappeared. Jen slowed Gallant's descent

"Netting meant to camouflage from the air," she said grimly. Below them, on the southern tip of the island, someone had erected a net tarp woven with twigs and leaves. Bigger tree branches were nailed to wooden beams. If her sword hadn't warned her, she'd likely not have noticed it as they flew over. The fact someone had gone to all this trouble told Jen the builder knew a Fae would disapprove if they were spotted.

"Mondred," Ethan growled.

"You didn't see him here?"

"No. But he could be here. See-the Future tells me of the next big attack within five minutes. There could be a hundred more in six minutes."

"That camp isn't big enough to hide a hundred men."

"Your assuming it's just that small island there. They might be on the shore too."

"I could take a hundred."

"Unprepared men, yes. Who knows what they've prepared? For all we know, this is where they make the ether. Not only is that explosive, but it will knock you out. It's smarter to wait, Jen."

"Alex…"

"Isn't here."

"You don't know that." She yanked Gallant's head around and headed to the trees lining the riverbed as she spoke. "I agree we should wait, but he could be here."

"Why would they go to Paris, sail up the river Seine, turn around and come back here?"

"To confuse us? It'd be smart to hide so close. We'd never have thought to look here. What are the chances we'd just happen to fly over?"

"Was Danu pulling you here?"

"No. I don't think so." Jen sighed hard and slipped from her horse's back to rest her forehead on his warm flank. "I'm so tired; I'm not sure."

Joash appeared above her head. This time he was quiet and hovered before her until she took the paper he clutched. The bird fluttered to Gallant's back and began to preen himself.

Ethan took the paper from Jen and said, "Jon says wait. He's coming with Brandon. He wants us to go further south out of sight and get high enough Maria can see us. He'll already be in Marcia. Alberic has taken a squad of his men and some Lesser Fae to work with King Cynwald, and they'll have summoned him. Just a few more minute's Jen."

"You really don't think Alex is here?"

"No. I agree it'd be smart of them to double back, but I doubt they'd risk staying so close. A ranger would spot the kids immediately."

"Do they know that though? Sure, they've seen rangers track, but wouldn't they assume that if there were no prints that a ranger couldn't spot them? How would they know a ranger senses people near them?"

"I don't—"

Joash cawed as Flynn appeared. Ethan snatched the note Flynn carried. He grabbed a charcoal stick from the pouch on his waist and scribbled a second, handed Flynn the note, and both birds disappeared.

"I told him we're waiting. We *are* waiting," he said firmly and mounted Gallant.

Jen mounted behind him and squeezed her eyes closed. Danu was angry with her. She felt it like needles under her skin. Sharp jabs of pain grew progressively worse as they flew away from the source of evil.

"Stop," she finally gasped out and laid a trembling hand against Ethan's cheek.

"Idiot! Why didn't you say something? What's hurting you?" Ethan yelled. "Heal yourself!"

"Danu. She needs this. I must—" Jen groaned against the pain. Needles had been replaced by fire.

"Take me back, Ethan. I'm trying to ask her to wait, but she doesn't understand. I have to go back!" Her voice had risen to shrill.

Danu pressed so hard she thought her skin might combust if she didn't give in. That she was able to hold out amazed her, but she wouldn't be able to hold back much longer. The pain was too intense, and when it overcame her, she'd give in. In moments, Danu would take control of her body and force her.

The idea terrified her, and she began to cry. Ethan cried out as thunder rumbled overhead. Jen screamed as Danu burst from her body. Dark blue and dense, Jen's magic swirled about them. Skeins of electricity flickered through it, zapping their exposed skin with painful jolts.

Gallant screeched an equine shriek of defiance and spun on his hind legs. The fire inside her faded and her sword appeared in her hand.

"I'm going!" she shouted.

Ethan laughed, surprising her.

"She certainly is persistent, isn't she? We'll kill them all!" he yelled and pulled the dagger from his waist.

The blue swirling around them settled to their skin and lightened but didn't disappear.

"No one seems to have noticed us," Ethan said. "We'll drop straight down. Try not to kill them all though. Leave us a few to question."

She grunted in annoyance. They flew above the trees so close leaves and branches brushed their feet. The ground passed beneath them with dizzying speed. She kept her eyes forward, peering through the glare from her sword. She thought they were flying about fifty miles an hour or so. Gallant had stopped responding to her control. Danu was using her magic.

"I'm still in control of me," she muttered, more to herself than to reassure Ethan.

Gallant disappeared from beneath them, dropping them toward the rocky shore of the small island in the center of the river.

"Wasn't me," Jen said as she flicked her fingers and encased herself in a protective shield. She casted a lesser shield on Ethan, getting the cast off right as he leapt to the ground. She landed a second after him. Her sword pulled her, not to the right where the canopy lay, but to the left. She ran across the rocky shore and into brush that reached her knees. Large rocks and a few trees formed a windbreak right on the high tide line. Someone had built a crude hut beneath the trees.

She kicked the door open.

A naked woman was tied to a post. She sat on a heap of moldy straw and stared with blank eyes. She would have been beautiful if she wasn't so lifeless. Wounds marred her body, bruises, burns, and slash marks. A man slept on a ratty blanket beside her. He jerked up and screamed when Jen entered, scrabbling backward using his hands to pull himself away. His gaze darted about the small room, landing on a wooden chest beside the door.

"Get face down right now!" Ethan shouted.

The woman laid down but was unable to turn. Short ropes on her feet and arms prevented her, but she kept trying. Ethan disappeared and hit her with his sap. She stopped moving. The man lunged to his knees and reached for the box.

"One more twitch, and I'll cut your fucking head clean off," Jen warned.

The man glanced around and clenched his fists. He licked his lips and tried to reach forward. Jen swung. The head toppled from the body. Blood splashed across the woman and soaked into the straw. The smell of feces burst into the air as the corpse voided its bowels.

Ethan untied the woman. She neither resisted nor helped.

Jen opened the chest. Inside, glass globes full of a murky liquid were nestled in straw.

"Yeah, he was prepared for a Fae. These are the same glass globes they used in the attack, but the oil looks different, cloudier. Do you recognize her?"

"No," Ethan said as he shrugged out of his shirt and dressed the woman.

"You're safe now. Can you tell us your name?" he asked.

She didn't reply.

Jen laid a hand on Ethan's shoulder. "Bring her outside. There's no point in questioning her. Maybe Arden can help her," she finished doubtfully.

The woman's blank stare unnerved her. It was clear to Jen that this woman wasn't in the here and now.

Ethan frowned and withdrew a healing potion from his belt and flicked the top open with his thumb. "Drink this," he commanded, and the woman obediently opened her mouth.

The bruises and cuts marring her body faded away.

Ethan frowned at the woman and grabbed the blanket to wrap her in. "Those goddamned assholes. How could they?"

"Was that the man you saw?" Jen asked.

"Yeah. I think he was here alone. Well, except for her. We weren't exactly quiet, and your sword is normal now."

Jen flicked a glance to her sword and dropped it, letting it return to mist. "Danu was right. He was an evil bastard."

"I still think Mondred's involved." Ethan knelt before the chest and examined the contents. He rose and flicked his fingers. "They hid something that way." He pointed in the direction of the camouflaged net.

Joash appeared and dropped a set of bangles at Jen's feet.

Mondred Exposed

Jon leaned over Jen's shoulder at the edge of the pit and growled. The low sound rose the hair on her arms. The odor emanating from the shallow grave made her gag. Tears filled her eyes as Warren revealed another rotted face screwed up in a horrified rictus. These women had died terrified. From the wounds so far revealed, they'd all been murdered to steal their unborn children.

"Dear God, so many… Why?" Arden fell to her knees, pressing her hands to her face. "Is this my fault?"

Jen stood and yanked Arden to her feet. "Don't be stupid. How could this be your fault?"

"If it's anyone's fault, it's mine." Anger vibrated in Jon's voice.

"We should've fucking killed him," Warren muttered.

He stomped to the edge of the small island in the river and turned away from them.

Ethan laid a hand on Jen's arm, then hugged Arden. "Never think you caused this. Mondred did this...this atrocity. He, Callahan, Ewan, and Bruno.

"Not just them!" Warren snapped. "There are at least seven other sets of prints I can't identify.

"We can't leave them here— like this," Arden said.

"No." Jon laid a gentle hand against Arden's pale cheek. "They deserve decent burials..." He pinched the bridge of his nose a moment. "Jen, go get Kuan. Tell him to bring drawing supplies. Maybe we can locate some of their families. Send Joash with a note to Alberic in Mercia to beg one of the priests there to return and preform burials. We'll need a list..." He stopped speaking to hug Arden who'd made a soft sound of distress.

She pushed away and grabbed the shovel from Ethan. "Bring back clean cloth to wrap them in and something to store their effects in. Their families and loved ones will likely recognize their clothing."

"All a hundred and twelve won't be here, Arden." Jen took the shovel from her and gestured her back. "I'm sure most of the babies were left by their parents."

"How are you sure, Jen?" Look at this! This is our fault for making no effort to find out who left babies on our doorstep. We assumed they were unwanted, that the parents left them with us because we could teach them so much. Our pride killed these women!"

"Don't be an ass! Mondred fucking killed them!" Warren returned to glare at Arden. "This isn't Jen's fault either. How the hell where we supposed to know he was murdering women to steal their babies? And how do you know he gave them to us? Granted it seems likely, but you don't know for sure."

"Stop it. All of you!"

The anger in Jon's voice felt like a punch. Jen lifted her hands to her face, then dropped them. Jon gave her an apologetic grimace.

"Accept we made a mistake but that we meant well. None of us intended for the mothers to be hurt. Our intent was to save unwanted children."

"Jon, we can't assume they were unwanted. If he killed these women to steal their children and give them to us mightn't he have stolen them from other women too? How in the world will we ever make this right?"

"This can't be made right," Ethan said sadly. "We can only do our best, Arden, and we meant well. Now, we'll do our best again and bury these poor souls. Hopefully, we can inform their families—"

"And if their families want the children back?" Arden bent to tug a scrap of embroidered fabric from the dirt. "This is a well-made piece of clothing. I'm betting she had a husband. Someone out there lost a wife and child. By what right do we keep his child?"

Jon sighed in exasperation. "Arden, what do you want from me? There are one hundred and seventy-two children in the new orphanage…. Sure, I'd give them back if I could, but who's to say which-is-which?"

"Maybe the wizards could help?" Ethan said thoughtfully. They can see the auras that connect us."

Jon pursed his lips. "I'm willing to ask them to look. I do want to do the right thing here, Arden. We'll change our procedures for accepting abandoned babies, but I can't turn them away completely."

"No, I don't want that either." Arden let

the muddy scrap of fabric fall to the ground.

Jen lightly touched her shoulder. "We assumed the babies were left because we'd provide a higher standard of living for them. We thought their families wanted them to have a shot at becoming our nobles." She turned to Jon. "You need to make it very clear no new children will ever receive any rank. They'll be clothed and fed and sent to school, but that's it.

"More than that. They'll never be Fae. Danu must be content with the ones we have," Arden said firmly. "We must stop thinking of them as our children. I recommend we send them away. Maybe to *Cear Gwinntguic* or Mercia. Let Irminric or Cynewald provide for them. We could give a tax break or something to make it worthwhile."

"That could work," Jon said, the lines on his face lightening. "Only the royal orphanage will be in Camelot. Every kingdom will be expected to fund an orphanage. I'll make the changes at once."

"Make sure the women know they're entitled to child support from the child's father. If every man must take care of all the children they sire, it should encourage them to use birth control."

"I agree, but proving who the father is…" Jon turned from the grave and peered out over the water. "We can worry about dead-beat dads later. Warren, keep searching. My guess is Mondred headed across the channel from here. See if you can find any tracks on shore that lead to the coast. But don't linger. The search for the children takes precedence. A man like Mondred won't be content to hide. He'll show himself sooner or later, and we'll deal with him when he does."

Warren said, "You have to ask yourself why he did it."

Jon said, "Maybe the women's clothing was left on purpose to identify them and he planned to demand we return the children when they were grown with magic of their own. If these dead women were of noble birth, he'd have his own Fae. And maybe he thought the world would believe we'd done it. He could uncover this pit and blame us."

"We can worry about why later. My wife needs rest," Ethan said.

"I know; I feel her exhaustion." Jon ran a gentle hand across Jen's cheek.

"Jen, I'm so sorry." Arden bit her lip and took Jen's hand. "I know you told me the strength of Danu's urges, but I never imagined…"

"Don't worry about it." Jen withdrew her hand to rub her face. "I'm not subjecting you to my feelings on purpose." She waved her hand through Danu that still swirled around her.

"She's too tired to hold it back," Ethan said anxiously. He pulled her tighter to his side. "Jon, we wanted to wait. We tried to wait, but Danu was hurting her. Not mental pain but real physical pain that I could feel. My wife needs rest or she's going to lose control."

"Take her home. The border of Mercia is just three miles or so away where the river curves in a ninety-degree bend seaward. You can be summoned home from there. Visit Diana and rest."

"It'll be good to see Sam," Jen said. "I'm worried about taking advantage, leaving Diana with her so long."

Jon winced.

"Is she okay?" She bit her lip then blurted, "Is taking care of Diana too much for her?"

"Sam isn't there. She left with Vicky to go search Metz, Bishop Maximus's hometown. King Totila rules there now, an Ostrogoths king."

Jen staggered and moaned, sinking to her knees as she fought Danu. Ethan grasped her arm and pulled her upright as Arden and Jon reached for her.

"Samantha Quinn is fine," Jon said forcefully, and Danu subsided. Jen lost her balance at the abrupt cessation of pressure, only Ethan's tight grip keeping her upright. Arden flicked a heal on her. The small golden sphere did nothing to ease the pounding in Jen's head. Arden and Jon's worry came to her clearly, and she grimaced and motioned them away.

"My daughter?"

"Is fine too," Jon said.

"She's fine," Arden said. She held out a hand, then withdrew it to wring her hands together. "Kuan is watching her. They're staying in the castle with us. Agnes hasn't left their side. Sam wanted to go. All the rangers are searching. Maximus grew up in Mediomatrix, an Ostrogoths holding, what we'd call Germans. In the future we call it Metz, and it's a French city but Austria owned it for a while in the future too. Cass thinks it'll be its own zone now. Father Dom tells us it's a rich city in the here and now and two major rivers border it. If they're traveling by water, Sam and Vicky will find them."

"We planned to go there ourselves," Ethan said.

"I don't know what to do." Jen could hear

the panic in her voice and tried to speak more calmly when she said, "The boat we were tracking was headed north into Germany, but the woods are so thick, and it branches so much and whose to stay they even stayed on the stupid boat?"

Ethan pulled her into an embrace as she began to cry.

"I miss him so much," she said through her sobs. Danu's fear magnified hers. Jen didn't know if Danu was now worried for Sam or the children or both.

"Me too; we'll find him," Ethan said in a voice thick with tears.

Jon said, "Go home first; see your daughter, and rest. Sam and Vicky are perfectly fine. They check in every eight hours and sleep in the woods."

Jon authoritative tone settled Danu. Jen's fear eased, and she slumped in her husband's arms, so tired it took effort to remain standing. She wished she could just sit at Jon's feet and sleep. His angry presence soothed Danu.

"She needs you, Jon," Ethan said unhappily. He frowned and waved his hand through Jen's magic. "I'm not jealous you need him. Well, I am, but I know it isn't a sexual thing. I just wish I could comfort you like he does."

"That need she feels is for Jon?" Arden asked in dismay.

"His magic," Jen said hurriedly. "Ethan can feel how much Danu subsides when Jon is near. It's relaxing to not feel her push me."

"And this unease— your worried I'll be jealous?"

"A little," Jen admitted. You're a new Fae. I'm worried you'll misinterpret my feelings."

"I sense them much clearer now than when I was human and stood in your magic," Arden said.

Jon pulled Arden to his side and kissed her cheek. "You've barely recovered from the transformation. I sense them better now than a month ago too. I don't know if it's because we're all so upset, or if that's a permanent change." He turned to Jen. "Don't worry about Arden. She knows how much I love her. If you need me near to rest, then sleep in our room."

"Are you going home?" Ethan asked.

"I know your worried and afraid but why does that scare you more?" Arden asked. Her expression tightened and she bit her lip. "I'm sorry, I don't mean to embarrass anyone. Am I supposed to pretend I don't feel it? I don't know the rules for this."

The question was asked so sincerely that

Jen laughed. Arden wasn't trying to be sarcastic, she honestly wanted to know.

Jon laughed too as he said, "There are no rules. Maybe there should be. I'll need to think about that, but we're all friends here. If you're concerned for a friend, it's okay to ask them."

Jen said, "Ethan is worried I'll lose control and start killing the humans. He wants me to rest but is afraid to ask Jon to put off whatever he's busy doing so I can sleep. I won't be able to rest easy if I think Jon is doing something dangerous. So, he's worried asking will worry me more."

"Pretty close," Ethan admitted and tweaked her ponytail.

She batted his hand away.

"We planned to be home just one day. Can you come home for one day?" Ethan asked.

"Yes." Jon clapped him on the shoulder. "I'll go with Jen to the border here, and we'll summon you."

"What about the woman?" Aden asked.

Jen smacked herself on the side of the head. "I forgot all about her."

"I'll get her." Ethan shooed her away. "I'll wait for Alberic and leave her with him."

Jen summoned Gallant, and she and Jon mounted.

"Was Arden angry?" she asked Jon as

soon as they reached treetop height.

"No. Not really. Don't worry about that. We have enough to worry about. You can't recall your magic?"

"It isn't worth the effort. She's so angry and afraid." Jen shrugged. She didn't want to try. The thought of another fight with Danu made her groan. And she couldn't afford to fight her and lose. Danu would take her as she had in Limenware and who the hell knew where she'd take her too. She didn't think Danu knew where to go either. Her sword glowed, but she felt no pull. Danu could kill her or get her so lost it took her weeks to get home. Just thinking about weeks without her family made her groan again.

Jon hugged her, resting his chin on her head. She leaned against him. His broad chest against her back felt like safety. By the time they reached the bend in the river, Danu had reabsorbed. Jon hugged her a minute before stepping away and reaching for a summoning stone.

Father Dom Speaks to the Holy See

Meanwhile, in Italy

The meeting room quieted, filling with a hostile silence when Father Dom entered. Men wearing white robes prodded each other and glared at the doorway. The guard who'd escorted him bowed deeply and retreated, shutting the double doors behind himself.

Candles spaced evenly across the wooden table flickered, sparking light from gold jewelry and gemmed rosaries that the gathered men wore. Windows open to morning breezes barely freshened the room that the crowd made close and dank.

Bishops and cardinals lined a thirty-foot

table in the center of the room. The four Cardinals sat two abreast at opposite heads. Lesser clergy lined the walls three deep, some with open Bibles or clutching sheaves of paper while others carried writing implements and wrote with ink-stained fingers on ledgers they balanced across their knees.

Father Dom bowed his head. "Thank you, your eminences, for agreeing to meet with me." He strode to Cardinal Pelagius and knelt to kiss his hand. "Your eminence," he murmured.

"Rise. Take a seat. The Holy See is in session and will remain in session until we can come to an agreement."

Father Dom glanced at the gathered men who glowered at him as he sat in the indicated wooden chair. The closest bishops shuffled their chairs further away as if afraid his mere presence would contaminate them.

"His presence pollutes this company!"

The florid face of the man who spoke darkened still further.

"Bertram, we will be civil," Pelagius said.

Bertram gathered the folds of his robe tightly around his corpulent form and glared. "Allowing a devil worshiper to attend our conferences—"

Pelagius rapped his knuckles on the table

and cut Bertram off. "It hasn't been decided yet that they *are* devils."

Bertram flicked his fingers, the small motion rife with contempt. "Of course they are. They freely admit they use magic. We ourselves have seen them do it."

"They're sorcerers and sodomites. Fornicators with no respect for law or God's holy word!" Bishop Umfrey shouted.

His tirade was met by loud assent.

Father Dom straightened in his seat. Before he could decide to speak, Pelagius again banged on the table.

"We're met here to decide if charges of witchcraft will be brought. Emperor Justinian is planning unprecedented meetings with Kings Germanus, Agila, Alduin, and Khosrow. We, ourselves, have been invited to hold this conference in Constantinople. Representatives from all over will be arriving. What we decide here will affect the entire world. Our decisions must be in accordance with God's law."

"And God's law clearly states men or women who use magic must be put to death. They are evil and an abomination!" Bertram thundered.

"But they are *not* men or women— they are Fae," Father Dom said.

The men turned to stare at him with shocked eyes. He wondered if the shock were for his words— or that he dared to speak in this august company.

The bishop to the left of Bertram nodded thoughtfully and fingered a gold cross dangling from a thick chain around his neck. "Can we judge them by rules of man? Do we have the right?"

"Don't be ridiculous. They're as human as we. The devil empowers them, nothing more," Bertram said.

"You're here at our behest to answer questions, not put yourself forward!" Umfrey snapped at the same time.

"They are *not* human!" Father Dom half rose from his seat and placed both hands flat on the table. "The Bible speaks of angels and demons. It is a book intended for the enlightenment, the betterment of man, but those words cannot apply to others. If Archangel Michael appeared with his sword of fire, would you burn him for a witch?"

"You're claiming they're angels now?" Bertram curled his lip and rose an eyebrow.

"Not at all. My point is there *are* other beings. To judge a Fae by human standards would be foolish."

"Not Fae. They're simply men possessed

of a demon."

"You're being stubbornly short sighted!"

"And you believe the lies they spout with suspicious ease!"

Pelagius stood and waved his hands. "The situation we find ourselves in is dire. The souls of mankind, our very way of life is at stake."

"Our lives themselves," a graying man seated beside Pelagius said.

It took Father Dom a moment to recognize Cardinal Tilly. It had been years since he'd seen him and Tilly had aged much during that time, appearing sick and frail. As the senior clergy present, he sat in a place of honor to the right of Pelagius at the head of the table.

"Yes." Pelagius nodded and resumed his seat. "To fight the devil will cost many lives."

"Lives we could spare. Give them their children and let them live in peace. Send emissaries and assure them the church played no part in Bishop Rufus's betrayal," Father Dom pleaded.

Bertram snorted in disgust. "We have no children, but if we did, we wouldn't make the mistake of trying to harness a demon but would instead burn the body to destroy the demonic host and force it back to Hell!"

The men began to loudly argue over the

merits of Bertram's response.

"Please…" Father Dom glanced over the arguing men and despaired. They'd already made up their minds. He closed his eyes and prayed for eloquence while the heated debate continued around him. When he opened his eyes, he stood.

"Your eminences, please, for this one hour consider that King Jon Arthur speaks truly. Consider what it will mean to the world if we declare them humans possessed by the devil and demand their deaths. If Jon told the truth, that Danu, the spirit of the Earth itself, empowers him, that she has chosen her champions to prevent her destruction and with God's help brought them here where they might save her, and we kill them…what have we gained? Is your certainty in your interpretation of God's word so strong that you'd risk murdering the Earth itself? The Fae have offered us no violence and are instead doing their utmost to improve our lives. They offer medicines and foods. If you saw how they live, you'd see it's different, yes, but they follow their laws and most believe in God."

"A trap to draw you in," Umfrey said, glaring at his fellow bishops as though daring them to disagree.

"No! That assumes they're lying, and I

swear on my immortal soul they're not!"

Pelagius rose a calming hand. "Maybe they believe it to be true, but that doesn't make it so. God has warned us of the danger of allowing those who use the devil's evil power to live."

"He warns of men, not Fae!"

"Exactly!" Bertram snapped triumphantly, slapping the Bible before him. "Show me where the Fae are mentioned in these Holy Words! Why has God not warned of them?"

"God states he created invisible things. Colossians tells us, 'For by Him all things were created, both in the heavens and on earth, visible and invisible, whether thrones or dominions or rulers or authorities—all things have been created by Him and for Him. And He is before all things, and in Him all things hold together.' Daniel speaks, warning of the future so does John the Baptist. God see's the future, what is and what will be. There can be no doubt of that. He speaks of the morning star singing together with angels giving praise to his creation. In Isaiah he says, 'For thus saith the LORD that created the heavens; God himself that formed the earth and made it; he hath established it, he created it not in vain, he formed it to be inhabited: I *am* the LORD; and *there is* none else.'

Father Dom nodded his head slowly as the gathered bishops began to look thoughtful. Angry glowers were replaced by pursed lips and hands reached for Bibles. A surge of hope filled his voice with renewed vigor.

"We interpret God's words as fits our knowledge of the world, but couldn't he have meant he created the heavens and earth with spirits?" Father Dom continued to beseech them. "God claims the Earth to be living and breathing. It is our hubris that translates the word of God as we will it. We assume he meant the life upon the Earth, but it could be translated as the life *within*. He makes winds his messenger, flames of fire his servants. God sent angels among men to show them the error of their ways or guide them. And oft times the angel was denied, turned away by doubting men. Hints abound in the holy word of other types of beings. The prophets speak of cherubim and seraphim. The Bible speaks of messengers and watchers, not men, but beings from his heavenly kingdom. To deny he has other creations and loves them… will you let the devil tempt you to power through hubris and the destruction of God's creatures?"

A frown built on Pelagius's face as Father Dom spoke. "You speak with feeling. I believe your sincerity, but sincerity doesn't equate truth. They too might believe they're other then what they are, but God has warned us of them."

"Not them," Father Dom pleaded. "If Danu had sent us human men and women, would we listen? If God himself sent a prophet who preached as they did, would we listen, or are we so wedded to our ways we'd blindly continue this path we trod, insisting we're right? Would we point at the Holy Words and insist we've deciphered their meaning correctly? I believe the power that the Fae possess is given to them for just this purpose. We cannot silence them. We cannot stop them. They're not angels but beings with freewill able to choose wrongly as are we. Without our guidance, they'll flounder, and the world will suffer.

"Instead of fighting, we should guide them and let them teach us. Consider why Danu sent them to this time and place. Surely, it would've been easier to leave them in their rightful time, and yet, here they are. God loves us. We're at a fork in the road, and he's sent a messenger; one we can't ignore. One with power to make us see and consider His words."

To the father's relief most of the bishops

were nodding thoughtfully now.

Pelagius scanned the table and his lips tightened.

Tilly stood and placed a hand on Pelagius's shoulder. "This decision shouldn't be rushed. We have much to consider and pray on, but in one thing there can be no doubt; the Fae, whether misguided or demons, are powerful. I propose we send assurances none of the missing children are here. Further, I propose we spend our resources searching for the children. Our church has been smeared in the illegal attack. Our name used; our honor besmirched. Send for the Diaconus Episcopi and demand an accounting be made. Find who has misused our funds and our name. If the Fae are indeed not human, we'll need to find a way to live peacefully with them. As the father says, God's law applies to humans. If they are human, then it is our duty to see to their destruction despite the cost. To attempt to keep their power, no matter the reason, is blasphemy. Bishop Mina paid for that blasphemy with his life and no doubt now resides in the fires of Hell."

Bertram said, "I've just this day returned from Constantinople and I'd heard naught of an attack on the supposed Fae. It was they who attacked. One of Justinian's senators was strongly advising that Justinian turn the Fae away and the man was most foully assaulted in his own home. Mina was a devout man. It's blasphemy of the rankest sort to condemn him on the word of a demon!"

Pelagius rose, shrugging off Tilly's hand. "There will be no more attempts to subvert their powers. If God-given or derived from Hell has yet to be determined, but either way, that power is not meant for man."

Fools!" Bertram stood and snatched his Bible. "Be swayed by these demonic words. Only Hellfire awaits you!"

The echo of his fist pounding on the door for release seemed to linger in the room.

Father Dom squirmed uncomfortably. Even as they spoke, King Jon was attempting to give their power to others.

Rising the Fae

Soft snuffling snorts from Diana woke Jen.

"I've got her," Ethan said. "Go back to sleep. We don't have to leave until you're rested."

"I'm good," Jen said as she sat to swing her legs to the side of the bed. She held out her arms for her daughter. Ethan handed her Diana and a warmed bottle of milk. Diana stared at her from baby blue eyes as she sucked, and Jen was angered all over again that this child had been stolen from her and she had to resort to a bottle to feed her. Diana's eyes widened and she scowled and kicked her feet, working up to a cry. Jen hastily smoothed her expression and crooned nonsense words until Diana relaxed.

"Good thing Jon has such a big room," she said, giving her husband a rueful grimace.

"Sleeping in here with them is weird, but I can feel it settle Danu. I don't want to make a habit of it, but if you need him near to relax, then that's what we'll do."

"I feel better. More myself. Has there been any word?"

"Nothing new. Cass thinks, and I agree, Maximus wouldn't trust Fae children with strangers. He'd leave them with family or his own men. Cass thinks it's more likely he'd use family allies, men he trusted, not his kin, in case we track them down."

"Do we know where his family lives now?"

"Mediomatrix. His wife was from Mediolanum Italy though, and his son is still there."

"He has a wife? I thought they couldn't marry?"

"Had. She died, and he joined the priesthood. It's unusual for a first son, but he comes from a wealthy family." Ethan settled to the edge of the bed beside Jen and rubbed Diana's toes as he said. "I think it was a political move. He had a legal heir so still controlled his estates even though he formally renounced his title and estates in his son's favor. He rose so rapidly in rank in the church, it's clear he bought his way to the top. And we know he isn't a Christian…"

"How do they not see?"

"I'm sure they do. But most of the Bishops are from good families and rose the same way. Rank is so engrained in them that they don't think it's wrong or dishonest to promote a ranked man above a peasant. They truly believe in a God-given right to rule."

"Father Dom is in Italy, isn't he?"

"He is, and Flynn goes daily. The father has spoken with the Holy See and they claim they have none of our children. He believes they don't but warns the clergy is divided and he can't guarantee some aren't acting outside of the church's policy.

Jen kissed the top of her daughter's head and lifted her to her shoulder to gently pat her back.

"He thinks some might be involved but doesn't wish to accuse without proof?"

"I don't know, but that's how I read it too," Ethan admitted. He took Diana from her, kissed her cheek, and continued to burb her. They both smiled at the unladylike belch that emerged. Jen casted a heal, not because Diana needed one just to assure herself her daughter was well.

"Let's go to Italy," Jen said.

"I agree."

"I feel bad leaving Vicky and Sam alone in Germany, but I think Italy is more likely."

"They'll be fine," Ethan said.

Jen didn't need magic to feel his guilt. He didn't like the idea of them being alone there either. "I wish she were with Brandon though.

"I'll ask Jon to send him. He knows Sam is timid and Vicky impetuous though. He wouldn't have sent them if he thought they'd find anything. He's just covering all the bases. Danu pushes all of us. We all want the children back."

Jen bit her lip and rubbed her daughter's back. Danu would make Vicky attack if Sam found the children, she was sure of that. And Vicky would attack without thought or skill. Sam would try, but she hadn't the skill either to support an untrained paladin in a major fight.

"I don't know what to do. I'm risking Sam's life. Damn it, Ethan!" Jen jumped to her feet and began to pace. "Vicky could find them, but if she does, she'll attack, and they'll be prepared for her. Neither Sam nor Vicky are experienced enough to survive an attack prepared for them!"

Ethan lowered his head, hiding his face

behind Diana's small body.

"We should recall them or go there," Jen said.

"Alex is more likely in Italy."

"Then recalling them won't matter."

"He might be there…" Ethan lifted his head. Tears shone in his eyes.

Jen whirled away, not wanting to see his pain. "It's selfish to risk them."

"They chose, Jen. They knew the risks. No one forced them to go."

Jen laid her forehead against the cool glass of the window and gripped the sill hard. "I don't know what to do. Was Arden able to get that woman to talk?" She turned to peer over her shoulder when Ethan didn't answer.

A red flush climbed Ethan's cheeks. "She killed herself."

Jen gaped at him. "What?"

"She threw herself in the river while we were digging up the corpses. Or, hell, maybe she fell in trying to clean herself, but I really think she killed herself."

Jen slumped against the window and put her hands over her face. "Dear God, what have we done?"

"We couldn't know she was tied like that to prevent her from hurting herself. Those bruises and burns weren't self-inflicted.

Someone beat her, Jen. Whether that man, or another; and even if he never laid a finger on her, he was guilty of hiding all those murders. He was evil. Danu wasn't wrong."

Tears sprang to Jen's eyes.

She forced a calm expression, rubbing her face and pulling her hair back. Ethan had meant to help too, and she was certain he was feeling as guilty as she was over the woman's death, but she didn't have time to beat herself up over it. There were children in danger who needed them to remain focused.

She tied her hair as tightly as she could with a strip of rawhide she took from her wrist. She wore a bunch of strips on her wrist, some wrapped a few times to have varying lengths handy. At least one pink bead dangled from all of them to send messages with firebirds. She smoothed the bracelet with the black beads interspersed with the pink, which so far no one had ever used. She dreaded receiving one from a firebird. To receive a message that all hope was lost would rile Danu unbearably; she was sure of that.

Ethan rubbed his bracelets, the red beads adorning them clicking slightly. He tucked the black beaded bracelet he wore beneath the others.

"Let's go talk to Jon," Jen said.

Ethan gestured with his chin to their packs beside the door. "Freshly restocked. Hot food and beverages are on the left, cold on the right. There's more bracelets in their usual pocket."

Jen nodded her thanks as she grabbed the packs. Ethan followed her from the room.

She found Jon pouring over maps in the meeting room behind the dais. He smiled when he saw her and gestured to the table. "Cass has worked out a route he thinks you can follow using existing landmarks. You can be in Germany in two days.

"We're going to Italy," Ethan said.

Jen took Diana from him and sat beside Jon. "Recall Sam and Vicky. It isn't safe for them there. Getting them killed won't help anyone."

"Is Danu telling you Italy?" Cass asked.

"No. But priests there know something. I'll make them tell me."

"How?" Cass held up a hand as Jen started to speak. "I'm not arguing against it. I'm legitimately asking how you'll get them to talk. These men are fanatics. Torture won't work on them."

"I wasn't going to torture them!" Jen snapped. She took a deep breath and rubbed Diana's back as the baby began to fuss. "I'll ask them."

Ethan glared at Cass. "We'll ask, beg, bribe, and spy. And, yeah, I'll torture the fuckers if I think they know where my son is."

Jon glanced at Ethan and winced. Jen rose to kiss her husband's cheek. "Did you get any rest?" she murmured.

His red-rimmed eyes glared, but it was the blue glow that alarmed Jen. Ethan normally had no problem controlling himself.

"Italy is a thousand miles away. It'll take you four days or so to get there—"

"One and a half. Two tops," Jen interrupted Cass to say.

He leaned back and pursed his lips. "And then you'll be exhausted when you arrive."

"Don't worry about that." Ethan pushed passed Jen and flipped through the maps on the table as he said, "I'll make sure she rests enough. But how do we get there? We aren't fucking following the coast like we did to reach Constantinople. What landmarks should we be aiming for?"

"Go straight west. The alps will be impossible to miss." Cass rummaged through the papers on the table and removed one, which he handed to Ethan. "If you hit ocean, stop. You'll have to follow the coast then. Bring a set of clothing they'd wear and ask someone where you are. I've made a list of all the major cities that I could remember with their modern names below it but most of these people won't have traveled very far and will only have limited notions of how to get anywhere. If you can pinpoint if you're north or south of the city though, all paved roads lead to it. The Romans built roads everywhere they went. I drew in where I remembered them being, but this is just a rough estimate."

"Try to stay hidden," Jon interjected.

"We will," Jen assured him. "We don't want them to know we're coming."

"They have to know we'll come," Ethan said and slumped, supporting his weight with both hands on the table. "I can't take this. I really can't. First my daughter, and now my son." His shoulders shook with silent sobs

Jen pressed against his back, not knowing what to say.

"Chelsea is safe," Jon said and laid a hand on his arm.

"You don't fucking know that!" Ethan batted Jon's hand away and spun to take Diana from Jen, speaking with his back turned. "For all we know, the entire world ended when we came here, or Team Valor caused a war. We don't know what the fuck happened to our families!" He took a deep gasping breath, kissed Diana's cheek, and whispered endearments to her.

"I'm sorry," Jon said in a tortured voice.

Ethan sighed hard before turning and saying, "No. I'm sorry. It isn't your fault, but you can't know, Jon. To lose a child... I tell myself Chelsea is well and happy with people who love her, but Alex— they'll twist him, and if he won't bend, they'll break him. They'll teach him to hate, and his own mother will be compelled to hunt him down and kill him."

"I would never...." Jen trailed off, struck with horror at the idea. "Oh, God. Oh God, Ethan! No! She wouldn't..." Sobs choked her as she fell to the floor to clutch Ethan's legs. Danu would force her. Mike had been one of her children, and Danu had killed him with neither a spec of remorse nor sadness. Danu had seen evil and wanted it dead.

Ethan crouched and tried to pull her up. "We'll find him. I'm sorry I said anything."

"I kill them, Ethan. Danu won't let us try to help him if she thinks he's evil. I won't do it! I'll kill myself first!"

"Calm down. Your scaring our daughter. Alex is innocent, and Danu loves him."

Diana began to cry. Jen tried to stop but couldn't catch her breath. Cass jumped over the table to hug her. He took Diana from Ethan and rocked her. The baby stopped crying and cooed, grabbing at the buttons on Cass's shirt.

Jen couldn't let go of the horror. Struck by a new thought, she grasped Ethan by his collar and shook him. "You didn't see that, did you? Tell me you didn't!"

"I didn't," he said as he pried her hands off. He kissed them and hugged her so tightly it hurt. "I didn't," he repeated. "I'm sorry I said it."

"That will never happen, Jen. I swear on my soul," Jon said. He lifted a glowing blue hand. "I, Jon Arthur, swear that Genevieve Frey will never be sent to harm her son, Alexander Frey. If he becomes a danger that needs to be stopped, I'll do it if every other means of stopping him has failed.

Thunder crashed, but lightning didn't manifest.

"My word is my bond, Jen. It doesn't matter if Danu didn't manifest. It was likely too complex for her to understand. We'll find Alex and raise him to be a good kind man like his father."

Jen shivered. Alex had two fathers and one was anything except kind.

Ethan said, "I'm his father, Jen."

She nodded and wiped her burning eyes.

Ethan sat and pulled her into his lap.

"Let's see these maps. We want to get going."

Jon said, "Stay until after the meeting. We're asking volunteers to become greater Fae."

Jen said, "I want to, but the sooner we start…"

"The meeting shouldn't take long and will begin as soon as Arden gets back."

"Where is she?"

"She went to speak with her EMT's"

Cass snickered, then kissed Diana's nose. His aura had soothed her, and the baby gurgled happily. "The Empties. That's what our citizens call them no matter how many times we explain what the acronym stands for."

Jon smiled but it was a tight, tired smile. "She's arranging a summoning chain the length and breadth of my realm, which is getting bigger ridiculously fast." He glared, then sighed and laughed and threw up his hands in a what can you do gesture. "She plans to build local hospitals, but the plague is spreading. Kirk is giving her all the healing potions she wants, but she still has to find them and reach them in time. It's a complicated project, but we can handle it. She should be back within the hour though."

To Be or Not To Be

The Lesser Fae had gathered in the main hall and spoke excitedly amongst themselves. Gwen had set up a buffet on the stage the musicians used but it remained mostly untouched. Glass decanters Dillion had conjured sat on every table and sparkled in the sunlight streaming in from the wide windows only a bit distorted from the glass.

Their craftsmen were growing more skilled by the day, Jen thought and was suddenly angry all over again that the church tried to keep this from the people. This room was comfortable now and beautiful. Fancifully carved goblets and plates sat beside colorful cloth napkins on the tables. Cushioned chairs interspersed the swings and benches. This was a good place.

Nothing about it was evil. Only small signs of the recent battle remained on the building, but the people were still afraid and downcast.

They picked half-heartedly at the food and frowned and gestured as they spoke. Jen had been so caught up in the search that she'd forgotten her friends were dealing with their own horrors. They'd lost friends and their hard work had been destroyed. But worse, the people they'd been helping and thought friends had betrayed them.

A hushed silence fell over the gathered men and women as Jon rose

"After much discussion we've decided to attempt to rise eight of you to greater Fae. Doing so will give us a full raid."

Jon waited for the murmuring to die down before continuing. Jen was relieved to note most of the Lesser Fae appeared interested and eager.

"To optimize our raid, we've picked classes that we hope will give us balanced parties if we need to spread out into smaller groups for our protection. The events of the last week have shown that our allies can be used against us to force us to spread ourselves too thin. With that in mind, in the future, our militia will be undertaking the training of a small, standing army. This army will be responsible for monitoring our borders. All of our borders. Never again will men march on us unawares."

The crowd murmured and shifted. Jen's gaze darted to Galahad and Dante who sat together behind the Lesser Fae. Galahad had been asked to train the army; Jon's theory being he knew how to relate best to the military class in this era. Jen wasn't sure where Dante's loyalties lay. He'd appeared genuinely horrified over his prince's betrayal but had asked to return to his king after seeing to Chrodesinde's safety. She'd fled her father, returning to Camelot days after she'd left. Jon had asked him to attend this meeting.

"We're too few to adequately monitor the borders ourselves. Those of us with abilities that allow for swift travel are busy elsewhere. Most of us now have children to care for." Jon held up a hand to still the mutters. "We'll speak of that in a moment. These are the classes we need. Please consider carefully before approaching a sponsor. I know the fighting here has upset everyone. Our lives in the future hadn't prepared us for the sort of violence the people of this era live with. If you choose to become a Greater Fae, you can expect to fight again. Your life will become more dangerous. As you've seen, the people of this time hate with a fanatical hatred. Even if the church does eventually accept us, you can expect to need to live cautiously for the rest of your life. You'll feel Danu speak to you. She can be very forceful when it comes to our protection. Especially for protection classes.

Kuan stood and said, "Because magic makes us so powerful every new Fae will be expected to take an oath to do no harm with their magic except in defense of the realm, not for personal gain. If we raise you to Greater Fea and you refuse to take an oath, you'll be considered a fugitive."

Jon clasped his shoulder and nodded. "We've learned our lesson and won't let new Fea bully the humans. We will use deadly force to stop you, but I trust that you can see the benefits of working together and force won't be needed."

Kuan resumed his seat.

Jon said, "We'd like three volunteers for paladins. Assume you'll be spending most of your time over the next few months learning your class and taking leadership classes, and that afterwards you'll be sent on missions across the length of the kingdom and possibly much farther. That means all personal projects and town works will be put on hold.

Jen stood. "For those of you considering

becoming paladins, keep in mind our armor is a spell. If you prefer an armor set, ask that paladin to become your sponsor."

"You're just trying to get out of extra work!" Brandon called in a laughing voice.

Jen grinned and winked at Trent who sat in the front row and had spoken to her before about becoming a paladin. "While I'm willing to sponsor you, Trent, you show great aptitude for leadership in my militia classes, I don't think you'll appreciate wearing my high heels. But hey, I'm game if you are."

A man sitting beside Trent punched his shoulder and laughed.

Trent reddened. "*Ha*, I'll ask Brandon. Thanks though, Jen. I'd forgotten."

Jon waited for the laughter to die down before continuing. "You'll need a sponsor and that person is in charge of your training. All aspects of it. If you consistently disregard their advice, or ignore their commands, fines will be levied. Serious fines. We're going to implement an apprentice system and until you're a master of your craft, your sponsor is in complete charge of you, including setting you work. You won't be paid for this service, and in fact, any money you might earn while doing tasks set by your sponsor will go to them."

Jon rose his hand to quell the mummers that erupted. "This isn't meant as punishment but control. There's danger in going off on your own, not only for you but for the normal humans. Your sponsors will be dedicating large portions of their time training you and deserve some recompense for it. If you're having a problem with your sponsor, you can come to me or Arden, but please reserve that for serious issues. I'll try to arrange things so everyone is happy, but your teacher gets final say. If they don't think you're ready to try something, then you don't get to do it. The classes will be at their convenience, not yours, and you could be set tasks you don't like. We expect your cooperation. When your sponsor thinks your fully trained, you'll be on your own, so pay attention!"

Jen was happy to note everyone looked thoughtful and most nodded along as if they agreed.

"Arden has successfully become a Sun Priest. Her healing spells appear to be a bit weaker than Tony's and some priest spells she hasn't mastered yet at all. Tony has agreed to sponsor her and hopefully she'll be able to learn to cast every priest spell but there's no guarantee that it's possible."

The crowd began to mutter uneasily.

Jon said, "Arden hadn't spent much time learning about the different classes and wasn't really prepared. Kuan thinks if you go into the change already knowing the spells that the chances are very good that Danu will gift you the correct magic to cast them."

Kuan said, "None of us started at level fifty. It makes sense you'd need practice to become proficient. I can't guarantee it will work but I really think it will."

His words seemed to comfort them because the mutters died down, replaced by thoughtful nodding.

Jon said, "We'd like two others to consider becoming a healing class. Preference will be given to shaman healers. We want at least one more. Ramiro will try to become a wizard. Rob will be his sponsor. That leaves two DPS class slots open.

"We hope Danu recognizes the bonds we have and agrees to the changes, but she might deny them. One successful transformation doesn't mean all will be successful. To help with future transformations everyone who attempts one must agree to disclose their thoughts and feelings about this process both during and after. Arden will keep these reports private, but it will help tremendously if someone's transformation doesn't take and they felt it beforehand. To suffer so badly for nothing…well, we wish to do everything we can to avoid that.

"No one may approach Dillion. Those wishing to become mages must wait until he's fully grown. Please approach your chosen class sponsor as soon as possible. For those of you who have a class firmly in mind, and can't be swayed from it, it's doubly important you let us know so we can attempt to balance the raids. Also, keep in mind being turned down now doesn't mean you won't get your preferred class. It just means that it won't happen right now. Your sponsor will be considering your suitableness for the class you've chosen and might recommend you pick another. Try to listen with an open mind. They've had years of experience judging who can become effective fighters or healers."

"That was a game though!" someone called out.

Jon nodded his agreement. "It was, but the personality types remain the same. Maria plays a DPS druid and not a healing druid for a reason. The spells aren't the only things that decide the type of caster you become. When she first joined our guild, she played a healing druid but asked to switch specs. I immediately agreed. Maria was always a skilled player, but healing bored her, and it showed in her lack of attention and initiative. She played well, but without the enthusiasm love of a spec gives you. Her playing, her love of the game increased dramatically when she was free to be herself, which made her much happier. Locking yourself into the wrong class or spec will make you unhappy in the long run. So, every one of you will need to pass first your sponsor, then me, and then Kuan. Once all three of us approve your choice, you can formally begin training."

"When will Kuan try to transform us?" Trent asked.

"Ramiro will be first and that happens today."

The crowd gasped.

"Keep in mind we don't even know if it will work. And if it does work, we don't know if that means Kuan could do it again. Maybe it worked once because I love Arden. We picked Ramiro because Rob loves him, and he's clearly so suited for the class he picked like Arden was. There can be no doubt Arden was a healer before her change."

Jen smiled at Arden who looked nervous. Jon ran a hand over her bald head, and she flushed and rose a hand to grasp his. The crowd all nodded their acceptance. No one doubted Arden's healer's soul.

"We won't attempt to change the next seven until Ramiro is fully recovered and we can judge whether the experiment was successful or not," Jon continued.

Jen rose and waved her hands to quiet the crowd. "This is hurried but we need the help. France is mustering its armies. We don't know what the church is doing, but it's likely doing something. Our citizens are afraid. Already some are leaving. They know war is coming. Our allies are afraid the church will fall on them while we're busy elsewhere. If we fail to protect them, I'm certain none of the others will sign treaties. It's imperative that we keep our word and honor our contracts. We'll need to leave some casters with our allies to protect them and some must remain here to protect Camelot. Those of us who leave our zone will be unsummonable. And while we have firebirds to remain in contact, it'll take us time to return to help.

"Danu demands we protect the healers in our group. She's especially concerned with Kuan. The newly made will need time to learn how to manage Danu's impulses. Ideally, they can remain here and learn in safety, but we can't wait. The church has our children and every day that passes those children get farther away."

"Only two of the missing are Fae though," Garret said as he jiggled his adopted son Mason on his shoulder.

"They're all Lesser Fae. The same as you," Warren said before Jen could answer.

Jen lifted her glowing sword. "Danu demands we retrieve them. For those of you with no magic, I can't explain it any clearer than that. To her, they're her children, the same as you are. She wants them safe. No, she *needs* them safe. She's terrified for them. Even now, while I stand here speaking, I hear her begging me in the back of my mind. I know she wants them back. I know they're in danger."

Warren nodded along with Jen and said, "Danu's voice grows louder each day that passes. The push to find the children becomes harder to resist. I think it's only our fear of leaving you undefended that lets us resist it."

"Some of my knights feel this push stronger than others." Jon glanced at Dante as he spoke. "I've decided to send another small group to France. They'll escort you and Princess Chrodesinde home. The princess will be bringing a message for her father. If he wishes to save his men and himself, he can abdicate and live out the remainder of his life in Divona on his estate there. Chrodesinde will become the queen of France and our ally. My knights will be searching France for the stolen children. You may warn your king that those found in possession of such will be dealt with harshly. But those who return them will be forgiven."

"And those who aid us in their retrieval will be rewarded," Jen added.

Jon scowled at her but said nothing.

The crowd began to speak amongst themselves as Jen sat.

"You should rest another day," Arden said.

Jen took Diana from her husband and kissed her daughter's forehead. "We're leaving after this meeting. Send us word if you hear from Father Dom.

"I warned him you're coming," Jon said.

Diana squeaked. "Sorry, sweetie," Jen whispered, easing her grip and kissing her daughter's head again before turning to glare at Jon.

"I've asked him to keep it quiet. He's a good man, and we can trust him. When you arrive in the zone, send for a summons and let him introduce you."

"Maria and I will go with you," Warren said.

"No. It'll slow us too much. Carrying three people will mean much more frequent rests," Ethan said before Jen could. He plucked Diana from her and rubbed his cheek on hers.

"It won't slow you at all. Kirk has made Maria a hundred summon stones. Every time you stop to regenerate magic, she'll summon me."

"We could pass over a border and you'll be stuck."

"Then she'll come back for me, and we'll catch up."

"Warren—" Jen gave him an exasperated glance.

"He'll be fine," Ethan said. "They both will. If they fall behind, they'll catch up. Maria can fly farther then you when you're carrying double. We can ask for extra stones too."

"As many as you can carry," Kirk said instantly. He stood and waved his hands, summoning his cauldron.

Jen pressed the heels of her hands against her eyes. "It isn't just that. I can't worry about them too."

"Then don't. We can take care of ourselves," Warren said.

"I can't help worrying!" Jen threw her hands in the air and reached for Diana.

Ethan handed her back.

Jen said, "Fine. Come. But you better be ready to travel fast. I don't plan on stopping."

"Stop when you reach the Alps and make sure your well rested to cross them," Cass warned.

"We will. And we won't try to cross ocean; we'll follow the coast."

Ethan laid a hand on her arm. "If we guess wrong and head out to sea, we'll die."

She nodded and breathed deeply of Diana's newborn smell. A grimace crossed her face and she laughed ruefully. "Our little princess needs a change."

"I'll take care of your daughter," Kuan said as he held out his hands.

Jen kissed her and handed her to Ethan who closed his eyes and rocked her a moment before giving her to Kuan.

Kuan's eyes flared blue and thunder rumbled. "I'll keep her safe."

The power of his words shivered across Jen's skin. She smiled gratefully and stood to fill her bag with summon stones.

Angels-Demons

"Thank you for meeting with me, your eminence," Father Dom said as he bowed over Cardinal Tilly's hand.

Tilly waved Father Dom to a seat beside the fire where he sat clutching a thick, woven shawl closed over his red robes. Sunlight streaming through the wide windows further warmed the room and sparkled on Cardinal Tilly's ruby ring

"That I should live to see this day…" Tilly rose a hand to cover a cough. "I'd never thought to see such before reaching Heaven's gates. Angels— demons… God's work is indeed mighty and mysterious."

"I assure you, they're neither angels nor demons," Father Dom said as he settled into the offered seat.

"No, but they *are* proof that such exist." Tilly smiled happily and reached for a cup that steamed on a side-table. "They must be very strange."

Father Dom snorted with laughter. "More than you can imagine and they grow stranger by the day." Uneasy now, he rubbed his hands together. "When I left, they were in the process of rising more like themselves. Beyond being upset over the attacks and the loss of their children, the transformations themselves agitate them. Danu flits about the castle and shows in their eyes. In the months I spent with them previously Danu was seldom seen. Now, she makes her presence felt to even those without magic."

"*Ah*, Danu, have you spoken with her?"

Father Dom smiled at Tilly's eager tone. At least this man didn't consider the Fae an abomination. "No. But I've seen her."

Tilly rose an encouraging eyebrow.

"She manifests as a blue mist. In that state, she's present, but the Fae can retain their human feelings. When she fully manifests as lightning, they cannot. She forces them to do her will. I've seen Sir Clark attempt to hold her back and fail. By all accounts, Kuan is the most powerful of them, the closest to Danu, and even he cannot deny her when she manifests as lightning."

"The church will never accept them. Everything about them— possession, magic… not to mention their ideology, is too much in conflict with traditional church doctrine," Tilly said sadly.

"They know and have decided to form their own church." Father Dom hesitated and Tilly set his cup on the table and folded his hands.

"To worship Danu?"

"No. I've been asked to beg permission for the wizards to examine the Holy Words so they might make a transcription. I've been assured they'll take oaths to transcribe accurately without bias."

"The church will never agree."

"No." Father Dom sighed heavily. "I believe the Fae will force us."

"And you think it'd be wise to offer them access?"

"I think we'd be wise to heed all their words. If you accept the premise that they're not demons, but Fae as they claim, Fae with souls, you must also consider they speak the truth of the church's future. They wish to give their people an alternative, a more approachable God. A God of love and acceptance."

"I see."

Tilly remained quiet for so long Father Dom thought he might've nodded off. The two men sat before the crackling fire deep in their own thoughts for many minutes.

Tilly finally stirred and said, "I'll speak to my brethren and pray. Please remain in the priory and keep yourself ready for questioning." He gestured about the room with a trembling hand. "The church has already made concessions beyond what I believed possible to meet and hold their conference without His Holiness present. Don't give up hope in us."

Father Dom rose and bowed again over Tilly's hand.

"Your eminence, I have healing potions. If you'd like—"

Tilly closed his hands around the vial, gently pushing the offered potion away. "Thank you, my son. I'll consider and pray. I'd looked forward to joining our Heavenly Father, but maybe my work here is not yet finished. I've argued against the hostilities our differing views have caused in the past. This seems to me a clear sign God too is dismayed his words cause strife among his flock. But the devil is tricky and can fool even learned men, tempting with honeyed words and hints of knowledge. I ask you to pray for enlightenment and beg you to speak truly."

"On my soul, I swear it."

Tilly brought their clasped hands to his lips and kissed them before releasing Father Dom and waving him away.

"Go in peace, my son."

No Time for Beauty

Jen sat with her back against a tree and her eyes closed. Thick snow mounded the base of the tree and partially covered her. Maria and Matt sat beside her while Warren and Ethan rummaged in their packs.

"We're camping here for the night," Ethan said.

She nodded her agreement. Steep sided mountains towered over them. Snow-covered peaks cast deep shade, seeming to block the starlight. And it was cold. So cold she could feel it despite her buffs. She didn't think it was cold enough to hurt her, but it was unpleasant.

"I'll make us a camp," Ethan said.

She smiled but didn't open her eyes. She'd assumed he'd take care of them.

"I love you," she said.

He paused in his rummaging, and Jen opened her eyes to see him smile at her.

"I love you too. Sleep if you can. I'll wake us at first light, and we'll cross."

"Where do you think we are?" Maria asked.

Warren said, "I think we managed to travel pretty straight. It should take us, say, two to three hours to cross. Maybe longer if the weather saps your strength and we have to rest more often."

"Will we be able to fly in the thinner air?"

"I think so," Matt said. "You use magic, not oxygen to fly. Warren can air bubble us if we start to have trouble, but it isn't that high." Flynn rustled his wings and made an odd sound that sounded more like a growl then a coo.

Matt said, "He hates the cold. I'm sending him to Jon. He can make his rounds from there. Anyone have any messages?"

"Just tell them we're fine and on track," Ethan said. He stood and handed Matt a tiny wood and canvas building.

Matt shook his head and handed it back. "Mine's nicer. I have enough magic."

Ethan accepted it and tucked it back into his bag, saying, "Fine, but keep in mind using all your magic makes it regenerate slower and the effect seems to last. Jen is tiring much quicker."

Jen spoke without opening her eyes. "I think some of that is caused from the effort of holding Danu back. But Ethan is right; don't run yourself down. It won't hurt us to sleep in a smaller tent."

"You do most of the work," Matt said and continued to remove tiny items from his bag. "With Flynn's help, maintaining a flying disk isn't too difficult."

"I'll make us a fire and get some tea brewing," Warren said.

Jen dozed off as they set up camp. She woke when Ethan picked her up.

"I've got you," Ethan whisper when she tried to walk on her own.

She relaxed and let him carry her to the tent. Lanterns threw shadows against the blue walls and the oil burning in the brazier in the center of the room gave off a nutty smell. The tent was already comfortably warm. Straw mattresses supported by vine rope woven between posts held thick furs over clean sheets. Ethan set her down on the edge of the bed

"Heavenly," she said, as she fell backward, making Ethan laugh.

"There's water to wash in when you wake, and tea is in the pot if you want some," he said.

"I'm good, thanks. She stretched out on the bed and plumped a feather pillow behind her head. "Wizards make excellent travel companions.

"Glad you think so." Matt handed Ethan a large wooden barrel of oil. "Think that's enough?"

"Yeah. It should be plenty. I'll get this all set up. Get some sleep."

Warren and Maria entered, letting in a cold draft. Warren tied the tent flap as Maria asked, "Which bunk is ours?"

"Any one you want," Matt said.

Jen rolled to face the wall and closed her eyes, letting their soft talk sooth her, and drifted to sleep again.

She woke on her own, feeling refreshed but having to pee badly and climbed carefully over Ethan who slept beside her. He'd undressed down to boxer shorts and lay on his stomach. She regretfully resisted running her hands over the muscled planes of his back. Everyone still slept. She wanted to go pee but didn't want to wake them by opening the door.

While she dithered, Maria sat and stretched, waking Warren.

"Is it morning?" she whispered.

"No idea. My bladder woke me, but I'm not tired."

"I'll come with you," Maria said as she reached for her sweatshirt. Jen waited for her to dress before untying the flap.

She rubbed her arms as she examined the thick snow drifts piled around their shelter. "*Brr.* It snowed and it's almost morning. The sky is gray but clear. I think we'll have clear skies today."

"I don't mind flying in the snow. I'd rather do that any day then fly in the rain," Maria said as she peeked over Jen's shoulder. She stepped outside the door and sank three feet. "Holy crap! It sure did snow."

The snow reached Jen's thighs now and covered the trees. Maria transformed to her eagle form and soared to the nearest trees. Jen leaped after her, laughing as she wallowed through the snow.

When they returned, Matt was putting the shrunken tent back into his pack. He nodded toward a basket on top of the snow. "Breakfast, and the tea is still warm if you want any. Ethan refilled your jug and there's enough in the pot to fill yours, Maria."

"I wish Warren could use my pack like Ethan can yours," Maria said as she opened the basket.

Jen summoned Gallant with a thought. His breath misted in the frosty air and he shook his head and stamped his feet.

"Ready when you are," Matt said and flicked his fingers to conjure his floating disk.

"Will it hold you without Flynn?" Maria asked doubtfully as she eyed the much smaller disk.

"Yeah. It'll be fine. He really hates the cold. I can manage for a few hours if Jen pulls me." He handed Jen the ends of a vine rope that clipped to his belt. She tied an end to each of her stirrups and straighten the ropes behind Gallant until they lay straight and even.

While she was connecting the ropes, Matt had removed a small pouch from his pack. He flicked his fingers and waved his wand and the tiny furs he removed from the pouch became full-sized fur coats.

He handed one to Jen as he said, "Maria, I'm not sure a coat will actually work for you. When you transform, your clothes might really disappear, and birds can get cold. If you get too cold, tell us, and we'll take a break to warm you up, or you can wait with Warren."

"The cold isn't bothering me. It feels cold but not painfully cold, if you know what I mean. I want to go and see the top. I bet I can see for miles up there."

Matt and Maria exchanged quick grins. Jen wished they could just be here for fun and enjoy the magnificent scenery, but she couldn't enjoy anything for more than fleeting moments. Her soul cried out for her to hurry. The children called to her and Danu's anger and impatience grew whenever they stopped moving.

"It might grow painfully cold at the top," Ethan said as he buttoned a thigh length fur jacket over his pack. He plucked Jen's pack from her and swung it over his arm, then mounted Gallant.

"Gallant can carry her too if we have to," Jen said as she shrugged on the coat Matt handed her. "I'm tempted to ask you all to wait, it would be quicker for me to go alone and summon you but if I fly out of the zone it might take longer to backtrack and find you."

"You aren't going alone," Ethan said. "We stick together as much as we can. I hate even leaving Warren behind like this."

"I'll be fine. Maria will summon when you reach the top and even if you left me there, I could make my way down."

"Let's get going," Jen said.

Ethan slid back to let her mount in front of him and Gallant soared into the air, his wings stirring up clouds of snow until they rose above the trees.

Matt's disk dragged for a moment, and then she couldn't feel the pull as Gallant gained speed. He flew upwards at a steep incline. She wasn't worried about Maria catching up. Maria could fly farther then her without resting and had eagle vision. She'd see them if they were in the sky.

At any other time Jen would've enjoyed the scenery. She'd never seen the Alps before and they awed her. Enormous pines, bigger than any she'd ever seen, covered the foothills. The air smelled fresh and clean and she wished they could explore the forests and shadowed gorges. *Sam would love it here,* she thought and then worried over Sam's welfare.

"Here." Ethan handed her a paper wrapped sandwich and a rough pottery jug of hot tea, pulling her thoughts from Sam. She accepted, grateful for the distraction.

He said, "When we get Alex safe at home, we should work on communications and storage containers. We need something better than paper and these crappy jugs to store hot food in."

Jen took a big bite of her sandwich, chewed and swallowed before saying, "I'm just glad we have Dillion's packs. I was thinking about that yesterday. Do you think Danu transformed him now because she knew we'd need him? This would be so much harder if we had to worry about food and water."

"I don't know," Ethan said thoughtfully. "We should bring that up in a meeting and see what everyone else thinks. Or ask Kuan," he said a moment later in an even more thoughtful tone of voice. "I'm sort of glad now Kuan doesn't feel any push to transform more of us. At least, I don't think he does.

"He doesn't. That was all Jon's idea. And it's a good idea for lots of reasons. The Lesser Fae could come to resent us. It's good they know we want them to share in our blessings."

Ethan snorted.

"They are blessings.... mostly."

"They are," Ethan agreed in a soft voice and ran his hand over her cheek. Gallant turned, startling Jen. "Look," Ethan said and waved his arm. The sun rose behind them, a golden line growing brighter on the horizon and tinting the day in rose and blue. Green rolling hills spread as far as she could see. The nearer hills were tipped in white, stained gold and mauve by the rising sun.

"Beautiful," Jen said, but she swung Gallant around and continued galloping across the air.

Burn the Corpse

Booted feet and loud voices woke Father Dom. He sat right as his door burst open. From the manner of entrance he knew this wasn't a polite summons to speak.

"Father, Cardinal Bertram has ordered your arrest. We're to confine you until your trial."

"On what charge?" Father Dom asked as he rose from the bed.

"Numerous charges." The man speaking waved the lance carrying men behind him back. The men muttered and complained. A few loudly proclaimed Father Dom a demon worshiper and the complaints grew louder.

The man in the doorway turned and bellowed, "Out! He's offered no resistance.

We'll treat him with the respect his rank is due!"

The men shuffled backward. The man placed both hands on his hips and turned back. "You're to be confined to this room. I can allow escorted trips to the baths and short walks outside."

"Your name, sir?" Father Dom asked.

"Tedesco. I'm sorry, but I have my orders."

"May I keep my Bible?" Father Dom asked as Tedesco grabbed his pack and cloak.

The men in the hall had begun to argue with each other, some urging violence and others restraint.

"I'll bring one. I've been ordered to confiscate all of your belongings. Even your clothing, I'm afraid."

He snapped his fingers and a young man stepped forward and handed him a bundle of cloth.

"Meals will be served twice daily and a guard will be on the door. They haven't forbidden books or writing implements."

"Thank you," Father Dom said as he removed his clothing and donned the offered garments. "If you'd be so kind as to bring me a quill and paper?"

"At once." Tedesco bowed slightly. "I'm

sorry but I must also take" – he pursed his lips, gesturing to the translation stone Father Dom wore around his neck.

Father Dom didn't know if the translation stone offended him or if he was just unsure what to call it.

"I've worn it so long, I'd forgotten it," Father Dom said as he reached for the rawhide thong and slipped it over his head.

Tedesco snapped his fingers again and the same young soldier handed him a wooden box.

"If you'd be so kind?" Tedesco held the box open and outstretched.

"Were you ordered not to touch it? I assure you, it does nothing except translate."

"Not ordered." He glanced over his shoulder at his still arguing men, then leaned closer and spoke in a low voice. "Contact with sorcerous items earns one hours of prayers."

Father Dom smiled ruefully and gestured to the clothing Tedesco held. "That clothing is enchanted as is the pack."

Tedesco held the clothing at arm's length, an expression of dismay on his face.

"It will repel a strike better than plate mail, and I feel neither winter's chill nor summer's heat when wearing it, but it only works for me. The pack will only open for me and nothing we possess will harm it."

Tedesco sighed heavily and tucked the cloth under his arm. "Have you any other enchanted items?"

"The pouch there." Father Dom pointed to his pouch hanging on a hook by the door. "It contains my healing potions and two summoning stones."

"The Fae have been generous with you. Although it is already forbidden to use them, men will sell such a potion for exorbitant amounts."

"The Fae are generous to all in their kingdom. I have more potions and stones in my pack."

Tedesco held out the pack he carried to examine it. He traced a finger over the glowing guild emblem, then stared at his hand as if amazed to not be burnt. "I'd heard of these magical packs and thought them an exaggeration. Is it true they keep things both hot and cold indefinitely?"

"Yes. And hold many times their size in items. The Fae themselves have no explanation as to how it's possible."

"I thought it was magic?"

"It is magic. I meant they have a great understanding of scientific principles. They can create wondrous things with no magic at all."

Tedesco stepped closer and lowered his voice to a whisper. "Is it true, then, they're from the future?"

"I believe it to be so. I believe everything they told me was true. They possess relics from their time, and they all tell the same tale. But what convinces me most is their goodness. Believe me, they have no need to lie. They could easily overpower any kingdom they choose."

"Except the kingdom of Heaven!" Bertram barked, startling both Father Dom and Tedesco. "Don't fall for his lies. See how the demon spawn have lulled a true believer? They pretend to goodness to lull the unwary and laugh as they gather souls for their master."

Father Dom bowed deeply. "I swear on my soul, they're not evil or of the devil."

Bertram curled his lip. "Your soul is already forfeit. Consorting with sodomites and fornicators. Condoning such behavior." His sneer deepened. "Or will you now claim they don't attempt to thwart God's will and prevent the conception of children, but instead swive whoever they chose, be it man or woman, without the sanctity of marriage?"

"No, that is true," Father Dom said

slowly. "They don't consider sex a sacrament between a man and a woman, but learning isn't all one way. We can teach them too."

"*Faugh*!" Bertram cut the air with his hand and spun, grabbing his long skirt with one hand and pushing past Tedesco "They revel in their debauchery and give you trinkets to bless them in it."

Tedesco stepped into the hallway, his troubled gaze on Father Dom.

"Being wrong doesn't make them demons," Father Dom pleaded. "There are tribes of men in Africa who practice cannibalism, and we send missionaries. The orient is full—"

"Enough! I forbid you to speak to these men. You will *not* corrupt them with your lies. Soon—"

Flynn appeared above Father Dom's head, clutching a rolled parchment in his talons.

"Demon spawn!" Bertram yelled out and tried to push through the soldiers who blocked the door. "Kill it!"

"No!" Father Dom shouted as Tedesco stepped forward, reaching for the sword at his hip. The young soldier who'd handed Tedesco the box drew back and threw his spear.

Flynn screamed and fluttered to the floor. Father Dom bent to scoop him up, still yelling for the soldiers to stop as a sword passed his ear so close it almost sliced it off. Hot blood gushed over the father's hand and soaked into his new robe.

"Flynn! No, he's just a pet, not a demon! Give me my bag. Maybe I can save him."

"Burn the corpse!" Bertram shouted triumphantly from behind his men as he snatched the bag Tedesco held. "See, they can be killed! Act swiftly and—"

His men exclaimed and pushed from the door as a blue cloud lifted from the bird. Father Dom moaned and fell to his knees.

"What have you done? Dear God… they'll be so angry!" He pulled himself to his feet, holding his bloody hands to Tedesco. "You don't understand. That was Danu's child, and she loves her children. They will come… You must go. Let me speak to them, and maybe I can stop them."

"You will speak to no one," Bertram said with vicious satisfaction. He strode into the room and nudged the bird corpse with his toe. "I said burn it!"

Knowledge is Pain

Needles of cold air jabbed against Jen's exposed skin. Her panting breaths froze into ice crystals as she exhaled, and even hot tea froze within minutes. Ethan was a spot of warmth against her back and she worried Matt and Maria were freezing, although neither had complained. The cold and thin air sapped Jen's strength. She'd have to land and rest soon and began scanning for a likely spot.

Bright sunlight reflected off the snow-covered crags below and to either side of them. Last night's storm had left a crystal-clear day behind with only the wind to gust the snow in swirling flurries, and she was grateful not to be navigating these mountains in a snowstorm. Sharp granite peaks jutted through the fresh snow, lining the rock face below them in black shadows. Gallant flew between two peaks that rose sharply on either side, offering no flat spots, but the gorge they flew over curved and twisted sharply between the mountain spires and there might be a flat spot around the corner.

Matt screamed, a loud wail of pain and despair.

Jen halted in shock and turned in time to see him fall. His disk had disappeared, and he plummeted toward the sharp peaks beneath them. She ordered Gallant to turn, knowing it would be too slow. Above her, Marie screamed. The eerie sound of the eagle scream seemed to echo in the thin air.

Maria's wings shadowed Jen's face as she craned over her shoulder, her horrified gaze on Matt's falling body. By his limp posture, it was clear he was unconscious, and if he landed in the deep snow and rolled into one of the gorges, they might not find him in time to resurrect him.

Ethan jumped, leaping thirty feet in an eye blink. The two men fell faster than Gallant could gallop. Jen leapt too.

She grabbed the hood of Ethan's coat and twisted, wrapping her legs around Matt who hung limply. "I got him. Get on Gallant." She summoned her steed who appeared directly below them. A rumbling roar grew, and Jen realized she'd heard it for a few seconds already.

Maria screamed again, the sound cutting off abruptly. A wall of white hit and tumbled Jen. She kept her grip on Matt, but lost sight of Ethan and Gallant. A finger flick encased her in a Greater Protective Shield as they tumbled in the snow, crashing down the steep mountainside. Rocks and debris mixed with the snow and in seconds she tumbled in blackness.

Something hit her left arm hard and she knew by the sharp spike of pain her shield was gone already. She casted another and gritted her teeth, hoping they'd slide to a stop soon or be summoned. The tumbling stopped, but she slid hard against a rough surface. Bright lights sparked on the edge of her vision and her breath came in gasping pants. She was going to suffocate and leave her daughter an orphan and her son… She prayed her husband had managed to fly to safety, although she knew he hadn't. He'd have summoned her if he could. He was likely crushed to death already and she'd never find him to resurrect him in time even if she abandoned Matt and tried to dig her way through the snow.

"Flynn," she gasped, and Matt moaned. And she knew. She sobbed out, "Jupiter Astor Shani."

Something hit her hard and weight built. Bright sparks bloomed, and she flicked her fingers in a heal but darkness took her.

She woke to a bird battering her face and thought she'd been out mere seconds. She'd stopped sliding, but a heavy weight crushed her chest and the air lacked oxygen. She casted her last shield, she was using them faster than the timers could reset, and strained to speak to the bird stuck between her and Matt. "The black bead, Joash, to whoever is closest. Go before you're crushed." She tried to shout but the lack of air and building pain from her crushed ribs made her words the barest whisper of sound.

Joash disappeared. A split second later, Warren called her. She sobbed and thought *yes* and a moment later she lay at his feet. Matt appeared and lay panting hard beside her.

"Ethan," she gasped.

Blood matted Maria's hair and the back of her sweatshirt. She shook in Warren's embrace. Jen scrambled to her feet. "Ethan?"

"Not answering," Warren said grimly.

"Did his magic…" She trailed off unable

to finish the thought.

"Haven't seen it." Warren knelt, pulling Maria down with him, to feel Matt's pulse.

"Flynn is dead," Jen said.

Maria peered over her shoulder at her. "You sure?"

"Yes," Jen said as she summoned Gallant. Gallant surged into the air and flapped hard, sending snow gusting into the air. Wind froze the tears on Jen's cheeks. It would take her twenty minutes to get back to where they'd fallen, and she wasn't even sure she could find the exact spot again. Tears dulled her vision as she scanned the ground below them, hoping to spot a familiar landmark and dreading seeing a blue cloud.

She fumbled for a summon stone, cursing herself for letting Ethan carry both packs. She only had the ten stones on her belt.

"Ethan Frey!" she screamed, clutching the stone hard in both hands, balancing easily on Gallant's back. The stone warmed in her grasp and disappeared three minutes later. She sobbed and yanked out another.

"Ethan Lance Frey!" The stone glimmered in her hand, sunlight sparkling off the deep red orb. She willed it to turn to blue mist, the sign of a successful summon. It stayed a shining stone. Below her, an outcrop of rock in the shape of a crooked diamond caught her eye and she headed Gallant to it.

"Yes, we went this way," she said and leaned low on her horse's back. An eagle's scream echoed from behind her. She peered over her shoulder at Maria but didn't stop. Unable to resist, she tore loose another stone and shouted Ethan's name into the thinning air. Gallant flew almost straight up, climbing at a sharp incline, heading to the narrow gorge they'd traversed before. Even from this distance, Jen could see where the avalanche had started. Freshly broken rock littered pristine white snow on the peak. The width of the avalanche had grown as it slid, and it had ripped loose smaller rocks and then trees when it hit the tree line. Miles of devastation lay before her. Her heart caught in her throat. She'd never be able find him beneath it. She didn't even know where to start.

Danu burst from her and swirled, buffeting her skin with sharp static shocks, and she screamed in total accordance with Danu's wild need. She should be protecting her party.

Danu raged within her as she flew above the path the avalanche had made. Sun directly overhead reflected off the white snow, making her eyes tear more. Snow gusted, tossed by the wind, obscuring and revealing patches of stone and dirt. Each one made her heart thump in hope and loss as she realized it wasn't him just another rock or clod of dirt.

"Ethan Lance Frey," she shouted as she pulled another stone from her belt. "Please, Ethan!"

Maria followed as she crisscrossed the snow, searching for any sign. When she could fly no further, she brought Gallant down on a freshly formed ledge on the peak and dismissed him. Maria landed beside her and immediately began shivering. Jen shrugged off her coat and placed it on her shoulders.

"Jen… I don't know what to say."

"Did you see where it hit him?"

"No. It hit me first. I'm so sorry. If I hadn't screamed…"

"It's not your fault," Jen said dully. "I keep expecting his magic to find me. Maybe I could follow it back to him. How come his magic hasn't come to us? He must be alive. He must!" She pulled out another stone and called his name again.

"Maybe it couldn't reach us beneath the snow and went to Jon." Marie began to cry and hid her face in her hands.

Her distress angered Danu who again appeared around Jen in a swirling vortex of blue clouds lit with sparks of static and small skeins of electricity.

"How will I find him, Maria? We have less than two hours until his spirit releases."

Maria's magic joined hers, coating her in Maria's guilt and sadness.

She'd never find him, never see him smile or hear his voice again. Pain like she'd never known brought her to her knees. She shrieked in fear and anger and Danu answered. Thunder rumbled overhead, and lightning flickered across the sky. *Protect*, Danu screamed inside her mind, and with all her soul Jen wished too.

"Where is he?" she shrieked and summoned her sword. It glowed but had no pull. Thunder rumbled again, and another chunk of snow fell from a neighboring peak. The snow tumbled, growing bigger each second until another wide swath of destruction marked its passing.

Jen screamed again and threw her sword. It flew in a glittering arc. Lightning impacted it and froze it in place as Jen yelled her husband's name and yanked the last stone from her belt. The lightning and her sword vanished. She cried as she clutched the stone to her chest until it disappeared three minutes later.

"Maybe Warren can find him?" Maria said hesitantly.

Jen nodded although she knew Maria didn't think he could.

"Twenty minutes to get back to him and twenty more to get back here. And I haven't the magic to do either." Jen crouched against the cold rock suddenly freezing and more tired than she'd ever been. She huddled beneath her cloak and hid her face while she cried.

Maria withdrew a summon stone from her belt and held it aloft. "Warren Hale."

Warren appeared a moment later. "Matt is recovering. I've informed Jon, and he's sent Kirk with Brandon, but it will take them days." Warren cleared his throat and rubbed his face. "Matt says he'd sent Flynn to Father Dom in Italy."

Thunder rumbled making Warren jerk.

"Jen?" He laid a hand on her arm. "I'm so sorry."

"What did Jon want us to do?" Maria asked.

"Wait for Kirk and Brandon. Jen, he wants you to come home. Rob has forbidden Joash to answer any summons except within the castle grounds. He's afraid he'll be killed too… Jon thinks you should come home for Diana. She began crying when…" Warren knelt beside her to hug her. Tears filled his voice when he said, "She knew and is very upset. Go home to your daughter."

The meaning of this words eluded Jen, sounding as if spoken in a foreign tongue.

"We should search. You might be able to spot him," Jen said.

"He's dead, Jen. I'm so sorry, but we'll never find him beneath all this," Warren gestured to the snow-covered mountain. "I can't spot the dead, only living things."

"He isn't dead, I know it. We can find him and heal him. I could resurrect him. We have to look!" She grabbed for another stone from her belt and swore when she realized she had none left.

Warren wrapped his hand around hers. "Maria lost her pack too. We don't have many left."

So what? What good are they?"

Warren nodded, plucked a summon stone from his belt, and called Ethan's name. They all stared at the stone until it faded to nothing.

"Jen, go home. We'll continue with Brandon and Kirk," Warren said kindly.

Jen rubbed her temples where a headache raged. Her thoughts felt slow and it took a second for his meaning to penetrate.

"You'll continue? You think…" Rage

flushed her skin and left her trembling. Warren took a step back from her and moaned as Danu left him to join the whirling blue cloud around her. Jen's sword appeared, floating before them, glowing a brilliant white.

"Your eyes," Maria said and reached for her. She screamed as Danu left her and merged with the wild blue cloud churning about Jen.

Jen grasped her sword, not caring if Danu took her.

I'm Still Human

Jen flexed her fingers and moaned. She lay face down on something cold and wet. Pain sang along her nerves. Hunger and thirst assaulted her, and her muscles ached as if she'd strained them all. Fire traveled her veins in increasingly painful waves. She groaned and pushed herself upright to grab her throbbing head.

Light snow fell around her. She lay atop snow-dusted ground in a field, dormant now, but clearly used for crops. Smoke rose from a thatched roof about half a mile away on a low hillside. She had no idea where she was or how she'd gotten there. She rose to her feet and casted a heal on herself. It took her two tries, and when she finally managed it the heal was faded and weak. Casting it made her head throb harder. A headache raged behind her eyes in time with her heartbeat. The aches and pains disappeared, but the fire beneath her skin remained. Hunger cramped her stomach and the cold air burned her sore throat. She knelt to cup the snow into her hands.

She gulped snow for a minute before the pain in her head faded enough for her sit back on her heels. The liquid cleared her head, and she remembered Ethan with shocking suddenness. She spun, searching for the mountains, and was horrified they were so far away. The white peaks glittered in late afternoon sunlight. The fire beneath her skin grew.

"I'm fucking going!" she shrieked, angry with Danu for pulling her away, angry with herself for not taking better care of her party— angry with the world.

Summoning her sword eased the fire beneath her skin but her headache redoubled.

"I'll fucking handle this! You stay out of it!" she shouted, feeling stupid for shouting to thin air but so frustrated she didn't know what else to do. She sheathed her glowing sword and began jogging to the house. She was afraid to call Gallant and be taken again without her will. Danu would kill her. She wouldn't mean too, but Jen's human body couldn't withstand this abuse. She needed food. *She needed Ethan.*

She pushed the thought away and picked up her pace. A feeling of vengeful anticipation grew as Jen grew closer to the house. Danu wanted Jen to force truth from these people and didn't care if they knew nothing. Jen staggered and fell to her knees, straining to push Danu back. The effort left her weak and shaking. She lay panting in the snow.

A man opened the door and halted at the sight of her.

"Lady," he said hesitantly as Jen pushed herself to her knees. She growled as Danu surged and tried to force her to rise and fight. Jen strained against the pull until darkness edged her vision. She laughed a dry cracked sound as darkness claimed her. She had no magic left for Danu to use.

When she woke, the man hovered over her. She didn't think she'd been unconscious long.

"Fetch another blanket and send for Fulvia," he said.

"She be a noble's mistress. Look at her clothing," a woman answered.

"Whoever she is, she be half frozen and needs help," the man said and tried to lift Jen.

Jen groaned, and he released her. Anxious brown eyes peered at her as she tried to sit.

He hovered uncertainly. "My wife will go for help. Come you inside and rest a bit."

"I have no time," Jen said as she pushed herself to her feet. Her headache threatened to blind her. Every movement sent a shaft of agony through her skull. "Water, please. A short rest and I'll be on my way."

He took her arm and half dragged her to a wooden bench beside his front door.

"Marisal, fetch water and be quick!" he called.

Jen leaned against the sun-warmed stones and closed her eyes. She batted the man away as he tried to tuck a patched blanket around her.

"I'm not cold just tired and thirsty." Jen's stomach rumbled.

"Marisal, bring food!" the man called and again tried to wrap Jen in the blanket. "It be freezing out here."

Jen groaned as she sat to take the blanket from him. She wasn't cold but didn't have the energy to argue

"Are you injured?" he asked.

She didn't reply, all her attention was on her throbbing head. The small movement of siting forward hurt so badly she thought the headache might kill her after all. Marisal returned and offered a cracked wooden cup of water.

"Thank you," Jen managed and drank it all in one long gulp. "May I have more, please?"

The woman scurried away and returned with a wooden bucket. Jen drank the entire thing.

"You'll sicken," the man said disapprovingly.

Jen laughed weakly.

"A man would sicken, but I'm no man." She handed the bucket to Marisal who bowed and hurried to the back of the house where Jen presumed the well was. Marisal and the man both watched in consternation as she drank another entire bucket and asked for more.

The spikes of pain behind her eyes had subsided to a dull throb, and she was ravenous now.

The man laughed as her stomach rumbled and said, "You'll be sick from all the water. Don't say I 'ner warned you. It be a shame to waste the bread too," but he handed her half a loaf.

She ate the entire thing and sipped a new bucket of water.

"Thank you," Jen said.

"Can we send for your kin or…" he trailed off.

A red flush climbed his cheeks and he lifted and dropped his hands as if not sure what to do or say. Finding a half-naked woman on his doorstep was likely a shock the quality of her clothing, as outlandish as it was, magnified. "You're welcome to sleep here, or I can borrow Mario's horse and cart and bring you to Papia.

Jen glanced down at her skimpy armor and grimaced. It was obviously richly adorned, the black gems and silver trim glittered in the sunlight, but it was also obviously not something a proper lady would wear even as undergarments and this man was trying not to give offense. "Thank you, but I must go. If I could beg some food for my journey? I have no means to pay for it at the moment, but I swear I'll return your kindness tenfold."

Danu roiled within Jen, pushing with renewed strength for her to go as soon as she mentioned leaving. Heat built in her veins, fiery lances that grew as she sat.

Jen rose and stretched, removing her helm to brush her hair back. The fire subsided when she rose and began building again when she remained still. "I'm going," she mumbled, speaking to Danu but the man answered.

"You be in no condition to travel and need warm clothing. I wish I had some to offer but we only possess what we wear," he gestured to Marisal who watched with an anxious expression.

"I need nothing besides food," Jen said with a meaningful glance at the door. Marisal bobbed her head and hurried inside.

Jen handed the man back his now dirty blanket. The touch of his hand made Danu flare from her. A light blue cloud, barely discernible, wound about her hands. She winced as she pushed it back, small though the effort was it left her head throbbing again.

"What are you," the man gasped as he jumped away and motioned Marisal back from the doorway.

"I am Lady Genevieve Lance Frey," Jen stumbled over the words, wanting to add wife of Ethan Frey and her voice caught on a sob. She had to clear her throat and wipe her eyes before saying. "I am a Fae and a knight of the Round Table."

"A fairy?" the man said incredulously.

He stared at her with wide eyes a moment, then hesitantly stepped forward.

"It's best if you don't get too close to me," Jen said, waving a hand through the blue cloud that began to swirl around her. "Danu is very upset." Danu was gaining strength by the moment, the water refreshing her as it had Jen.

"Danu— why are you here? How are you here? Dear God, have I gone crazy?" He called over his shoulder, "Marisal, can you see her?"

Marisal peeked over her husband's shoulder and bobbed her head. She handed the man a simple knife and a small pouch.

Despite herself, Jen smiled.

Danu subsided so suddenly Jen sagged into the mud of the path.

"Iron and salt won't harm me. Please, if you could spare a meal?"

The woman nodded nervously and ducked away. The man goggled.

They stared at each other a few minutes. The man finally blurted. "How are you here?"

"Where am I?"

"You know not?"

Jen pushed herself to her feet. The man made an abortive attempt to help, then stepped away and smoothed his beard.

"I've lost my companions and my way." The words tore a sob from her, and the man frowned.

"Bring back the blanket!" he called to his wife.

"I have no need of one. Thank you. Just food if you can spare it. And directions."

"This is Po, a province of Lumbardia, on Earth," he finished as if she might not know.

She tried to smile, and he took another step back.

His wife handed him a ratty sack and a damp rag. He motioned her back and sidled to the left of the door where he placed the items on the bench.

"Those be the best we have!" Marisal called.

"And I thank you for the kindness. What is your name, sir?"

"Gianni," he said as his wife hissed, "No tell her that."

"On my honor as a knight, I mean you no harm. I'll leave you in peace and won't forget your kindness to me," Jen said as she picked up the sack. She eyed the damp rag thoughtfully. "Might I trouble you for a piece of charcoal?"

Gianni nodded and a moment later Marisal handed him a handful of burnt, charred sticks. Danu had ceased pushing her to fight but urged her to travel with increasing heat beneath her skin until it was all Jen could do not to moan with the pain.

Jen backed away so he could place the charcoal on the ground without touching Danu.

"Which way lays Rome?"

He pointed southeast. "What do you there. "

"The church has stolen our children and has much to answer for," she said as she summoned Gallant.

Gianni exclaimed and Marisal shrieked.

"I won't forget your kindness," Jen called back as she mounted and urged Gallant into the air. She slung the food over her shoulder and used the damp cloth on her face and hands, then drew lines across her face with the charcoal as Gallant followed the man's pointing finger. All who saw her would know she was at war. The fire within her eased and Danu receded, leaving her alone with her grief.

She cried into Gallant's mane as she flew. She'd abandoned her husband to his fate and had left her friends without a word with no idea on what peak to look for them. The mountains looked different from this side and she'd flown for hours.

"Or maybe Danu transported me here?" she asked Gallant. She thought it more likely she'd flown on Gallant. Hours had passed. Twilight was upon her. Unless she'd been transported instantly and laid insensible in the mud for hours, which was always a possibility, but surely someone would've seen her? She shrugged irritably, annoyed with her senseless musings but not wishing to think of anything at all.

"It doesn't matter."

Gallant flicked his ears but didn't stop. Broad wings flapped in a steady rhythm southwest. Flying exhausted her and she'd gone less than five miles when she had to stop. She landed beside a trickling stream, more bogey ground then a true water way, and lay prostrate on the ground to open the sack.

Marisal had given her dried sausages, dried apples, raisins, olives, cheeses, and bread, likely thinking it enough for a few days travel. Jen ate everything, wishing there were more, and scooped water from the stream.

Danu wished for her to go but she felt sick with exhaustion and grief. She curled on her side and cried herself to sleep. She slept late into the next day and mounted as soon as she'd drunk her fill and relieved herself.

The air grew warmer the further south she went despite the darkening sky. She stopped every thirty minutes or so to let her magic regenerate, landing beside water when she could and amazed herself with the amounts she drank before her thirst was quenched.

Tears filled her eyes again as she remembered asking Ethan to get her salty foods, and she again turned to stare northwest at the now invisible peaks.

The voice of Danu grew louder and insistent, her nagging impossible to ignore.

"I'm fucking going!" she snapped as she summoned Gallant.

Every mile she flew from the Alps felt like a knife in her soul. She'd never be able to find his corpse. Father Dom had betrayed them. Sam and Vicky had flown to Germany using directions supplied by Father Dom and likely ridden into another trap. Danu's fear and anger surged, and Gallant spun without Jen willing it. Her horse shrieked and pawed at the sky.

"You stupid…" Not knowing words harsh enough, Jen screamed every swear she knew as she fought Danu for control of her horse. The blue surrounding her had grown so dense it dimmed the sunlight.

Danu wanted with a need beyond desperate for Jen to protect, but she couldn't seem to make up her mind on where the danger lay. Her sword pulled her northwest and southeast with equal intensity. Gallant came to a gasping standstill. His sides heaved with every breath he took, and he blew hard, shaking his head and stamping his feet.

Thunder crashed, and lightning began

striking around Jen. She tipped her head back and laughed. "Go bother another paladin! I can only go in one direction at a time! I'll get them back! You don't need to force me." The storm faded away but the hair on Jen's arms remained standing. "I want the enemy dead too! I hate them all," she whispered.

Saint Elmo's fire appeared and flowed over her, lighting each strand of hair on her and Gallant in a purplish-blue glow. Gallant's mane fluttered from the power of the magical vortex swirling around them, and he shrieked and pawed the air. Thunder rolled in continuously peals.

Jen turned southeast. The wind died, and the thunder stopped mid roll, leaving an eerie quiet behind. With shocking suddenness, Danu dissipated.

Jen laughed and drew her sword, pointing it southeast and began to gallop. Father Dom would pay for killing her husband. She'd kill them all for taking her son.

Fighting Danu

Jen's sword led her to a stone house with a thatched roof.

Danu grabbed her, and Jen killed the man inside before she could question him. The woman in the house cowered, crying on the floor. A half-grown boy ran into the house and tried to pull the woman outside as Jen screamed and threw her sword from her. She kicked the table and stool, then grabbed the stool and smashed it to pieces. Panting with rage, she destroyed everything in the house before she'd calmed enough to rifle the corpse's pockets.

Another man ran in the door. This one didn't pulse red, but he carried a sword and advanced boldly. She wanted to kill him and shocked herself motionless with the strength of her desire. Her sword glowed but didn't pull. This man wasn't evil. She still wanted him dead. She wanted them all dead.

Danu flared from Jen, and the man jumped away. The woman and boy peeked in the door. The woman screamed. The boy ran.

The man gathered his courage and straightened.

He'd fight her and die. She'd be a murderer, and Ethan would still be dead.

"Go," Jen said tightly and waved him away.

To him, she likely appeared uncertain. She stood unmoving by the corpse, but internally she struggled with herself. The struggle harder because Danu wanted her to fight.

He swung, and she ducked, grabbed his blade, and twisted. She threw the bent metal from her and again pointed to the door.

"Go! My patience isn't endless." The understatement made her laugh. She felt like she would fly to pieces Danu was so impatient for her to kill this man.

Her moment of amusement lightened Danu's grip and she laughed again. She'd fight to be herself, the woman Ethan had loved. A sob tore from her, and she rose her hands to wipe her eyes. She could hold back until she reached her enemies and spend her rage on Father Dom and the corrupt priests he sheltered with.

The man took a step back, his gaze darting from his ruined sword to Jen and then to the doorway.

"He was an evil bastard." Jen summoned her sword and the man shouted a breathless profanity. "Danu leads me to evil." She pushed past the man, leaving him gaping after her. Gallant coalesced from blue mist before you could blink, and the man cried out. She flew away without looking back. She'd barely gone half a mile when her sword flared again. This time, she kept it sheathed. Danu whirled around her in a storm of magic, little skeins of lightning biting her skin.

I must be a terrifying sight, she thought in one corner of her mind as she strode inside a small tavern.

Men exclaimed and jumped to their feet. A woman screamed. Something metallic fell with a thunk that sounded loud in the sudden silence. Jen's eyes fasten on the man pulsing red.

"Where are the children?"

He held out his hands and stepped away.

Without meaning to, Jen leapt forward

and swung her sword. She screamed in anger as she killed the man.

"Damn it!" she shrieked and threw her sword as men shouted to each other and reached for their weapons.

Danu disappeared with a whoosh of air that made Jen's ears pop. A man grabbed her arm, and she pivoted and threw him, sending him crashing among his fellows. So angry she trembled, she stomped from the building.

"Damn you!" she screamed into the sky and jerked as an arrow hit her back. She turned and snarled, and the bow wielder ducked down, hiding beneath the open window. Men argued, some wanting to chase her, others saying they should call the guard. Jen ignored them, concentrating on Danu.

She called Danu out and stared at her glowing hand. "This is pointless. Let me have control." She yelled a wordless cry of annoyance as another arrow hit her.

"Knock it off!" she snapped as two more arrows tumbled from the magical shield surrounding her. She summoned Gallant and her sword.

Her sword led her to a church, the biggest building in the small town, one street away from the tavern. Made of stone with a timber roof, it sat in the center of the small village.

Danu swirled about her. Danu's need and fear pressed on her. Her every thought seemed to agitate Danu. Pain stabbed her soul when she thought of Ethan, and Danu answered with a spike of angry defensiveness. Thoughts of Alex made Danu swirl faster and static flickered in the blue cloud. She dropped her sword to wipe her eyes. Men yelled in the distance and galloping hoofbeats approached.

"This is my pain, not yours!" Jen shrieked and summoned her sword. She pointed it at the church and her sword pulsed. It pulsed faster as her emotions raged.

Jen sank to her heels and cradled her head in her hands, trying to get her raging emotions under control. Alex needed her to be calm. Her anger and pain incited Danu. If she couldn't control Danu enough to question the men Danu lead her to, Alex would be lost to her too. A murmuring crowd grew, but no one approached her. The blue cloud surrounding her slowed.

"We'll work together," Jen said and tried to project calm acceptance to Danu. She stood, and Danu swirled faster.

"Soon, but we must have patience." She stepped forward slowly and Danu swirled faster. Jen closed her eyes and took a few deep breaths. She tried to think happy thoughts, but every memory brought her pain, pain that incited Danu and infused Jen with a fierce protectiveness. Picturing Ethan's smile or Sam dancing made her eyes burn and her head throb. It was worse thinking of her children. Jon would be angry. And Danu wanted him with a desperate need when she pictured his face. She quickly pushed Jon's image from her mind and pictured Kuan sitting in the fields and communing with the trees just enjoying being a druid. Danu calmed. When Jen finally opened her eyes, Danu had settled to a light cloud of blue, barely noticeable against her bare skin.

She took a step forward. Danu remained quiescent.

"She's going into the church!" a woman yelled, sounding horrified.

Jen glanced over shoulder and was surprised by the size of the crowd that had gathered. Night had fallen while she'd communed with Danu. Armed men milled uncertainly. Only a few women had come into the street although more gazed from windows. Jen wondered what they thought, if they'd even heard the Fae had returned.

She shrugged, this time in perfect agreement with Danu. She didn't care about them at all. Danu hummed against Jen's exposed skin when Jen turned back to the church. The hum grew as she stepped forward, but Jen was able to keep Danu contained. She pushed the half open door fully open and stepped inside.

Two men holding pitchforks stood before the priest. The priest clutched a Bible and swung a censor on a silver chain.

"Begone, demon, back to the hells that spawned you!"

"Give me my children and I'll go."

The men lowered the pitch forks as Jen walked down the aisle. They exchanged puzzled glances, appearing confused by her calmness and request.

"There are no children here," the man on the left said.

"He knows where they are or who has taken them."

"Kill it!" the priest shrieked.

Jen paused, pursing her lips and cocking her head as she examined the priest. "You know they cannot. Why order them to their deaths?" She turned to speak directly to the man on the left. "Danu senses evil, and I know he's lying. Will you die for a man who steals babies?" Guilt made her wince. She was a hypocrite who'd stolen another's child but would kill to retrieve her own. She tried not to hit the man when she hacked in half the pitchfork that he jabbed at her. He grasped the broken shaft tightly and took a step back.

"I have no wish to harm you." Jen threw her shield, knocking the man down and leaving him stunned on the ground. A flick of her fingers placed her lowest level Deadly Ground beneath the priest. He screamed and writhed unable to pull himself from the glowing red circle on the floor. She canceled the spell and stepped closer. "I could kill him in an instant, but I'll have mercy if he confesses and tells me where the children are."

The priest grabbed for the other man's pitchfork.

The first man rose, shaking his head as if he was dizzy, and jabbed at her with the broken shaft. She kicked him, and he fell back with a shriek. The priest thrust. The tines of the fork scratched across her armored shoulder with a sound of metal-on-metal although to the human eye it appeared as if the forks had touched bare skin. Jen grabbed the priest by his robe and shook him.

The other man grabbed her arm and yanked, then reached for a dagger on his waist when he couldn't budge her.

Jen punched him. Bone cracked, and the man screamed shrilly as he held his hands to his bleeding face.

"Where are the children!"

"I know not! But even if I did, I'd rather die a martyr than—"

Jen threw him as hard as she could. The priest's head impacted the wall with a wet splat, and he crumpled, unmoving. She drew her sword and stabbed. Lightning flickered through the open door behind her and the crowd outside yelled.

"He wasn't a martyr but a liar who wished to steal my children's gifts for his own use!" She nudged the corpse with her toe. "I'd burn him. If anyone was a demon, it was him." She flicked her fingers, casting Lay Evil Spirts. A reddish-gold glow suffused the ground beneath the corpse.

The man whose nose she'd broken ran from the church and yelled for the guard to attack. The man she'd kicked watched her with wide, terrified eyes but didn't try to rise.

When the red glow dissipated, Jen strode from the church and summoned her mount. She followed her glowing sword.

War Has Already Begun

Father Dom stared from his window at the brown robed monks crossing the plaza beneath him. No statues or artwork yet graced these grounds but Sir Rob had shown him visions of what would be. He could see the bones of the Vatican as it would be in the half-crumbled walls before him. Long years of fighting had left these once elegant buildings in disrepair. Construction had started and halted, leaving stones mounded in piles before the obelisk that dominated the main plaza.

Father Dom believed the visions Sir Miller had shown him to be true visions, including the giant fire ball that had destroyed an entire city. He believed the Fae truly wanted to preserve the Earth and the people on it, but he also thought they'd lost their way a bit and fallen farther from God. The weakness of the future church worried him, and he'd begun to think God had chosen this time and this place to give the church a chance to do it right. The Earth didn't just need the Fae, the Fae needed God. It would take patience and love to turn them to a righteous path. Force would just be met with force. Their beliefs were as deeply ingrained as his own, and he was just beginning to see how different those beliefs truly were.

His breath misted the cool glass, and he used his sleeve to wipe it. His door opening startled him.

Tedesco stood stiffly in the doorway. "Cardinal Tilly has requested your presence."

Father Dom inclined his head and went where he was bidden.

Tedesco led him without speaking to Tilly's apartments across the compound and knocked lightly at a wide oak door.

"Your eminence, Father Dom as you requested." He gestured Father Dom into the room and bowed himself from it, closing the door quietly behind himself.

"Sit," Tilly said, gesturing to the seat Father Dom had occupied just yesterday.

"I argued against your arrest—"

Father Dom waved a hand in dismissal. "It matters not. Have you been informed of the murder of the firebird?"

Tilly's reaching hand halted halfway to the cup beside him. "I have not."

"The bird arrived while the guards and Archbishop Bertram were present, and Bertram ordered them to attack. The Fae will know and mourn the animal, and I'm afraid it will convince them we're all enemies."

"Did the bird offer violence?"

"Not at all. It was a tame creature and visited me daily bringing letters from far away friends. It liked me and would rest by my fire… It was easily killed because it trusted me."

"*Ahh*, you worry the Fae will now believe you're untrustworthy and trapped the bird apurpose."

"I guarantee Sir Biddle will seek vengeance. For all their talk of the sanctity and equality of all human life, they're extremely vengeful. I've personally seen a party of five kill a hundred men in under five minutes when two attacked."

"The rumors of their might aren't exaggerated?"

"I couldn't say as I don't know to what rumors you refer, but they're mightier than you can imagine. The ships sent were destroyed with no loss of life on their side. The only deaths were those caused by poison and trickery and only good Catholics died. Innocent men, women, and children."

"Ships?" Tilly set his cup on the table and leaned back in his seat. "I think you had best tell me everything, leave nothing out. We authorized a ship to seek out the Fae but didn't authorize an attack. Only one ship should've been sent. We certainly didn't tell them to poison anyone."

"I believe the schisms in the church are deeper than you think," Father Dom said.

➞

"That is quite the tale," Tilly said when Father Dom finished speaking. "I see now we have enemies among us, not misguided or misinformed but men lying for foul purposes. Men who care not what damage they cause to the church."

"And you've heard naught of these attacks?"

Tilly steepled his fingers beneath his chin a moment, then tapped his lips thoughtfully. "Only what you'd told us on your arrival here. We'd heard rumors of the doings in Justinian's court. Rumors that most disbelieve. The emperor has sent an emissary and offered to bring us to his court to hold our meetings, but we've heard nothing from France. We're sequestered here with little contact with the outside world. Perhaps, in time, word would reach us. The question is, who has authorized the use of church funds and usurped their power? Very few men would have the authority to order our limited troops or remove funds to pay for others. The encounter you describe would've cost a hefty sum. The pilfered amounts will be greater than I'd thought and likely better hidden. The truth will be difficult to ferret out."

"What is true and what is believed to be true are two different things," Father Dom said dryly.

Tilly smiled sourly. "The Fae will believe the church sent the ships and ordered the deaths?"

Father Dom nodded.

"The church will not admit it happened at all."

"But—"

"There's no proof. You say they've sunken the boats and there are no survivors. It'll be years before official word of the attack reaches here and years yet before any credence is given to it. It's unthinkable Archbishop Mina would attempt to harness a demon for his own use or that the church would order poison used against its own congregation."

"Are you saying the Fae lied? I assure you, the attack happened. I was there and saw it myself. The dead killed by poison, the ships…"

"Not at all. I'm saying whoever orchestrated the attack will say such is the case and there's no proof to refute it."

"The soldiers are dead. Surely their families will know where they went and wonder when they don't return?"

"And storms are simple things much easier to believe than the truth."

Father Dom shrugged irritably. "And nothing we say, no matter how many believe it to be true, will matter in the least. Danu will speak and her Fae will listen. The death of the bird… they argue amongst themselves. Some wish to go into seclusion, others wish to destroy the church completely. King Jon tries to balance both sides. He wishes to build a world with fair laws and safety, for not just his people, but the Earth itself. Even now, they make plans to rebuild the Vatican and form it into the church of the future."

"And this might tip them to hate us?"

"If we could find and return their children…"

"*Ahh*, yes, the missing children. I'm not without resources and connections. I shall see what I may find, but even the fastest ship wouldn't have arrived here yet."

"And, meanwhile, the Fae grow angrier while we debate endlessly. If we don't take action soon, the matter will be torn from our hands. They have no respect for rank or privilege. They won't spare the nobles or clergy. To declare them demons is to declare war on the world."

"And if they *are* demons?"

"Then that war has already begun."

Vatican City

Jen flew until she tired, then crawled into a haymow to sleep. Bird song woke her. A mere half mile from where she'd rested, the obelisk that defined the Vatican rose into view. It towered over the stone buildings that jammed the narrow streets beneath her. Men and women screamed and exclaimed as she flew overhead, but she paid them no heed.

Slate roofs rose in varying heights, quickly blocking her passing from view. The city was more crowded and built better than she'd expected. Paris had led her to believe cities in this day and age were formed crudely, but these homes were elegant and graceful, much like Constantinople had been. Carvings lined doorways and statues adorned interior gardens hidden from street view by tall walls. It was clear this had once been a prosperous city although by the state of disrepair and rebuilding it was also clear the city was recovering from a period of strife.

Wide cobbled streets encircled a thick wall with a crenelated top. She paused to examine the buildings, recognizing the terrace that would one day be the plaza of Saint Peter's. Thin columns held up a portico that encircled the plaza but the church itself was much smaller with two small doomed buildings attached to a two-story dome adorned with a wooden cross.

No statues lined the plaza, but carvings of winged women adorned the walls of the smaller domed building. To the left, a bell tower rose before a wide, gated pathway. The gate was open now and men led wagons pulled by shaggy horses through the gateway. Women with black shawls tucked over their heads scurried into a side door of another building where smoke rose in vigorous plumes from four chimneys. Her sword pulled her to the west where a three-story building of graceful arches and wide windows sat on manicured grounds. Only the topmost windows sported glass, tiny squares in wire frames. Shutters on the second floor, folded back now, bordered the windows she'd have called French doors if they'd led anywhere. The bottom floor windows were smaller and remained shuttered. She followed her sword, flying directly through one of the wide windows and into the building onto the second floor.

A wide stone corridor lined with closed wooden doors lay before her. Statues and artwork were tucked into niches lining the walls and torches glittered on gilded paint. Every inch of the walls and doors was carved, painted or plastered in fanciful designs. She dismissed Gallant with a thought. Her sword led her forward. A man in a black robe halted at the sight of her.

Another man, who stood before double doors as if guarding them, swung to face her and yelled, "Halt!"

He hadn't noticed her enter. His expression was shocked as she approached.

"Step aside," Jen said and waved her glowing sword.

He drew his sword while the man in the black robe screamed and ran.

Jen ducked under the swing and hit the man hard with the flat of her blade, knocking him to the floor. It was hard to hold back. She wanted to slay every man here for causing Ethan's death, and she had to take a few deep breaths as she reminded herself that she needed them alive to question. She could kill them when she knew where Alex was, she told herself firmly.

While he moaned and tried to push himself up, she kicked in the door. In the distance, a bell began to ring. Men shouted, distance muffling the sound, but she assumed they shouted about her. It would take them time to muster a sufficient force to be a threat to her. If she were quick, she could find and question whoever she wished before they could gather enough men to stop her.

The sword in her hand pulsed. The men in the room jumped to their feet, all exclaiming. Jen's vision sharpened, Danu manifesting in her eyes, and a feral smile appeared on her lips. She'd found her evil. Two men outlined in red stood to her left. It was clear they'd been seated at the table.

Jen's gaze scanned the room. It was furnished sparsely but finely. Frescos decorated the walls and thick curtains framed narrow glass windows on the eastern wall. A fire smoldered in a hearth big enough to roast an entire pig. Gold and silver candlesticks sat on the table and lined a carved and gilded mantle. Every chair was carved in different patterns and sported thick cushions. Jen smiled in satisfaction that the room only had one door and the windows were too narrow to jump through.

"Shut up!" She waved her sword and pointed at the loudest screamer with her free hand. "And sit the fuck down!" She kicked the door closed with her foot. "Call the guards if you wish. Their deaths won't stop me for a minute."

The men backed away from her as she strode forward. Jen almost laughed. Danu hummed eagerly but made no demands, working with her, not trying to force her. Jen's shoulders relaxed, and Danu hummed harder, the sensation pleasant now and not painful. Danu was with her, and Jen embraced her nature.

Cooperation with Danu increased the effects of her flaring eyes, and Jen wondered if they shone white now instead of blue. Danu's eagerness made her feel powerful, and she welcomed the sharpness and clarity of her sight and hearing. Even her sense of touch seemed magnified. She could feel the unevenness of the boards beneath her feet and gauge movement of the men by air currents against her skin. She didn't try to stop her feral smile from widening.

"Demon!" a man yelled shrilly, grabbing for his Bible.

He began to pray in a loud sonorous voice. Jen jumped onto the table, scattering parchment and writing implements, and kicked the prayer. He yelped as he flew backward into the black robed man behind him.

"I said silence!" Jen bellowed, her magically amplified voice echoing in the stone room. "I'm no demon! I'm a Protection Paladin!" Jen laughed, loving what she was, and Danu responded with a wave of satisfaction. The hum against Jen's skin lessened, but she felt Danu's eagerness. "I'm a paladin!" Jen shouted again and placed the tip of her sword on the neck of the man who was outlined in pulsing red. Danu appeared about her, and the men screamed. Her target stood stock still and held out his empty hands.

"Where are the children?" she asked.

Although she didn't yell, her words held weight and reverberated off the stone walls.

"Sit!" she barked as men rushed for the door. A flick of her fingers placed Deadly Ground between the table and door. Men shrieked as they were pulled to the glowing spot of floor. She canceled the spell with another finger flick and bellowed, "Sit or I'll kill you all! Where are the children?" Lightning blew through a leaded glass window and hit the table so hard it cracked. The men screamed curses, threats, and prayers.

The door opened, and Jen threw her shield at the man who entered. It knocked the man down, leaving him dazed on the floor, and men in the hallway yelled. Her shield returned to her hand.

"Last warning," she said and laughed as thunder rumbled.

The men in the room exclaimed and began pushing and shoving, some trying to go to the door and some to the far wall.

"Take your seats," an old man in a red robe said, half rising to gesture them to sit. The ruby ring on his finger caught the light, glittering with each movement.

The men began to sit, muttering between themselves.

The old man clasped his hands and inclined his head. "Might we know your name?"

"We aren't having fucking tea. This asshole is an evil fuck and if he doesn't tell me in three seconds where my children are, I'll cut his fucking head off!" Thunder rumbled again, emphasizing her words.

"You hear that?" Jen pointed to the ceiling with her glowing sword. "That's Danu and she wants you dead."

The evil man blanched, and Jen glared around the room. "She wants you all dead! Danu hates you for stealing her children. I only want the guilty parties like these assholes here—" Jen gestured to the man sitting beside her target— "Dead. But make me wait too long, and Danu will make me kill you all."

Her target yelled a wordless cry of fear as she leaned forward, her blazing eyes inches from his. "Tell me where my children are."

He darted panicked glances about the room but clenched his lips.

"One!" Jen drew back to poke him with her sword hard enough to draw blood. He tried to back away but the men behind him blocked him. They scrambled over each other, and he stepped back. Jen stepped forward, lifting his chin with her sword. It glowed so brightly it casted shadows.

"When I get to three, you're going to wish you'd spoken. Two!"

The man turned pleading eyes to his companion and licked his lips.

The man beside him glared and crossed his arms.

"They've been sent to—"

"Shut up, fool!" the man beside him yelled.

Jen swung, and men screamed as the head rolled across the table.

"You were saying?"

Her target blinked rapidly and rose a trembling hand to his bloody face.

"I don't know where they are now. I swear it!"

"My sword wouldn't be glowing if that were true. Danu can sense evil, and you're as evil as they come." She flicked her fingers, hitting him with her lowest level Wrath spell. A dark purple ball of light burst from the tip of her sword and hit the man in the chest. He shrieked and swore.

"One. Two—"

"Please, may we speak civilly?" the old man begged.

Jen drew back and prepared to swing. "Thr—

"Barcelona! They'll go to Bishop Sanzo. King Agila has consented to hide –"

The door burst open and two men with bared swords rushed in.

"No!" the man in the red robe yelled as they swung at Jen.

She caught the first sword on her shield and swung, cleaving through the man's sword and into his companion's shoulder. He screamed as he dropped his sword and clutched his bleeding wound. Her backswing sliced the first man across the chest, killing him instantly. She threw her shield at the door and jumped after it.

"No!" the old man yelled again. "Lay down your arms; I command you!"

"He has been bewitched!" a man yelled from the hall. "Attack!"

"No! Please, they're innocent men, have mercy!" the old man begged.

Jen ducked under the spear aimed at her heart and stabbed upward as she rose, catching the spear wielder in the throat. A flicker of red caught her eye, but the man in the red robe outlined in pulsing red ran through a door before she could leap again. Glittering swords appeared around her and she laughed as she spun, sending them whirling. Men cursed and screamed and died.

"Guards! We need more guards!" a man yelled as Jen hopped forward and threw her shield.

While it knocked down a tight grouping of men, she spun and attacked the men hitting her back. Small spikes of pain disappeared as she casted a heal followed by a Protective Shield on herself. The men exclaimed as the small wounds they'd made disappeared. They swore as their swords hit the magical shield surrounding her, making it flare whitely,

"I command you to lay down your arms! I am the senior monsignor here! Do as I bid or be forsworn!" the old man shouted.

When Jen turned, the old man stood with his arms outstretched between her and the soldiers beginning to rise from the floor. She threw her shield behind her without looking and smiled as men cursed as it hit them. A finger flick placed Deadly Ground behind her. She didn't turn as the men began to scream.

"Your book can't stop me." She gestured with her chin to the Bible the old man held, but she canceled her Deadly Ground spell. Men moaned and sobbed behind her.

He glanced down and shrugged lightly. "I'd forgotten I carried it. It wasn't meant to stop you. I believe you to be Fae and an honest woman. Return to the meeting and we can discuss your concerns."

"My concerns? You fucking attacked my home, stole my children, and killed my husband!" Jen strode forward with every word and now glared nose-to-nose with the man. "I want nothing from you, except what you've taken. "

The man waved his hand and the soldiers

behind him backed away. They lowered their weapons but didn't drop them.

One of the men said, "Your eminence, word has reached us that she entered the Basilica of Santa Maria in Trastevere and killed the reverend father there."

Jen glanced over her shoulder at the man who spoke. He wore a blood-red cloak over bright chainmail and carried a sword it took two hands to hold. She smirked. She could kill him in seconds.

"He was fucking evil!" Jen snapped. She pointed her sword at him and waggled it side-to-side. "This sword can lead me to evil. It led me there and it led me here. "

The old man said, "Decurio DiAndrei, gather the troops and keep them outside the main gate. You cannot stop her. If she's determined to kill us all, so be it. We won't sacrifice our men too."

"Not all," Jen said stiffly. "Just the guilty parties and whoever stands in my way."

"Please, Lady— Victoria, isn't it?"

"Frey. Jen Frey."

The men behind the father took a step back. Hands tightened on weapons and nervous glances darted between them. Jen glanced at her black armor and pursed her lips. She'd forgotten she wore the black set. Her eyes narrowed. This man had heard of them and knew Jen generally wore white and Vicky to be reckless and not in control of her magic.

"Father Dom," she hissed.

"Lady Frey, we'll question Bishop Egas together. I've just recently learned of the atrocities committed against you and your kind. Please, this is difficult for all of us. Remember you were human once and have patience."

He half turned to speak to a man behind him.

"Tedesco, fetch Father Dom and bring him here."

"His eminence has ordered him—"

"And I'm ordering him brought before us. As I outrank Cardinal Bertram, you'll carry out your orders at once."

The man bowed deeply, saluted and spun away. He gestured for the soldiers to follow. Jen lowered her sword and strode back into the meeting room. A simple hop brought her to the tabletop.

"Leave or remain quiet," she said as she strode forward to again point her sword at the man who glowed red.

A few men scurried for the door but most remained seated.

The old man said, "Monsignor Egas, tell

us who ordered the attack and where the children are to be brought."

Egas said, "Your eminence, surely you see she is a demon?"

"I see a distraught Fae who wants her child."

"Fae." Egas curled his lip and glanced around the room.

Jen followed his glance. Most of the gathered clergy appeared terrified, but some nodded thoughtfully or glared at the man while others eyed her as if she were the devil incarnate.

"You've taken vows of obedience. Will you be forsworn?" the old man asked.

The sword in Jen's hand pulsed.

The man's lips tightened but he bowed slightly as he said, "The children were to be taken to Tolosa in France and then on to Barcelona, but I wasn't privy to the particulars."

"Why?"

Egas cocked his head.

"Why take them," the old man clarified.

"Too…" He trailed off and darted a guilty glance around the room.

"Go on," the old man said.

"We cannot fight them. They're too strong. You saw her!"

"Yes. She *is* strong. I think she could easily kill us all, and yet she doesn't. The only evil I see is the evil we did."

"But they're demons!"

"No; they're different. It's clear to me they're not demonic. I can see no earthly reason why she doesn't strike us all dead."

"She thinks to gull you."

"Ridiculous." The old man's eyes narrowed and he spoke in a softer voice when he asked, "And what were you paid to arrange the theft of the children?"

A red flush climbed Egas's cheeks.

"Nothing, your eminence."

The sword in Jen's flared and a smell of ozone built. She knew he lied. The old man knew it too. His eyes narrowed even more, and he tapped his fingers against the tabletop as if contemplating his next words with care.

"Danu will strike. Can you not feel her in the air?" the old man asked.

"The smell of Hell accompanies her."

Jen drew back her arm.

"She is the evil thing. Her and all—"

His words ended in a strangled groan as Jen swung. Blood dripped from her sword to the table, the soft pitter-patter the only sound.

"When my people come, tell them I've gone to Spain. Tell them what was said here."

Jen sheathed her pristinely clean sword. It no longer glowed. Danu was sated. Eagerness to be on her way hurried Jen's words. "I've killed others in your city besides these here and the priest your guard mentioned. Two, I'm not certain why Danu wished dead. I'm only certain they were evil. The Fae wish to live in peace, but we *will* protect ourselves and those in our care. Raise arms to us again, and I'll destroy your church."

"Blasphemy," a man muttered.

"Truth," Jen said. I believe most of you weren't aware of what was planned or done but the church *did* pay for the attack. There can be no doubt you harbor evil men." She kicked at the corpse slumped across the table. "He wished to steal my children's gifts for himself. If he truly believed me a demon, what does that make him?"

A timid knock sounded on the door.

"Enter!" the old man called.

"Cardinal Tilly, Father Dom, as you requested."

"He is innocent!" Tilly shouted as Jen leapt for the door.

You Can't Kill Pain

Father Dom held out his hands, his eyes sad. The soldiers surrounding him rose their weapons in white-knuckled hands.

Fury like she'd never known made Jen's voice tremble.

"Ethan died because we trusted you. Will you let these good men die to protect you? You know I can kill them all." She wanted to kill him, to kill all of them. Danu didn't care. Her sword didn't flicker. These men weren't evil, and Jen had taught Danu they weren't the enemy either. Just moments ago, she'd been proud and happy Danu had learned, and now she cursed Danu's new acceptance. She hesitated, caught by her own confusion.

"Where is Flynn's corpse?"

"Cardinal Bertram ordered it destroyed. I'm so sorry, Genevieve. I never meant the bird any harm."

Jen's trembling escalated. She wanted to kill him to ease her pain. She'd looked forward to it, imagining the relief she'd feel when Ethan's murderer was dead, but she knew the father spoke truth. "Who killed Flynn?" she asked in a strangled voice.

"They are innocent. They'd never seen nor imagined such an animal and its sudden appearance feared them."

Jen took two quick steps forward and screamed in anger when her sword refused to pull her. She threw it from her, and the soldiers straightened. Eager glances darted between them. They thought her defenseless without it. She laughed and crouched, wanting them to attack, wanting to kill them with her bare hands, wanting anything that would ease the pain in her soul.

A hum began to build against her skin, and she felt Danu straining for understanding. Jen's emotions flared without her control. Fear, pain, anger, everything she felt was magnified and examined. One emotion after another was plucked and discarded as Danu sought enlightenment.

Jen stood on a cusp. She could shape Danu to her will, convince her the murderous rage she felt was justified even if it caused Danu to hate the entire human race. Danu would help her kill and would treat them as the enemy, and Jen wanted to kill them.

She rose a trembling hand to her burning eyes. She wanted to kill her own pain. Right or wrong, she didn't think she had the strength to forgive, to stop feeling hate. A hate she'd thought to unleash on Father Dom when she'd believed him guilty of betrayal. She wanted him to be guilty to avoid this choice. Without her hatred, she'd only have pain.

"Killing them won't ease you," Father Dom said sadly.

Her sword appeared in her hand again and she took another step forward.

"Maybe not—"

Genevieve Lance Frey, her husband called.

"Ethan?" She rose trembling hands to her face as her soul cried out yes.

***

"A narrow escape indeed," Tilly said as he exited the meeting room.

He held his robes from the bloody floor and stepped to the side to let the other men exit. "Decurio DiAndrei, send to the kitchens and stables. The Holy See departs at dawn for Constantinople. Arrange for a fast boat. I wish to travel quickly." He smiled at the gaping man and waved him away. "If His Holiness won't come to us, we must go to him."

Love Returned

Jen found herself thigh-high in snow beneath towering conifers. Ethan smiled and reached for her. She fell into his arms.

"I thought you were dead," she sobbed as he kissed her check, then neck.

"I thought you were dead too." He took a deep shuddering breath. "Even when I found them, I thought you were gone for good, taken by Danu. I began summoning as soon as we reached the other side of the peak and you never answered…."

"Where were you? Why didn't you answer me? You're okay, aren't you?" She threw a heal at him and kept healing him until he glowed translucently. Tears streamed down her cheeks and her legs collapsed beneath her. "I thought you were dead; I thought you were dead," she gasped between sobs as he knelt beside her in the snow. She cried in his arms a few minutes before regaining enough control to wipe her eyes and speak. "I never would've left you. Never!"

"*Shh*," he said and rubbed her back. "I know. They told me. God, Jen."

"I don't know how I left. I didn't want too."

"*Shh*," he repeated as her voice became shrill. "Danu called you. And you listened. I don't blame you. There's no need to feel guilty." He kissed her brow.

"Jen, we all know you wouldn't have left. I thought you were gone for good too," Warren said.

She started in surprise just noticing the others.

"You touched the hilt, and the glow from your eyes spread until you became a glowing white ball and flew away."

"You were vaguely horse shaped," Maria said.

"The front half, anyway," Matt added and winced when Ethan moaned.

Danu swirling around them brought his fear and horror to all of them. Jen shivered and pressed closer.

She said, "I don't remember it at all. I woke starving and thirsty with a raging headache."

Ethan shuddered and groaned, filled with dread.

She laid her hand on his cheek and tried to sound reassuring as she said, "Danu is listening better to me now. But where were you?"

Ethan sat in the snow and pulled her into his lap. He kissed her deeply before saying, "Beneath a huge freaking pile of snow. I think that peak was the border of Austria and I landed out of the zone. Gallant almost got me out. A wall of snow pushed him into the peak, and we rolled, causing another avalanche. The snow crushed him but left a deep pocket with hard-packed snow above him when he disappeared. The fall knocked me out and broke my neck." He shivered and clutched her tighter. "When I regained consciousness, your black-beaded bracelet was draped over my hand." He cleared his throat and wiped his eyes before continuing in a firmer voice, "I'd landed in a deep crevice of almost sheer rock. The entire thing was filled with snow, except where Gallant had been, and a narrow crack in the stone near my head that ran up the rock face and let in light and air. It took over a day before I could move enough to reach a healing potion and it was another few hours to climb free. And all that time I thought…" he shook himself hard and continued, "Once I was free of the gorge, it took me another day to reach the zone where they were. I used almost all my summoning stones trying to reach any of you." He rocked them back-and-forth as she cried in a mix of remembered fear and loss.

She'd laid in the snow unconscious for over a day. Danu had almost killed her.

Danu swopped about them, adding her love and relief, fear, and eagerness to be away to Jen's wild mix of emotion. Her head began to hurt, and she tried to stop crying, knowing she was dehydrating herself.

"I spent a day staring at your bracelet unable to move to even try to summon you. Neither firebird would answer me. I pictured you dying, smothered, freezing all alone. God, Jen, that was the worst day of my life. I almost didn't try to climb out, but the children needed me."

He was quiet a minute.

"I thought you'd all been killed. Neither Joash or Flynn answered me," he whispered and shuddered, tightening his grip.

"Joash has been ordered not to go

anywhere."

"I know." Ethan wiped his face on her cloak, then pulled a cloth from his pocket and blew his nose. "I caught up to Warren and Maria."

"And me," Matt said.

She glanced over but made no move to rise from Ethan's embrace. She wanted to lay in his arms forever.

Warren and Maria sat together holding hands with their backs turned. Matt waved a greeting but didn't approach. He crouched before a metal brazier, warming his hands. The death of Flynn had aged him. His cheeks were sunken, and lines framed his eyes.

She said, "I'm so sorry, Matt. Father Dom told me they burned his corpse."

Matt nodded tightly. "Why'd they do it?"

"Because they hate us!" Warren snapped.

"I'm not really sure," Jen said. "Father Dom said Flynn startled some soldiers when he appeared and they killed him, but there must be more to the story. The soldiers would've had to have been close when he appeared and had their weapons out already."

"Unless he lied."

"No. I'm sure he wasn't lying." Jen touched the hilt of the sword peeping from the scabbard across her back.

Matt rose both hands to cover his face. His shoulders shook, but he made no noise. Jen wanted to go to him but couldn't bear to leave Ethan's embrace. Maria rose and hugged him.

Ethan ran his hands lightly through her hair and kissed her lips. "Heal yourself," he whispered.

"A magic induced headache. Heals won't help it. I need water."

"You need food and rest. We can camp right here."

She hugged him tighter when he reached for his pack.

"I'm fine. Stay with me." He nodded and kissed her again. She rested her forehead on his and breathed his air, so grateful to have him back it hurt.

"Matt and I will go make a camp." Warren stood and grabbed his pack. "Maria lost her pack too, but except for summon stones, we have plenty of supplies. Take all the time you need. There'll be a tent set up for you just over that ridge." Warren pointed and offered a hand for Matt to rise.

"We should go back to Rome. I think I know where the children—"

Jen jerked as Danu burst from Ethan and slammed into her. It knocked them over and rolled them.

"Sorry," he gasped as he struggled upright in the snow. They'd matted the snow near them, but it still reached her chest when she sat to grab her throbbing head.

Ethan patted her shoulder anxiously as she said, "I'd just reached Rome and only got one man to admit anything. He claims they're headed to Barcelona, and he wasn't lying. We were chasing the wrong boat. They must've switched boats before entering the river and traveled the coast. They didn't take the Seine. They plan to hide them in Spain. King Agila is working with them."

Warren knelt and withdrew a map from his pack. Jen scooped up handfuls of snow to quench her thirst as Warren traced his finger along the map and tapped thoughtfully. Ethan shrugged his pack off and rummaged one-handed, keeping his other arm tightly around her.

He handed her a flask of water conjured by Dillion. She took it gratefully and drank. It cleared the ache in her head, and she sighed in relief.

Warren said, "It'd take a minimum of three weeks and potentially much longer. They'll have to go either east or west to avoid the mountains, which will be uncrossable for a human at this time of year. I'm betting they go west to the coast and plan to take a boat along the coast to Barcelona. Cass has Barcelona marked as a major city. We might beat them there. Kirk and Brandon can wait there, and we can backtrack. This is great, Jen."

"Rome can wait," Ethan said. "It'll take at least a day to get there, and they'll be prepared now. The men who know will have heard Jen was there and will hide, and while I want to hunt them all down, it isn't worth missing the children. She needs rest. A day spent here resting before flying to Spain would be better."

"I agree," Matt said.

"Those fuckers will pay," Warren said as he stuffed the map back into his pack and offered Maria a hand to stand. "Rest, Jen." He pulled Matt up and slung an arm around his shoulder, and the three trudged through the snow toward a less dense stretch of trees south of where they sat.

"How's Matt?" Jen asked as she watched them leave. She rested her head on her husband's shoulder and enjoyed holding him.

"Heartsick. We're all sick over Flynn's loss. It's such a—"

Matt screamed as Warren yelled. Jen

jumped to her feet and ran toward them, floundering in the snow. She casted Valorous Leap and summoned Gallant. Ethan leapt past her.

"Flynn's magic," Warren said, holding out a hand to stop her.

Matt staggered, landing on his hands and knees. Warren pulled Maria away when she reached for him.

"Give him a minute. It's all he has left."

Jen sank to her knees. Adrenaline left her heart pounding but her knees weak. She was so tired she didn't think she'd have the strength to stand.

"Damn it!" Matt yelled and held his hands out. The blue of Flynn's magic darkened as Matt's magic joined it. The magic swirled and took shape, growing denser and gaining color. Within a minute, a dark-gold firebird hovered before Matt. Deep orange wings flicked, dripping sparks. A beady-blue eye stared into Matt's. "Be welcome, Finnian Lior Tyson," Matt said in a husky voice as he offered an arm. The bird settled, cooing softly. He tucked the bird beneath his coat, leaving just the bird's red and gold crested head peaking from the furs.

"He isn't Flynn, but he feels similar, like Flynn's son or something. He loves me already, an echo of Flynn's love." Matt's voice broke. "His public name is Flynt."

"He's beautiful," Jen said.

"I wonder what colors them?" Warren asked. "Did you choose the color?"

Matt shook his head.

Maria leaned closer to run a finger across the bird's cheek. Flynt cooed louder and tilted his head, obviously enjoying the caress. "We'll be careful when we call him," she said.

Matt exhaled heavily and reached inside his jacket to pet the bird. "I trust you, and it was my own fault. If you need help, call him. As much as I love him, I love you guys more. I'd ordered Flynn not to attack anyone there. I was afraid Danu would push him to attack and he'd be hurt. I didn't even think he'd see anyone except Father Dom. I'll make sure Flynt knows he's to protect himself.

Jen's shoulders tightened. It was her job to protect them all and she was failing.

Tilly Takes Charge

"Now isn't the time to play politics. The world has changed, and we must bend or be destroyed." Tilly turned from the window, letting the thick curtain swing closed, and stepped aside to let two servitors carrying a leather-bound trunk pass.

"You'd have us give up without a fight?" Pelaguis stood glaring beside the open door.

"How can we fight? Shall we throw our men away? And for what? Father Dom assures me the Fae will leave us in peace if we do the same. By what right do we impose our human law on them?"

"On the right God has entrusted to us to

save the souls of man!"

"Even when they don't wish to be saved?" Tilly settled into a chair before the fire and waved Pelagius to a seat. "Can we not be brave and go to the Fae towns and preach as we will? I'm assured the Fae won't stop us from forming any church we desire."

Pelagius huffed but sat, twitching his robe closer so the servitors might pass unobstructed. "And when we succumb to their blandishments and they show their true colors?"

"Then we've lost nothing. We'll fight as God wills, and we'll die. But if they speak truth, we gain the world. Consider what Father Dom relays to us of the fate of the church. Shall we rail against our fate, or embrace it, and in so doing, win the entire world."

Pelagius rubbed his temples. "But to give in…. to accept their immoral behavior and condone it…"

A small smile built to a grin on Tilly's face. "No. We won't condone it. The only requirement is to not preach against it. But we can and should preach for morality. While we cannot say they're wrong, we *can* say we are right."

Pelagius pursed his lips. "And how then do we offer communion to a man we know is living an immoral life, a sinful life of sodomy?"

"There'll be many things about them we dislike and disagree with, but *they* are willing to compromise. We too must bend."

"If we deny God's words for our own comfort, we become a tool of the devil whether they be devils or no."

"Then we shall search the Holy scripts and pray for enlightenment. All need not be decided at once, and God is clearly speaking. Can he not speak to Danu, his creation, as easily as he speaks to us? Can he not convince her to guide her children? He must love her as he does us. Is it not worth accepting the things we despise to give the Fae time to reach enlightenment?"

"And if they never do?"

"Then we'll have openly what we both know exists now in secret."

Pelagius made an unhappy noise and heaved himself to his feet. He bowed and kissed Tilly's hand. "Your eminence, I'll assure we're ready to leave on the tide. Don't expect the entirety of the clergy to accompany us. Already some retreat to their estates and prepare to wage war."

Tilly patted the hand he still grasped. "The Fae will see we're trying, and while I wish for a bloodless transition…" He sighed, released

Pelaguis, and made the sign of the cross. "Go with God, your grace."

Pelaguis bowed deeply and stepped backward from the room.

We Aren't All Bad

Firelight cast by the cooking fire outside danced across the canvas ceiling of the two-man tent. The interior was warm and cozy. Thick furs piled on the wooden floor cushioned Jen's weary bones. She lay naked across her husband's chest, the feel of his skin on hers easing her soul. She'd never forget the pain of losing him.

"We're okay," he murmured, trailing his hand along her side to cup her breast. She sighed with contentment and closed her eyes. Her bladder woke her, and Ethan woke when she untied the door.

"I'll be back in a minute.

He laughed as her heated gaze traveled him and lay back on his elbows. She returned, bringing warm tea and an entire pot of stew someone had left beside the fire.

"I'm so hungry," she said as she sat to wolf the food.

"You've lost weight." He ran a finger over her collarbone. She stopped eating with the spoon halfway to her mouth. He chuckled as he withdrew his finger and waved at the pot. "Eat first."

She set the pot aside and crawled across the furs to kiss him. When she woke after their lovemaking, he handed her the now cold stew. "I can go heat it," he offered.

"No, stay with me."

"Always."

Stew forgotten again, she got caught up in his kiss. His hands on her body, the love he felt as he caressed her, sent all thought from her mind, and she cried out his name, not caring who heard.

"I'm hungry now too," Ethan mocked complained as he held himself above her still breathing hard, laughing when she giggled. She ate the entire pot of stew before falling asleep.

The next time she woke, the sun rode the sky. Ethan handed her a green pouch, and she picked through the tiny paper-wrapped parcels of food, selecting one she thought held a roast venison sandwich and dispelled it with a flick of her fingers. She offered the pouch to Ethan, but he shook his head and tucked the pouch back into his bag.

"Better?" he asked as she licked the last crumbs from the paper.

"Yes. You don't know… When I thought I'd lost you.…"

"I know. I felt your loss as keenly. We were reckless in our haste."

"I'd never considered the landscape could be dangerous. The ocean, sure, we could get lost and drown, but the mountains? I'd never seen anything like that." She shook her head and pulled him closer for a kiss.

"Diana—"

Ethan's shoulders tightened, and he rubbed his face hard. "Cries incessantly. Only Kuan can soothe her, and he's worried."

"Those goddamned bastards."

Ethan sat and began stuffing bedding back into his pack. "We'll rescue our son and go home to our traumatized daughter." He glanced at her with glowing blue eyes. "I won't be able to stop from killing them."

"Good."

The smell of roasting meat drew Jen from the tent.

"I don't think I'll ever be full," she complained, making Ethan snicker. She rolled her eyes at him but couldn't stop herself from smiling.

"What's for dinner?" he called.

"Rabbit, vegetable casserole, and conjured bread." Warren waved them to wooden chairs set before a large fire. Marie and Matt nodded greetings but didn't stop eating.

"Jon sent us a letter," Warren said as he handed Ethan a sheaf of notes. "Rob is still worried about Joash and asks that we don't call him into danger unless it's life or death. He's lifted his flight ban but would prefer if we let him stay home. Jon says he's on edge over Ramiro and we shouldn't take it personally, that he's likely to let Joash visit like normal once the transformation is complete."

"How's Ramiro doing?" Jen asked.

Warren handed her a heaped plate. "Fine, considering. Jon also said Diana has settled but Kuan is worried about her."

"Matt, can you send a letter to Kuan?"

"Sorry, Jen, but Flynt can only go to people he's met or places he's been."

She bit her lip and glanced at the sky. She estimated it to be six or so. Only a hint of setting sun remained.

"I'm worried too, sweetheart, but Alex needs us more now."

"If she sensed our pain and fear…Ethan, we could've scarred her for life. No baby should feel that."

"If she can sense our fear, she can sense our love too." Ethan pushed her gently to a seat. "Sit and eat. We'll leave in the morning."

Jen sat, wishing for the first time Ethan could lie to her. His words might've comforted her if she couldn't feel his worry. She pulled Danu back, forcing her away from him.

Warren said, "Brandon is still coming and should be in range by midday tomorrow for a summon. If we leave at first light, we can be on the coast by then and summon them right to us."

Warren rose and withdrew a map from his pack. He opened it and spread it on Ethan's lap and leaned over his shoulder. "One of the paladins can take me back into France. There are very few roads in the here and now. It shouldn't be too hard to check them all."

"We're talking about thousands of miles," Matt said. "They could be going to the east coast, not the west."

"True, but I don't need to patrol the entire thing just the roads that lead to Barcelona."

Matt peered over Warren's shoulder with worried eyes. "If they hear we're looking, they'll go elsewhere."

"How will they hear? Even if a man left last night, we're still faster."

"But we have to search, and a message could be sent right to them."

Warren shrugged and began to roll the map. "Any message would still have to be sent on foot, and they have no way of knowing where exactly they are either. Sure, they could know the route the kidnappers planned to take, but not where they are on it."

"And we have my sword," Jen said.

Warren nodded thoughtfully. "Yeah, Jen should take me. Brandon can lead the rest of you to Barcelona."

"No. We should stay together," Ethan said.

Warren shook his head. "Barcelona is only an hour's flight from France. We can send for you and summon you right to us."

Ethan glanced between them frowning. "Jen won't be able to wait an hour."

"I can wait. If I think Warren and I can't handle it, we'll wait. I won't risk any of the children. Warren is right. You can do more in Barcelona. We need to know who's involved and what they've prepared. You and Matt can spy it out." Jen turned back to Warren. "Did you tell Jon we think we know where the children are?"

"Yes. He'll meet us in Barcelona. Arden will remain at home with Rob and Emilio."

Jen bit her lip and Warren patted her hand.

"He's setting up a summon chain to get us back home in minutes. If anything goes wrong in Camelot, he can be back there in seconds. The Fae are going to Spain in force. Jon has declared war on Spain as well."

"Jesus, we're at war with France, Italy, and Spain…" Jen trailed off.

Warren snorted in derision. "Just Spain and the church. After one minor battle, Childebert went into hiding. Chrodesinde is in charge and implementing Jon's policies. Jon has no intention of marching on Italy. He's rounding up the priests in France though and offering them a chance to leave his realm or join his church. Most are opting to leave. Some are hiding. There's very little fighting in France, but that could change."

Jen frowned.

"Those fuckers in Italy better get what's coming to them," Ethan said.

Warren slapped his shoulder. "We can handle that once we save the children. There's no rush."

"Cass says we should give the church time to find the men responsible and punish those fuckers themselves." Matt rubbed his head as if it hurt. "He didn't mean we do nothing, but letting the church handle it will show the world whose side they're on. Their methods will be more brutal than ours."

Warren said, "You're assuming they give a shit what's done to us."

"Jen told us they didn't know, and she knows they weren't lying. What does it hurt to let them handle it? It isn't like we can't go later and handle it ourselves if we don't like what they do."

Jen said, "I know there were more guilty parties there but not how many. I saw one man but didn't get a chance to question him. I'm assuming he was a cardinal by the red robe, but you called me before I could chase him down."

"You should go back for him," Maria said. Jen turned to her as Maria continued, "If the evil man you saw in the red robe was a cardinal, he'll likely know the entire plan. Who's to say if the man you spoke with even told the truth? I know he believed it to be true, but maybe all the kids weren't sent to Spain, or they told some lies, knowing we'd go to Italy and question them."

"Jeez, that's a cheery thought," Warren said sourly. He snatched the map back from Ethan and frowned at it. "We came off the mountain in the Alto region here. And that isn't Italy in the here and now but an independent kingdom. There's lots of small kingdoms in the north. I think we're in the Lombard region right now. We could be in Rome in five or six hours."

"Maria and I can go south to the coast. The Lombards control all of this. It should be the same zone. We'll summon Brandon and Kirk when they reach the zone and they can head to France. You could summon us if you need us, and if not, we'll summon you. We'll only lose a few hours. It's worth checking."

"Let's go. I'm rested enough," Jen said.

"I have two stones left," Ethan said.

"I have sixteen." Warren grabbed his pack and kissed Maria. "Stay with Matt, and if you need me, have him summon me."

"We'll be fine," Maria said. She rose to hug Jen, then Ethan. "Take them alive if you can."

Gallant stamped his silver hooves.

Matt handed them two green pouches he

took from his bag. "Put one in your pocket, Jen."

She flushed. "I have no pockets. My clothes disappeared when Danu took me. It pisses me off too. I only had that one pair of real jeans."

Matt held up a finger and rummaged in his pack again. He grinned in triumph and took out a light blue sack no bigger than a change purse. A moment's sorting of even tinier bags followed, and he handed Jen the bag, keeping only a few pieces back. "Women's clothing. I carry an assortment now since we met Anise. There are drawstring jeans and t-shirts and sweatshirts in there as well as gowns and plain dresses all made with the new looms and sewing machines. The numbers on the front of the bag is the approximate size, but they've been designed to tie at the waist so should fit just about anyone."

"I'm like a foot taller than these women," Jen said as she opened the bag. "Ethan, remind me to carry a few sets of your clothes when Dillion makes me a new pack."

"The pants should be long enough as they're meant for us," Matt said. "The underwear is our type too."

"Go dress. I'll make us tea for the trip." Ethan kissed her fingertips, then blew across them. "And food."

"— the tents," Matt was saying when Jen exited the tent. She wore her righteous armor over tan drawstring pants and a white shirt. Matt had even supplied heavy cloth boots with thick leather soles. She'd washed in the now cool water and emerged with wet hair but feeling clean for the first time in days.

"It'll be faster if we summon Warren to us," Ethan said as he vaulted to Gallant's back. Jen got on behind him and hugged him tightly. Gallant lifted into the air with a sweep of his broad wings and the campfire dwindled to a spec of light in the dark. "Matt's sending Flynt to us in forty-five minutes to be sure he can find us, and we'll rest for fifteen, but if you get tired sooner, we should stop."

"I'm fine. I wish we had granola bars though, or chocolate. I barely remember what it tasted like."

"We'll have it again. Matt gave me his energy bars. Want one?"

"Yes, please."

Ethan handed her a postage size bar that she dispelled with a flick of her fingers. They flew without speaking, just passing the tea back and forth. Jen rested against her husband's broad back almost overcome with the blessing of having him returned to her. She shivered as she remembered how close she'd come to losing everything. Not just Ethan, but her soul. She'd been seconds away from murder. She'd almost made herself a woman Ethan couldn't love.

He rose her fingers to his lips and kissed them. She vowed to herself she'd try harder to remember she was human once and show mercy.

⟶

"Not as impressive as I'd imagined," Ethan said as they hovered within a stone's throw of the eastern wall surrounding Vatican City. "Should we rest a few hours first?"

Jen urged Gallant to the ground. "I'm okay. Summon Warren."

She'd barely finished the sentence before Warren appeared in front of Ethan.

"Climb on. I'll circle and see if we can pinpoint the strongest source of evil."

"Can you hold Danu back?" Warren asked as he swung on behind Ethan.

"I think so. She's eager, but not pressing me. We've reached an understanding of sorts. I couldn't turn away completely now, but she'll let me proceed at my own pace."

"Danu hasn't pressed," Ethan added. He

pointed to their right. "Lights and lots of them. Odd for this time of night."

"Circle or check it out?" Jen asked.

"Check it out," Warren said.

"Might as well," Ethan agreed.

The lights lit a small courtyard before a long, low barn. Men and women scurried about loading bales and boxes on rough wooden carts.

"Rats deserting a sinking ship," Warren said.

"Not complete fools, then," Jen said. "I warned them you'd be coming. Let's see what they have to say for themselves."

Warren and Ethan jumped down. No one appeared to notice Warren, and Ethan was already invisible. Jen brought Gallant lower. A woman shrieked and men exclaimed. Everyone except a few men wearing chainmail raced for the exits nearest to them. Jen left her sword sheathed.

"Who's in charge here?" she called, adding will to her voice.

One of the chainmail clad men stepped forward. He gripped the hilt of his sword tightly but didn't pull it. "Monsignor Thomme has been left in charge in the cardinals absence."

"And where might I find him?"

"Ask him where the cardinals went," Ethan whispered.

"And where have the cardinals gone?"

"Cardinal Tilly has left for Constantinople and taken most of his excellences with him. Some have left for their homes and Cardinal Bertram travels to France with a small contingent to confer with King Childebert."

The sword on Jen's back pulsed, casting a shadow across Gallant's mane.

"That is a lie," Jen said softly.

The man swallowed hard. "In truth, I know not where he went but was ordered to say he travels to France although he left by the eastern gate with only a small party."

"How many?"

"Twenty-two."

"And this here?" Jen gestured about her at the half-filled wagons.

"Cardinal Tilly ordered the Vatican emptied of all except a few."

"Where has he sent them?"

"Most he asked to temporarily return to their homes. The Holy See has accompanied him to Constantinople." The man rose a hand, then dropped it.

"Ask," Jen said.

The man's troubled expression deepened. "Can you read minds?"

"No. Danu can sense evil and led me too it. She can sense truth from lie and shows me."

"The fathers put themselves in danger by traveling on your behest."

"Not mine. But I get your point. We offered to bring the pope here. He refused."

The man's frown deepened. Before he could speak another man strode into the courtyard followed by a line of pikemen. Horses whinnied in the distance and the sound of marching feet approached.

"So, the demon has returned," the new man said.

Jen rolled her eyes. Ethan glided between her and the new man.

"I'm not a demon, and I'm not arguing about that. Call me whatever you want. Piss me off at your peril."

The man's lips tightened.

The man Jen had been speaking too bowed low and said, "Primus Nefrimidi, your orders?"

"Continue in your duty. The demon is constrained from causing harm on holy ground."

Jen laughed. "Fool. I have free will the same as you, and only my will constrains me." She let her eyes flare blue and leapt from Gallant's back, landing lightly before the man.

"Shall I kill you to prove it?"

Ethan appeared and grabbed her shoulder. "Jen."

Men shouted and lowered their pikes.

"Who cares what they think?" Ethan said. "Where is the evil?"

"Northeast." Jen sheathed her sword and summoned Gallant. She offered Ethan a hand to mount. The watching men again exclaimed as Warren became visible and vaulted to Gallant's back.

"Shall we chase?"

Ethan snapped, "We're too late! He has a day's head start. I'm not saying we couldn't find him, but he could've gone anywhere. The children need us. Alex needs us."

"Compromise," Warren said. "Chase until midday. Maria can summon us when she calls Brandon."

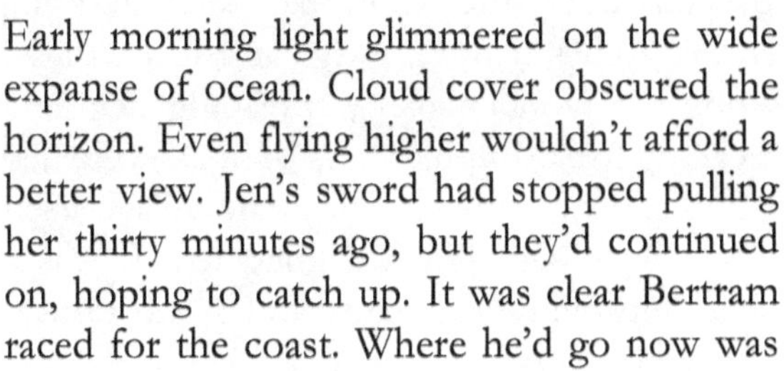

Early morning light glimmered on the wide expanse of ocean. Cloud cover obscured the horizon. Even flying higher wouldn't afford a better view. Jen's sword had stopped pulling her thirty minutes ago, but they'd continued on, hoping to catch up. It was clear Bertram raced for the coast. Where he'd go now was anyone's guess.

"I should've waited in Rome to see what those fuckers would do," Warren said angrily.

Ethan slapped his shoulder, giving him a commiserating glance. "I really thought we'd catch up."

Jen said, "I hate not having summon stones."

Warren pointed to thin plumes of smoke rising to their right. "Go back to that village there. Let's see if anyone knows where they're headed."

They flew over farmers bringing produce into town in horse drawn carts, and women carrying baskets who screamed at the sight of them. Ten-foot walls curved around the village. Armed men carrying pikes lounging in the shade beside open gates straightened when Jen flew overhead. She assumed they'd hear alarm bells any minute.

She headed to the docks where tall masts peeped over the rooftops. Men wearing simple tunics with bare legs and feet worked along the wooden piers, spreading nets and cleaning fish. Multiple styles of boats were tied off. This was a major port. The village itself was bigger than Jen had imagined. It was a small city with real roads and stone houses with slate roofs.

Jen guided Gallant to the cobbled street. Men and women bowed and ducked away as they galloped past.

"Meet back here in two hours," Warren said as he slipped from Gallant's back,

"Be careful," Ethan said and kissed her temple. She slowed Gallant to a walk and craned over her shoulder to watch Ethan leave. He was already invisible and mixing with a crowd peering from an open doorway of a warehouse across from the docks. The expected bell began to ring.

Jen yelled, "I've come in search of Cardinal Bertram, the Archbishop of Sicilia! He and his compatriots arrived within the last day and took a boat somewhere!"

The crowd remained silent with only the tolling bell to break the morning stillness.

"Someone must know something! I have no time to be diplomatic! I'll burn this city to the ground, starting with the boats in the harbor! Where has he gone?" Her shout echoed louder then she'd intended when the bells stopped.

She waited a minute, examining the crowd. No one would meet her eyes. All ducked away when they felt her perusal on them. Shutters up and down the street banged open and closed, and movement on rooftops told Jen some had gone to their roofs for a closer view

She felt like a bully and the hugest hypocrite. She'd just gotten through promising herself to be more human and here she was willing to terrorize these innocent strangers to force them to help her. But Alex was in the hands of madmen who thought nothing of burning children. She couldn't afford to be weak. *What good would being nice do Alex?*

She'd spun Gallant and had taken two steps onto the pier when a man hailed her.

"My lady, please, if you would?"

She swung back around to see a portly man with a balding head wearing floor-length robes in wide green and yellow stripes bow nervously. What hair he had left on his head was curled into tight ringlets and his beard was elaborately braided. By the bright colors and fancy hair Jen knew he was local nobility.

"Do you know where they've gone?"

The man bowed three times in quick succession. "The men you seek have taken ship to Crete."

Loud booted feet approached. The man darted a glance over his shoulder and licked his lips. "The guard. Please, Lady. They are good men. Captain Thais is a good man too.

Cardinal Bertram…" he swallowed heavily and fingered the braids on his face. "He isn't here," he finished and glanced worriedly at the men running into the street.

"Show me where his boat was," Jen said.

A man at the head of the armed men brought his troops to a halt by raising his fist. He waved his hand and the men stamped their feet once and unlimbered their shields. Jen almost felt bad for them. Ten men wouldn't slow her for a minute.

She said, "I have no wish to fight. I seek information. Cardinal Bertram, Archbishop of Sicilia, has stolen my son."

"They had no child with them," the fat man offered hopefully.

The lead soldier waved again, then approached slowly. His troops began spreading out and motioning the citizens back.

"Fools! Fight me and die if you must or do the decent thing and tell me where the cardinal went, where he might hide a Fae child! He has no right to them! His actions anger Danu so much I must fight her to keep from attacking!" Jen lowered her voice and held out her empty hand. "I realize you're afraid. That I'm unexpected and mysterious. But Danu sees you as enemies who'd take and harm her children. The Fae *are* her children and she is afraid for them. Why provoke us? Why not offer help instead and show Danu you aren't enemies but care for her children too?"

"Deal with demons!" one of the soldiers shouted in derision.

The lead man waved his hand again and the shouter clamped his lips together.

"I'm *not* a demon, but I *will* be your enemy if you persist in hiding our children."

"We have no child of yours," the man in the gaudy robe protested. "I've told you all I know."

"I believe you," Jen said. "I also believe others will have heard the men speaking and might know more. Was the captain of the ship waiting for them? Did he speak of his plans? If your son was stolen, wouldn't you do all in your power to retrieve him, or would you accept the word of one man when you'd tracked the villain and he'd escaped you?"

The man in the robe held up his hands. "Please, I can only say what I know. Captain Thais is a good man who deals fairly with us. He brings in goods and livestock from Greece and Egypt and the occasional passenger or two. His voyages generally last a season. I couldn't say if he'd bargained with the archbishop or not."

"Nay," another man said and stepped

forward.

He was dressed like one of the simpler fisher folk in a plain tunic with bare feet and legs. Gold beads dotted his beard and he wore a thick chain of silver, *so a well to do one,* Jen mused.

"Cap'n Thais be waiting on a shipment of mirrors from Basilicata. The cap'n would no break his word or mayhap he thinks he won't be gone long at all? If the archbishop only desired transport to Bari or down the coast a bit, the cap'n could return in time to keep his commission."

The man in the robe nodded eagerly. "That seems the more likely scenario. Captain Thais is an honorable man and even a great sum of money wouldn't entice him to go back on a bargain struck. I'm certain he'd have no truck with kidnapping."

"Show me where he docked. I wish to question the others near him who might've seen or heard."

The man in the robe glanced at the soldier who half bowed and stepped forward.

"I'll take her." He gestured to his men. "Return to your duties."

"We shouldn't let it wander freely," the man who'd called her a demon said.

"Leoni, return to barracks. She's a visitor,

and a distraught mother. We'll treat her with respect. Go!"

Jen sheathed her sword and dismissed Gallant. The men and women exclaimed as her horse disappeared. She made a real effort and her clothing turned white. Danu hummed harder for a second, then dissipated, and Jen relaxed her tense shoulders.

"This way," the soldier said and sidled past her.

"Thank you," Jen said.

He shot her a quick glance and pointed to the third dock. "Where that small red boat is now."

He followed as Jen strode down the dock and questioned everyone she saw. All gave her the same story with no additional details, although the man on the red boat told her Captain Thais had told him he'd deliver a packet of letters in Greece for him, and he could use his berth for four weeks. The captain had also made arrangements to postpone the delivery of the mirrors but had sent assurances it would be no later than six weeks.

"Can your horse not fly over water?" the soldier asked.

"He can, but I think Bertram leads me away. My son is mere weeks old and needs me…"

"A Fae child… it's so unbelievable. You're so unbelievable. I see you glow with my own eyes and your attire is so outlandish, and still, I can hardly fathom the wonder of it. I've heard you live in a city made of plants and you sing and dance and—" He abruptly stopped speaking as his cheeks reddened.

Jen sighed and smoothed her skirt. "We do have homes formed of living wood and more traditional homes too. We're pretty normal though."

He eyed her doubtfully.

She held out her hand. "I only have two armor sets, both gifts from Danu. The black set protects me better and while I wear it an attacker would have a harder time targeting anyone in my party. It manifests when I'm upset as does Danu. She's the blue mist you can see floating about, and she shows in a Fae's eyes when they're agitated." Jen traced the marks on her face with a fingertip. "These marks warn we're at war. We can't help Danu manifesting, but we can warn we're on edge and that to provoke her will lead to an attack."

He looked both horrified and intrigued by that. "She'll show up?"

"As more blue mist and lightning, but she can force Fae to do her will."

He frowned and stepped away.

"Normally, she doesn't wish for anything but is content to live inside us. But we *are* as she made us. I'm a Protection Paladin. Righteous anger empowers me. My sword leads me to evil, and then I must slay it as Danu wills."

He nodded slowly and pursed his lips. "I'd heard you raise demons to do your bidding and control the animals and plants of the forests, bending them in unnatural ways. I could hardly credit the rumors they were so outlandish, but we've been warned that when Fae attack the only way to defeat them is by fire. My commander reported the Fae attacked Rome last night and burned the churches and slaughtered the priests."

Jen snorted. "It was just me, and I killed five men; the rest attacked me. I warned them first... We aren't evil. We didn't start this war, but we *will* finish it. Whoever took our children will pay. We offered amnesty for the children's safe return. You can hardly blame us for seeking them out." She shrugged lightly. "The rest is true, I guess. Rangers can call animals to them and control them as can shamans to a lesser degree. Warlocks can craft constructs meant to terrify, and since you fear demons, they resemble them."

She broke off as Ethan approached. He glided up to them, not becoming visible until he stood beside her. "Warren is waiting," he said.

The soldier exclaimed and jumped back.

"My husband, Sir Ethan Frey," Jen said, a happy thrill that she could say it making her grin as she summoned Gallant. "Thank you for your help."

The soldier inclined his head. "It was interesting meeting you."

"What did you find out?" Jen asked as she urged Gallant to rooftop height.

"Bertram was accompanied by a group of clergy and Senator Gauis and his guards. They killed their horses getting here and bought passage to Greece. Rumors are flying that Rome is burnt to the ground and the clergy all killed. The populous is incredulous but firepits are being built outside the town walls. They have no real idea of what we're capable." Gallant turned and headed west without Jen's guidance. "I spoke with Warren and he's meeting us outside the west gate.

Jen said, "I learned the same things you did except for the fire pit thing. I'd have told him it wouldn't work."

"He wouldn't believe you anyway."

"Maybe not now, but if we found out they

lied and come back here, he'd believe it then."

Ethan made a vague sound of agreement then blurted, "This is so frustrating! With all our power and knowledge, we can't find them!"

"We will. I have to believe we will. Danu wouldn't give him to us and tie him to us so tightly with bonds of love just to take him away."

"She's afraid too…" he trailed off, resting his chin on her shoulder. She didn't need Danu to feel his unhappiness. His fear for Alex was clear in his slumped posture and desperate grip on her. She urged Gallant faster.

Pay Our Debts

"Finnian Lior Tyson," Warren said, holding out his hand.

Jen handed Warren one of her beaded bracelets. Warren wrapped it with his and Ethan's and tied them loosely around the bird's neck. "Thank you, Flynt. Return to Matt." He stroked the bird's crest until it disappeared a few moments later. "It doesn't understand like Flynn did. We'll need to be very careful with it. Matt calls." Warren disappeared.

"He calls me too," Ethan said and kissed her cheek before accepting his summons. Ethan's disappearance made her shudder. She waited anxiously for Matt to call her and accepted at once.

"Where are we?" she asked when she appeared. Snow tipped mountains loomed over the rolling hills. Light snow covered the ground and it was at least ten degrees colder than Rome had been.

Matt said, "Lombardia. We crossed a wide river ten minutes ago, which might be the border to Piemonte.

Flynt screeched when Joash appeared. Joash dropped a rolled paper at Matt's feet and disappeared before Jen could greet him.

"Damn," Warren muttered, staring at the sparks Joash had left.

"I hope Ramiro is well," Ethan said as Matt unrolled the paper.

"Kirk and Brandon are over the mountains. He reached for a summon stone and called Kirk's name.

"Jen!" Kirk said as soon as he appeared and hugged her tightly. "Sam was worried sick. We all were. Kuan wanted to come himself but Jon convinced him to stay." He stepped back and examined her, then hugged her again.

Brandon appeared and hugged Ethan, then Jen. A flurry of hugs and greetings followed as Danu flitted about them. When Danu disappeared, Kirk summoned his cauldron.

"What news?" Brandon asked.

"Nothing new," Ethan said and clasped his hand again. "Have you heard from home?"

"Ramiro's transformation was successful, but his firebird follows Joash and they worry it'll get lost. Kuan sent word we aren't to call Joash except in direst emergency for a few days to give Ramiro time to bond with his bird."

"That explains the quick visit," Warren said with relief as he grabbed a handful of summon stones from the cauldron by Kirk's feet.

Jen reached in and withdrew five. Brandon opened his pack and handed her a new belt and tabard that he dispelled. "Kuan called Danu and began the next batch of transformations. He's impressive and scary."

Jen snickered as Brandon dampened a rag from the flask on his belt and reached to wipe her face.

She took the rag from him as he waggled a pot of black makeup. "Let me fix your face. You look like a chimney sweep."

"It was the best I could do," she said defensively.

He snorted and took a small paintbrush from his pocket. She closed her eyes and let him paint her face as Warren and Kirk poured over the map.

Jen said, "We need to stop in Po quick. Its somewhere near Palia."

Kirk traced a finger across the map. "Let's see, Cass has Palia as north of Tuscany in the Lombardia region. What's there we need?"

"A family I need to thank. How far out of our way is it?"

"Not very. An hour tops. "

"An hour?" Ethan said doubtfully.

"It's important that the Fae keep their word," Jen said without opening her eyes. Brandon still painted her face. "It's also important we're seen as kind, not just bloodthirsty."

"Fine, let's go. Can you even find it again?"

Jen stepped back from Brandon, earning an annoyed huff, and gave him a quick kiss on his cheek, being careful to not mar the white lightning bolt edged in black that bisected his face.

Maria grabbed the pot and began painting batwings across Warren's eyes. "Summon us when you get there."

"We need stickers," Kirk muttered as he accepted a small container of white makeup from Brandon.

Ethan dabbed his fingers in and drew a

wavy line across his cheeks. Kirk sniffed and pursed his lips.

"Sure, easy for you, no one sees you, but I can't draw for shit, and I'll look ridiculous."

"Wear your armor," Jen said as she mounted Gallant. "You should keep it on. No sense taking chances."

Kirk waved her away, saying, "Go. I'll summon another stone cauldron every thirty minutes until you're all restocked. Brandon offered a hand to Kirk to mount Ed.

Ethan mounted behind her and they headed to Po.

***

Jen led Gallant to Gianni's door and knocked. This time she wore her white armor and Danu was content to remain within her. He jumped back when he opened the door.

"Peace," Jen said, stepping away from his door. "I've come to thank you." She laid a stack of cloth on the ground and dumped a small blue pouch atop it. A flick of her fingers sent white motes drifting over the tiny heaps of fabric and tools and in seconds they reached full size. She'd tried to pick things from Matt's store of goods Gianni could use that wouldn't get him killed by his neighbors.

The man's wide eyes widen further, and he nervously licked his lips. His gaze darted to Brandon and Kirk who wore full armor and then to Ethan who still sat astride Gallant.

"You weren't a dream…"

"No, we're very real and here to stay. Camelot lies across the mountains. Any are welcome there who follow our laws. Your church has split, some calling us demons while others accept we're Fae, children of Danu and not inherently evil. Use care who you mention us too as your church is without mercy."

"Demons," the man said and stepped away from the offered goods.

Jen sighed heavily.

"Let it go, Jen," Brandon said.

"We aren't demons. We're Fae, but do what you like," she said to Gianni, then craned over her shoulder to speak to Brandon in English. "He was kind, and we should encourage that. He deserves a warning though. Who the hell knows what these assholes will do to him?"

Brandon waved in agreement and turned Ed. Kirk jumped down and approached. The man glanced behind him and stepped forward, closing the door. He trembled but stood before his closed door.

"Be gone, demon!"

Kirk removed his helm. "I'm not a demon. It's just armor." He twitched his fingers and haze of green rose from the ground at his feet, thickening into blue mist that solidified into a green vial with a silver top. "This is a healing potion. It'll heal anything at all. It does nothing else and only you may open the top." He let the vial fall to the stack of clothing and dropped two gold coins. "Thank you for helping my friend. You remind us not all humans here are lying thieves." Kirk slapped Jen's shoulder and strode back to Brandon who offered him a hand to mount.

Jen glanced back as they flew away. Marisal stood beside her husband now. Two small boys held her hands and gaped after them.

"Thanks, Kirk!" Jen called.

"*De nada.*" Kirk waved his hand in airy dismissal. "You're right. Building goodwill is important. They'll hear of the killings, but know we aren't just that."

Jen winced.

Ethan nuzzled her neck, his warm breath making her shiver. She turned so she could kiss him, then turned all the way, riding backward so she could hug him.

"We're okay," he whispered as he stroked her back. "We know where he is."

The words made Danu manifest, but she didn't press and subsided in seconds.

"She's letting me handle it."

Ethan nodded and kissed her cheek.

"She knows I'll kill them all."

"You won't have to. I'm much faster than you," Ethan said.

———➤

Two days later Jen stood on the shore of an icy cold mountain stream that flowed down a rocky gorge into the sea. The stream separated France from Spain, a fact they'd worked out by trying to summon.

Jen clasped Brandon's mailed hand in hers. "Be careful."

"You too."

Starlight glittered across Brandon's mail and Kirk's armor, catching and reflecting off the lightning bolt bisecting the iron cross that was their guild symbol.

"Flynt will bring word," Matt said as he stroked his bird's head.

"I don't like you staying alone here," Warren said to Maria.

Maria hefted the crude backpack she'd made from fabric from Matt's pack to hold her summon stones. The sack bulged alarmingly but would be hidden when she transformed and wouldn't hamper her movements. "I'll be fine. One tree in a forest of trees, and you're a summon away." Maria kissed him hard, then pushed him away.

Warren's frown deepened but he climbed on behind Jen.

She leaned down to kiss Ethan one last time. The thought of parting from him made her feel sick. By his expression he didn't like it either. Gallant stamped his feet and Ethan stepped back, lifting a hand in farewell. He'd wait with Maria for a summon from Kirk when they reached Barcelona. Then he and Matt would spy.

Artemis

Four Days Later

A winding ribbon of dirt road disappeared beneath the trees in the distance. Cloudless skies made visibility good, and Jen worried the men they sought would spot Gallant before she spotted them.

They traveled to Bordeaux following Cass's advice. Ultragotha had family in the region, and Bordeaux had strong ties with Spain.

Men and supplies would be plentiful because Childebert kept an active armory there to keep the populous in check as Bordeaux was a recent acquisition.

Cass had sent copies of maps, marking

what he thought would be the most likely route. But it was all just supposition and guess. She hoped Ethan would learn more. He'd already found clergy who waited eagerly for the children's arrival.

She fingered her summon stone belt uneasily. They had stones too and might be able to get word to the kidnappers.

She urged Gallant faster, but she was already flying at her top speed.

"You need to rest, Jen," Warren said fifteen minutes later.

She nodded agreement and brought Gallant to the ground, dismissing him so that even the small effort of keeping him corporal wouldn't drain her limited reserves of magic. She lay back on the cold hard ground and closed her eyes while Warren made tea.

Warren woke her, and she sat irritably, annoyed with herself for dozing off. Warren handed her the tea and a paper wrapped sandwich.

"How long did I sleep?" she asked as she shaded her eyes to peer into the sky. The sun didn't appear to have traveled far.

"Not long. We'll beat them."

"If they don't have a summon chain in place."

Warren growled in annoyance. "They

might but even if they run, flying is much faster."

Warren shrugged irritably. "We'll find them, Jen. We're hot on their heels. Ethan will make them talk if we have too."

Neither of them mentioned the very real probability of the children being murdered if the men thought the Fae were close.

She summoned Gallant and ate while they flew.

The miles slipped by beneath them, and she wondered if anyone noticed their passage and what they thought if they did. The land she flew over was wild and appeared unpopulated. A river wound through dense trees that had replaced cultivated farmland although she could see clearer patches in the distance and grey smudges in the sky that told of a town.

"You should rest again," Warren said forty minutes later.

"I can make that town. I'll rest while you see what you can find out."

Warren nodded, and both stared with hungry eyes as the town took shape.

Gallant pawed the air, turning so sharply he almost unseated them. The glow of Jen's sword dimmed, deepened, and began to pulse as they turned. The hum of Danu against her skin grew louder until Jen could almost hear words in it. But she didn't need words. Her sword was very clear. Evil lay ahead.

"There," Warren said again and pointed, not toward the distant village, but to the river and a lone plume of smoke.

"A Fae child; I'm sure of it."

Jen's breath caught in her throat, and she urged Gallant faster toward the house that sat by itself over a mile from the town, which was unusual in this day and age where there was safety in numbers. Most people lived very close to the towns center and even farmers built their house adjoining others, two or three families sometimes sharing one house.

Horses filled two paddocks behind the house, churning the damp ground to deep mud. They milled so closely she couldn't count them but guessed there were at least fifty. The house itself was formed of a mix of stone and mud worked with straw and half built into a bank. Bright straw comprised the roof as though it had just been thatched.

"Newly constructed." Warren pointed to the half-cleared field behind the house. "The horses haven't been here long either, and I don't think they intend to keep them here. The paddocks and fields are too small and there's no guards or shelters. I think this is meant as a quick stop, a place to change out horses."

"But how could one of the Fae children be here then, or have we missed them, and the rest have already gone on?"

"Maybe, but the horses look fresh and frisky, not ridden hard."

Danu swirled about excitedly, an excitement Jen shared. The Fae child might be her son. Warren hadn't said it was, and she knew he could 'see' Alex, but she couldn't give up her hope. This was her child, she knew it.

"Two in the house and no one else within my range," Warren said.

Jen growled low in her throat, wishing there were fifty riders to kill. Two wouldn't sate her anger at all. It shocked her how much she looked forward to killing, and Gallant stuttered in his flight. She wanted to fight, to ease her anger and fear in bloodshed. She thrust her doubts down deep and urged Gallant on. Alex needed her to be brutal, and she'd be everything he needed.

Warren called for Flynt as Jen dispelled Gallant and fell the last twenty feet to the mud of the road. The muddy track she landed on skirted a raging river that cut through low rolling hills. The Pyrenees Mountains dominated the southern landscape, snowcapped tops lost in the clouds, but the field beside the ramshackle house Jen ran to was clear of snow and muddy. Smoke rose from the home's chimney and a single goat wandered before the house.

The rickety wooden door shattered when she kicked it.

"Give me the child!" she bellowed.

A woman in a much-patched dress glanced at a cloth-covered wooden box beside the fire. She jumped to her feet, dropping her knitting as a man swung away from the fire to face the door.

Thick jowls covered with dirty whiskers quivered in rage as the men snarled, "Faugh, demon spawn! Your wretched child has brought them to us!" He backhanded the woman, knocking her into the wall, and reached for a pike in the corner.

Jen couldn't tear her eyes from the box. Her child; she knew it. Lightning flickered over Jen's skin. Danu knew too and rejoiced.

The man dropped his reaching hand and laughed as Jen jumped forward. He kicked the box into the fire as the woman screamed.

"I knew it be evil and should be slain!" he shouted as the woman and Jen scrambled for the fire. A thin wail rose in volume as the cloth covering the box caught with a whoosh and fell inside.

Jen reached for her son. Her pulse beat so hard in her ears it drowned out noise, but the red face screwed up in a grimace of agony was clearly screaming. Delicate flesh blistered and peeled, and the baby stilled abruptly. Jen flicked her fingers, bathing the baby in yellow radiance and used her cloak to smother the flames. The man hit at her, sharp stabs of pain that another finger flick stopped. She elbowed him hard, not willing to set the baby down to summon her sword.

"Jen?" Ethan called, sounding confused and hopeful.

His voice broke through her thudding pulse and all at once she could hear.

The baby shrieked, the woman cried, and the man swore. Gladness filled her heart as the child's cry grew in strength, and she shifted her grip to summon her sword. She clutched the child to her chest and thrust with her sword right as the man lifted the pike leaning in the corner. He gurgled and groaned, clasping the edges of his torn stomach in both hands as he sank to his knees.

"Should've killed them all. Dirty whores…." He gasped hard and his breath rattled as he thumped face first to the dirt floor.

The woman continued to wail and tried to

grasp the child from Jen. Jen backhanded her, sending her flying to landed on her ass beside the stool she'd occupied moments earlier.

The baby sniffled and screwed up its face. Ethan grasped her shoulder as Warren ran into the room. The woman pushed herself to her knees and used the stool to stand as Jen patted the baby's back. Hot and cold waves traveled her. Relief and fear collided. She'd almost been too late. He'd almost burned her son. He had burned him. Horror roiled Jen's stomach and she vomited.

"Let me have him," Ethan said and tried to take the baby.

"He's mine," Jen said as she wiped her face and turned to glare at the woman.

"Not yours." The woman scowled, her scowl darkening as she glanced at the dead man and then Jen. "I thought it an innocent, just a babe, a fair replacement for the whore I raised, a chance to do better." She clamped her lips closed and backed away as Ethan advanced.

"Wait," Warren called out. "I know you. You're from Limenware."

"Aye. We be from that demon infested hovel. I know what you are." She glared with pure hatred at Warren. "Take your demon spawn and go. You've taken everything from me! If I'd thought it as corrupt as its mother, I'd have burned it myself!"

Jen stared transfixed at the child she held. Blond curls had partially burned away, and true-blue eyes stared up at her. It wasn't Alex, but it was her child. She knew it. A shiver raced over her, and she began to tremble. "Why are you here?"

The woman cocked her head, clearly not anticipating the question.

"Why are you here in this place!" Jen shouted and slashed at the woman, not meaning to connect.

The woman gritted her teeth, baring them in a soundless snarl before saying, "The French prince offered my husband employment in exchange for the babe, and so we went where he bid. I convinced my husband to keep the child. I thought her normal and convinced him it were evil to give a child to the French to raise as a demon. We planned to leave this foul place when the men arrived for the horses with his pay and raise it as a Christian. We should 'ner have come here to this den of demon worshipers, gold coins or no."

"Where is her mother?"

"Dead!"

Jen jerked back. The woman smiled

viciously, clearly happy that her child was dead.

"In childbirth?" Ethan asked mildly.

His tone encouraged the woman who smiled at Ethan as if they were friends, as if he'd agree with and condone her actions. Jen knew Ethan's mildness was tight restraint. He was on such a ragged edge it surprised her the woman couldn't see it. Or maybe she could and taunted him. Jen turned away from her hatred and cuddled the child who still cried. She flicked her fingers, sending balls of golden light to the child until she glowed softly from the heals.

"She was a whore who deserved her fate. A filthy animal who rutted with demons, and I should've killed her demonic spawn too. Instead, I saved it and so doing killed my husband, a good man." She started to weep and fell to her knees beside the corpse. "A good man. A good man," she repeated as she rocked and moaned.

"Jesus," Warren said, sounding sickened. "She killed her own daughter."

Jen held out the baby and unwrapped the singed rags. "We have another daughter." She offered the girl to Ethan who took her with trembling hands. The baby shrieked indignantly, and he laughed in a tear-choked voice. "She's so fierce. Thank God we found her." He closed his eyes and cuddled her close. The baby stopped crying and pulled at his hair.

Jen glanced at the crying woman who knelt with her head bowed over the corpse. She shook her head and turned her back. How that woman could cry over such an evil man she didn't know. She couldn't imagine killing her child for any reason, but to kill her for being the victim of a crime? No wonder her sword pulsed, warning of evil.

"They're so fucking evil," Warren said.

Jen let lose a bark of half-hysterical laughter.

"Did her mother name her," Ethan asked the woman.

"It be an evil thing." She glared at them and rose her bloody hands. "Take it and go!" she shrieked suddenly. "I curse it! To think, I thought to raise that demon spawn!"

The baby began to cry again. Ethan gazed about the room, then reached for the homespun blanket on the bed.

"Leave it," Jen said, wanting nothing to do with anything from here. She removed her cloak, releasing her sword to do so, and handed the soft cloak to Ethan. "Use our supplies—"

"Stop!" Warren yelled and drew back his

arm. His fingers flicked, and the woman screamed as Jen turned.

The woman flew backward, knocked back by Warren's spell. She dropped the pike she held, and her head hit the mantel as she fell. Her loose shawl caught, and in seconds fire flowed over her. She screamed and beat at the flames. Jen placed Sanctuary beneath her and grabbed the blanket. She tried to roll the screaming woman in the cloth, but the woman thrashed harder, trying to push her away.

The woman rose her hands and yanked at her burnt hair as she hopped about the glowing floor, screaming shrilly as if the yellow light emanating from the dirt floor hurt her. Fire still crawled over her but did no damage to either her clothing or skin. She reached for the pike and stabbed. The blade passed through Jen without doing any harm.

"Curse you! Curse you!" she shrieked as she stabbed repeatedly.

"Take our daughter away," Jen said as she ripped the pike from the woman's hand. She broke the thick haft over her knee and threw the pieces behind her. "You need help. I wish I knew how to help you. Can't you see how crazy you're acting?"

Her words fell on deaf ears. The woman continued to rant, growing shriller by the second. Jen stood in her Sanctuary undecided on what to do. This woman was crazy, but still her daughter's grandmother.

She grabbed the woman and shook her. "Shut up! I'll go as soon as the fire dies, or do you want to burn to death?" She pushed her away and despite her protests, smothered the remaining flames with the blanket before striding from the house. Warren had already unslung his pack and withdrawn a bottle, blanket, cloth diaper, and a simple cotton nightdress with a drawstring bottom. The two men crouched and dressed the baby.

"She's crazy," Jen said and rubbed her arms where goosebumps had formed.

"As a loon," Warren agreed.

The shrieks from inside the small hut grew louder. Loud crashes and bangs accompanied her yelling and she began screaming for help.

"What the hell?" Ethan rose as he wrapped the baby in the blanket and gestured with his chin. Jen turned to see flames licking through the thatch roof and black smoke begin pouring from the window.

Warren grabbed Jen's shoulder as she whirled to run back into the burning building.

"No. She did it herself. The flames were almost out. There's no way they traveled from your sanctuary without help. She likely thinks to burn you too."

"Leave her, Jen." Ethan handed her the baby. "Our son is close. Leave her to the fate she chose."

Jen shivered and hurriedly summoned Gallant. The shrieks had changed from crazed to pain filled but manic laughter interspersed it. She carefully cradled her daughter as the men mounted behind her and urged Gallant away.

"I thought it was Alex he burned. How could anyone…" Jen began to cry, the baby in her arms not comforting her at all.

Ethan reached over her shoulder, tucking Jen's cloak tightly around the baby and resting his hand on her back. "She's as much our daughter—"

"But I thought it was him. Dear God, Ethan, our son could be dead already! Burned—"

Sobs clogged her words in her throat and remembered horror, the baby's screams as she burned, made her ill. Gallant descended to earth and Ethan lifted her from her horse's back. "We need a minute, Warren."

Jen continued to cry, hating her weakness but unable to stop. Ethan said nothing just rocked them in his arms until her tears finally slowed.

"I'm a bit overwhelmed myself. I hadn't expected another child so soon but there's no doubt she's ours."

Jen wiped her face on her cloak. "And she might have lived her entire life with that woman…"

"But she's ours now."

"How old do you think she is?"

"Three months or so. I'm guessing her biological mother went to Miguel willingly at first, but who knows, maybe he forced her or tortured her." Ethan threw his hands in the air and turned away, saying over his shoulder, "I don't want to know. We'll never tell her. Artemis will grow up believing she was always loved and wanted."

"Artemis?"

Ethan turned back and smiled as he ran a finger over the baby's cheek. She snuffled and opened her eyes, then began to fuss. "It suits her. She's so fierce, and we found her on a hunt," he said as he opened his pack to take out the bottle.

Jen took the bottle from him to begin feeding her new daughter. "Our children will have delusions of grandeur named for gods."

"We'll teach them right from wrong." He paused a moment then blurted, "I can't believe we have three children."

The dubious tone of his voice made Jen laugh although the thought of three children overwhelmed her too. Artemis made a soft sound of contentment that melted Jen's heart. She already loved her. The connection had been instant and unmistakable, and she wondered if all new parents felt this fierce love when they saw their children for the first time.

Alex

Jen had calmed by the time the other Fae began to arrive.

A horse whickered, and she glanced over her shoulder. Brandon stood with his glowing sword in hand, holding Ed's reins and gesturing east. Jon and Arden leaned over Warren's shoulder, staring at a map Cass held and pointed at.

Kirk glanced up and smiled a greeting but stayed by his cauldron. Firebirds flickered in and out, snatching and dropping bangles to Jon and Arden. Ling and Sota appeared. Both stared hopefully at the baby Ethan held and a wave of guilt flooded Jen. She shook her head. "I'm sorry, but it isn't Jia."

Sota grabbed Ling when she moaned and

rose her hands to cover her face.

"We better join them," Ethan muttered.

Jen took a deep breath and stepped forward. Ling's pain and fear buffeted her as she entered the blue cloud flitting between the Cheng's and Jon.

"I'm so sorry," Jen said again.

Ling straightened, dropping her hands. "It isn't your fault, and I'm happy for you." Her voice broke, and she began to cry.

Jen felt no blame only longing, but it didn't ease her guilt. Ling and Sota clasped hands and turned their glowing blue eyes on Jon.

Jon glanced over as she and Ethan approached and offered his hand. "Congratulations, another daughter. Warren tells us her family tried to burn her. Is she well?"

Jen kissed Artemis's head and nodded.

"Sam is still home," Kirk said and gave Jen a quick squeeze. "She, Rob, and Ramiro are guarding the children with the other new Greater Fae. Take a few more summon stones." He nodded to the cauldron at his feet.

Trent Vicky and Kuan appeared. "Trent…" She gave him a hard hug, running a hand over his bald scalp. He'd been recovered for barely a day.

"I'm fine," Trent said gruffly. He held her at arm's length and smiled. "Better than fine really. I love being a paladin. I'm still a bit weak and unsure of my spells, but I'm learning fast. The rest of the new casters are staying home, but we can have them here in minutes if we need them. We've taken our vows, and we're all eager to help."

"We better not need them," Kuan said as he gave Jen a hug. "They're hopeless right now. Complete noobs. Trent does good though if a bit slower than he should be. At least I don't worry about him falling to his death."

Trent laughed and punched Kuan's shoulder, wincing when Kuan rubbed it. "Sorry, not used to my new strength yet."

"Trent!" Jon called and beckoned him.

Jon and Matt conferred over the map for a few minutes and Jon said, "You and Brandon are taking Warren and Cass on forward patrol. I'm ordering you to report before engaging," he said in a voice laced with command.

Ethan said, "I'll leave Artemis with the EMTs," and he left them to approach the men and women appearing beside Arden.

Jen rubbed her arms. Danu hummed along her skin. Eager anticipation bounced between the Fae as Danu gusted in small clouds, twining about them in increasing agitation. Jon's commanding voice settled her, but Jen would have to go soon. As if he sensed her distress, which he likely did as she sensed his, he laid a hand on her shoulder. "You *will* wait with me. To rush in risks their lives. First, we'll get the children, then we'll attack."

Ethan hugged her from behind. "What'd I miss?" he asked Jon.

"You were gone like five minutes…" Jon rolled his eyes and made a vague gesture to the northeast. "Brandon and Trent just left. Arden, are the EMT's ready?"

Arden glanced up from a scroll she was reading and nodded. "Packed and ready. We can have the children examined and healed within minutes. They'll clean them and care for them until we can get them home." Arden's eyes flared blue. "God help them if they've hurt any."

Jen smiled a hard, satisfied smile over Arden's anger. Danu practically purred with contentment. This was how it was supposed to be. Arden was meant to be a Fae.

Arden grimaced at Jen and shrugged.

Jon lay a hand on her cheek. He too was satisfied with Arden's possessiveness and anger. Danu brought their feelings clearly to

Jen. Arden was a bit dismayed, but she was newly Fae. Jen knew Arden would grow less human over time, and for once, the thought didn't worry her. She wanted Arden to be their defender. She needed it.

"There will be an accounting." Jon lifted two fingers to his lips and whistled, gathering the Fae. "You'll be summoned by group. Group leaders will be assigning sectors, but I expect you to use initiative. The children come first before DPS targets. Sota, Ling, I want you in the first wave who arrive, but I expect you to hang back and give our stealth classes time to get into position. If you don't think you can wait, go in the last wave with Jen."

"Jon—"

"Last wave, Jen. We can't risk them."

"I'm in control."

"You are now, but Danu has no sense. She'll want you to rush in and doing so will give those bastards time to burn the children." His eyes softened when she shuddered, and he gave her a quick hug. "Sota, Ling, you guys good?"

Sota said, "Fine. Angry and worried, but Danu doesn't push us like she does Jen."

Dillion tugged on Jen's arm. "Here, Aunt Jen." He handed her a new pack.

She absently took it from him as she

kissed his cheek. "What are you doing here? You should be with Sam."

"Dillion is my knight and has sworn to obey. He'll remain with Arden, but we could use his invisibility and disguise and maybe his silence or Polymorph," Jon said as Dillion said. "I can help, Aunt Jen."

"Jon… he's too little to see this."

"I fought in Camelot. I'm not too little." Dillion rubbed his neck, then hastily dropped his hand.

Jon's eyes flared blue and Jen knew hers had as well as sight and sound deepened and gained depth.

"I'll be careful and stay with Arden. *Uh*, the queen."

"You can call me Arden, or Aunt Arden," Arden said as she smoothed his hair.

Dillion fingered the glowing dagger on his belt and ducked his head. A red flush climbed his cheeks.

"We're family, sport. We'll always be family," Jon said and scooped him up to give him a smacking kiss on the cheek. He handed him to Jen when he giggled. She kissed him too and crouched to be at eye level when she set him down.

"This is serious and might be very scary. Stay with Arden and do whatever she says."

"Healers set positioning," Dillion said and nodded, his face serious.

"If you do want to leave, I can call an EMT and have you back at the castle in minutes," Arden said.

Dillion said, "I hate them too."

Ethan made a soft sound of distress, and the worry Jen felt from Danu surrounding her intensified. The knights exchanged uneasy glances over Dillion's head.

Jon took his hand. "Not all of them, sport. Just the guilty ones."

"I wish I could see them like Jen can. Everyone should be able to see evil. It isn't fair it can hide. She should've killed Mondred."

Jen said, "We knew he was a bad man, you're right about that. We should've been much more careful of him. We never should've let him stay in the castle unsupervised. Nothing that happened was your fault, Dillion."

"If I'd been faster, if I knew he was bad… even when he stabbed Fredrick, I thought he'd offer a healing potion. He was a prince, and they're supposed to be good. It happened so quick. I was too slow," he finished angrily. He wiped his face on his sleeve. "I won't be slow again. I just wish I could see them."

"We all do," Jon said dryly.

"It's better to be slow than to kill an innocent man," Arden said.

"You aren't to kill anyone except in self-defense," Jon said firmly.

Dillion pursed his lips. Jon's eyes narrowed.

Jen laid a hand on Jon's arm and shook her head slightly. "Dillion is a knight, and even though he's taken no vow, he'll honor them."

The mulish expression left Dillion's face, and he straightened proudly. "I *am* a knight."

"You are," Jon said softly and kissed his brow. "Guard my queen well."

"Jon, we should go search too," Ling said impatiently.

Jon took her hand, then kissed her cheek. "We need to be patient and give no hint of our presence."

"And if someone goes to that house and sees them burned?"

"True." Jon glanced around, then waved at Vicky who stood by herself at the edge of the wood. "Vicky, take Matt back. He can wear a Cloak of Seeing and speak to anyone who comes."

Vicky glowered but summoned her steed.

"We'll summon you back before we engage."

Her glower faded, but she still didn't look

happy.

Jon sighed hard when she flew away with Matt.

"Problems?" Jen whispered.

"She was angry that I recalled them, said I didn't trust her. See how she stays away from everyone? She doesn't want us to feel her anger and embarrassment. I'm worried she'll try to do something to prove she's a good paladin."

Jen winced, all too familiar with the trouble players who tried to prove how good they were could cause by taking on enemies too hard for them and killing their entire group. And Vicky had almost done it once already when King Goswin had lured her into a trap.

"We have no low-level dungeons to learn in," Jon said, sounding frustrated.

Ethan said, "Let her lead a group, Jon. She *is* a Protection Paladin and being in the back during an attack will be hard on her.

"I know, but I worry she'll be hurt when she rushes in. She doesn't have the skill Jen and Brandon do to use her spells instinctively."

Arden said, "Her magic isn't as strong as theirs either. It's getting stronger but she needs more practice. The newly made Fae seem to receive power according to training. My healing spells are as strong as Tony's, but Jasmine's aren't. She had no medical training or experience. It works the same way for melee. Trent's spells are already more powerful than Vicky's, but he was a sergeant in the Army. I'd say he's about ten levels or so higher than her."

Jen said, "Put Vicky in charge of training Trent. She has a good grasp of spell timers. He won't be hurt by it, and she'll need to improve her speed to keep up with him."

Ethan nodded agreement and said, "Let her be as her nature bides her, Jon. Her soul tells her she's supposed to protect. Let her learn from doing. Experience is the best teacher. How many raids did you wipe while learning?

"Exactly. We can't afford for her to learn that way."

Ethan snorted. "Don't be stupid. Doing is the only way any of us learn. We can't protect her from life. She knows this isn't a game and people die in war. Commanders have always learned that the hard way. I'm not saying we should let her throw lives away to keep her happy but trust her to lead her party. You can't micromanage everything."

"I'll speak to her—"

Flynt appeared above Jon's head and dropped a rolled paper at his feet. Jen held up an arm for him to land on. The bird appeared excited. His feathers were fluffed, and he continuously flicked his wings, scattering sparks.

Jon grabbed her arm and turned his blue eyes to Ethan. "They've found them." His grip on Jen's arm tightened. "Stay!" Jon whistled and handed a beaded bangle to Flynt. "Brandon." The bird disappeared as Jon reached for a summoning stone on the belt on his waist. Everyone gathered around Jon. Danu swirled about them, growing darker by the second.

"Summons are incoming. Immediately summon your assigned sector." Jon held up the summon stone. "Victoria Chan," he continued speaking, "Brandon reports all but three of the children are accounted for."

A cold sweat broke out on Jen's brow. "Alex?" Jen asked as Ling said, "Jia?"

"Both are there. Stay!" he said again in a sharper tone.

Jen released her sword and rubbed her sweating palms on her cloak.

"They're traveling by horseback. Two riders per child plus fifteen men behind and before. Cass snuck in close enough to see the children all wear oil-filled globes and the men carry lanterns. We can assume—" he broke off as Vicky appeared. A second later Matt joined them summoned by Arden.

"We can assume," he continued after giving Vicky a quick nod, "they'll try to burn the children. Ethan, your target is the man carrying your son. Ling, Sota, get Jia then place AOE slow traps down on the lead men behind the main group. Vicky, you're putting your sanctuary beneath the first grouping of riders carrying children and then attacking the armed men in the lead. Your priority is men carrying fire. All wizards will be stealing the flames. Dillion, keep the officers, the ones in the fancy clothes, silenced and sheeped, and if you see fire, you're using freezing rain on it. Guard Arden. Arden, Dillion is a good player, so if he offers advice, listen."

"Groups two and three are under Vicky's command. Vicky, station your groups as you wish but Kuan is in group three. Danu will be worried for him."

"I understand," Vicky said eagerly.

"Jen, get your sanctuary beneath the rearmost riders carrying children. I want you to get an invisibility ball from Matt and drop us right in the center of the group. Emilio, you're keeping the riders in the rear contained, but don't worry about them running. Keep them from starting fires or hurting children if you can.

Anyone who gets a child free is to immediately get it inside a Sanctuary. Cami, you're inside Vicky's Sanctuary. Lou is inside Jen's. Just like in practice, your group leader will be assigning individual targets. When you see Cass's flare, the attack will start. Get your assigned target before helping anyone else or worrying about runners. If they're smart, they'll scatter, but we can track them all. Every one of you with a crowd control spell is using it. We want to question them."

Jon glanced at his watch. "Summons will start in one minute and twenty-eight seconds. Any questions?"

He glanced around at their eager faces. "Great. Dillion, when we arrive, cast invisible on Kirk. Kirk, place a doorway at either end of the line."

"Brandon calls," Arden said and disappeared.

Jen shivered in anticipation. She forced herself to remain mounted and still. It was hard when the Fae flickered and disappeared. In moments, she was alone in the clearing. Danu burst from her when Jon called her name. She appeared before Jon in a small clearing. Somewhere close water ran but she couldn't see it. Tall pines blocked the road she knew was near. Fae crouched and ran through the woods under Brandon and Cass's direction. Matt handed her an invisibility ball when Jon mounted behind her. She and Jon both clutched their swords.

"Wait for the signal," Jon whispered as Gallant leapt into the air.

Jen wanted to attack, the wait was agonizing, but Danu didn't push. She hummed with eagerness along Jen's skin, but made no demands. Jen didn't know if it was her control or Jon's presence keeping Danu so passive.

Gallant flew above thick trees bordering a narrow winding pathway. The river glittered to her left. Smoke rose in lazy plumes to the south, the edges of the village she'd passed earlier. Only the faintest dark smudge marked the spot where Artemis's grandmother had burned. Jen turned her gaze away, sure she'd have nightmares about that.

Brandon had positioned them on a sharp turn. Overgrown meadows bordered the road on the east and more thick wood and brush blocked the river side. The rangers had casted Imperceptible and waited unseen, lining the road with their bows cocked.

Jen hovered just above the trees, high enough to see the men coming. The men rode quickly at a fast trot with few supplies. All were heavily armed. Most wore health potions on their belts or dangling from leather thongs about their necks. The green glow showed clearly in the artificial twilight beneath the trees. A few carried summon stones as well. Jen's shoulders tightened, and she craned her head to see if Arden had reached her assigned position.

"We got this, Jen," Jon whispered.

"You see they have stones?"

"Yes. We'll hit them hard and fast."

"Fuckers," Jen muttered.

Gallant hovered above the treetops, slow sweeps of his wings keeping him in place. Kuan perched in panther form on a tree limb to her left. Cami in tree form sat before Arden who hid beneath a No-See-Um with Dillion, Vicky, Trent and Brandon. Her gaze skipped to Ethan who signed to Kirk. Glowing runes already lay at the far bend of the road visible only to those who could see magic. The jingle of tack and clomping hooves approached.

"Wait," Jon said, laying a hand on her arm.

She was in control of herself, but barely. Every nerve in her body seemed to scream her son's name. She gathered herself to leap as

Ethan glided behind a man's left stirrup, keeping pace as the man trotted. Her eyes fastened on a swaddled baby tied across the man's armored chest with rawhide straps.

"Alex," she breathed, and Jon tightened his grip.

"Wait until everyone has their mark and the men are in position," Jon whispered.

Jen's blood pounded in her ears, and she leapt as the first flicker from Cass's flare lit the darkening sky. "Attack!" she bellowed.

She casted Sanctuary as she fell and threw her shield as she landed, stunning the three riders and their horses at the back of the pack. Men exclaimed, the sound swallowed by the pounding of Jen's pulse in her ears.

She slashed and severed her target's head from his body and caught the corpse as it tumbled from the horse. She ripped the rawhide loose and took the now screaming child. Ethan reached for him, and she let him take him. Her cooldown for leap wasn't up yet so she ducked beneath the horse and slashed as she came up, catching a lantern carrier on his outer thigh and half severing his leg. She dropped her shield to grab the lantern from his hand and threw it as far as she could. A ball of fire streaked past her face as she leapt and hit a man across the face with the flat of her blade, tumbling him from the horse.

"Jen!" Dillion screamed, and she turned in time to see him run forward and hold up his arms. She followed his terrified gaze and ran to a burning man lying on the path behind her. Freezing cold rain began to fall around her. The riderless horse bolted. Another small ball of flame flew past her, a wizard capturing the flame, leaving a motionless corpse on the ground. She flipped the body and grabbed for the child. Before she could cast, brilliant white light infused the child, Arden was already resurrecting.

"Good, keep them there, Vicky!" Jon yelled.

"Clear!" Cass hollered and sprinted past Jen. Brandon reached a hand to him and the two men soared into the air on the back of Ed.

Jen leapt over the sidling horses to her husband and took Alex from him. The baby whined fretfully, taking deep gasping breaths as if too exhausted to scream as he wished too.

"Drugged, I think," Ethan said, sounding as angry as she'd ever heard him. Blood marred his cheek and dripped to his leather chest piece. She healed him even though she knew it wasn't his blood. Flickers of green and gold began to bounce between them as the rest of the healers began to cast. In moments, everyone glowed softly.

Jen ignored the shouted commands from the Jon and Cass and the curses of the captured men, content to hold Alex and let Jon handle everything. It had taken less than half a minute.

"Vicky, leave those men and take Jamal. Sweep for one mile to the west. Do whatever you think best if you find anyone. Trent, take Cass. Cass is in charge."

Jen glanced at Vicky's face and hid her smile in the blanket around Alex.

"Is he okay, Aunt Jen?" Dillion asked.

"Sleepy." She crouched so Dillion could see Alex.

"You did great, sport," Ethan said.

"I sheeped the guy in the fancy hat and silenced the guy on the black horse," Dillion said proudly. "Vicky caught a big bunch in her deadly ground. She used a low level because it didn't kill them."

"Smart," Ethan said.

"I better go see if Arden needs water." Dillion kissed Alex's forehead and scampered to Arden who stood in Jen's sanctuary.

Jen felt bad hogging Alex but couldn't make herself give him to Ethan. He rubbed his son's back and glared at the men Kirk was herding past them.

"He okay?" Kirk called.

"Drugged, I think."

Kirk nodded and prodded his charges harder. A small red imp cackled and capered at his feet. It flitted from man-to-man stabbing with its tiny pitchfork and belching small flames. The imp was a vanity item that did nothing except amusing tricks. Jen hadn't even known Kirk possessed one. He never bothered with petty tricks while raiding. She'd banned many players for using their imps to poke and prod, annoying players who were trying to eat or rest.

Kirk saluted her and winked. His charges were clearly terrified.

"They probably think he can bring them straight to Hell," Jen said not sure how she felt about terrorizing them.

"They deserve it and more," Ethan muttered. "Wonder if the imps can make you sick too?"

Jen shrugged and grimaced. In the game, red imps could make players who ate while within range of them vomit intermittently for hours. "Probably, although I doubt it will get the chance."

Ethan's expression lightened, and he put an arm around her. "Let's go see what these assholes have to say for themselves."

Pursuing Vengeance

Flynt flew in lazy circles above Jon's head, the bird's brilliant red plumage dripping sparks as he dove and rolled in an impressive aerial display. Another bird Jen didn't know but assumed was Ramiro's because it was the exact shades of Joash except inverted, sat on Arden's shoulder.

Joash cooed and muttered irritably from his perch on Jon's shoulder, flipping his wings and glancing at the bird behind him. Jen's eyes widened. She recognized a female firebird but had never seen one as a companion before. They were extremely rare spawns in the game and rangers sought them for vanity pets as they all possessed the ability to shoot flames like dragons so were a mild

DPS boost.

The female was a much smaller bird with coal-black, gold and red tipped feathers. The glossy black feathers glittered as if made of glass and the overall effect was of extreme heat. Jen imagined the bird would singe her skin if she touched it.

"The black one is Ramiro's bird. The one that looks like Joash is Sheila's," Kirk said as she approached. "Ramiro's can breathe fire too." He offered an arm for the bird to perch on and Flynt swooped down and landed so hard it staggered Kirk. "Someone is a bit jealous," he muttered as he petted Flynt.

"Showing off more like," Ethan said as he rubbed Flynt's head.

Jon shot them an annoyed glance when they laughed but kept talking to Nina. "Send us Sam and see if Ron and Ramiro will come. Get as much precooked food as you can from Gwen. I don't want you to stop at all." Jon turned to Jen. "Go with her. You can visit with your kids and help pull the *Enterprise* back here. Kuan and Cami will accompany you. With the new paladins helping, you should be able to fly back nonstop."

"No," Ethan said before Jen could open her mouth to agree. "Jen and I are going to Barcelona so I can spy. None of these fuckers is getting away. Matt and I found out they had three reverend fathers and two bishops working with them, and we were there only a few days. We need to know how invested the church is in our destruction. Is this policy? Or are these men acting outside church doctrine for their own gain."

Jon pursed his lips but nodded.

Ethan turned to Nina, "Ask Sam to bring our Diana with her, and Agnes to watch them."

"Sure," Nina said and handed her bangle to Arden.

Arden held out her other hand. "Two bangles, please."

Nina handed her another bracelet. Cass handed her a set too. Arden tied one set of bangles with hers and the other set with a plain strip of rawhide and handed it to Joash. She gave Shelia's bird the second set. "Thank you." The birds disappeared.

Ramiro's bird cooed softly, the sound so low and sweet Jen smiled.

"She's so cute," Dillion said enviously. "I wish mages had companions."

"Sam can train a pet for you. Maybe even a real firebird if Ramiro's can lay eggs."

Dillion brightened.

"I'll ask her when I see her," Jen offered.

She gestured to the men Matt was tying. The terrified eyes of the captives flicked from the greater demon who stood with hooved feet spread, holding a sword of flame and glaring from red glowing eyes, to Jon who glared from glowing blue ones.

Jen had seen Kirk's greater demon before. She knew it was a construct, not a real thing, and it still gave her the willies.

At least she hoped it wasn't a real thing. Her glance flicked to Gallant, and she frowned thoughtfully. Paladin mounts were also constructs formed from the minds of their casters but so real and lifelike she supposed they were real in a way.

She shrugged and dismissed the thought. Kirk rarely summoned a greater demon for more than moments to sacrifice it to form his armor. But real or not, it terrified the captives.

Kirk's small red imp still poked and prodded the captives and the ranger's pets hunkered behind them growling but all their attention remained on Jon and the demon.

Jon's protective aura felt relaxing to Jen, like sitting on a beach in the sun on vacation as if she could rest with no worries. But that same aura obviously terrified the men. None attempted to resist Matt as he tied them. A few prayed but most cowered.

Vicky had captured the entire lead group. Brandon had kept four from the rear group alive and two lantern carries had lived.

"What will we do with them?" Jen asked.

"Let my fucking demon have them," Kirk said and laughed when the captives moaned and cried out.

"It isn't a real demon, assholes. I wish it was. You fucking deserve to be tortured for a million years."

"Kirk, help my EMT's examine the bodies, please," Arden said.

Kirk rolled his eyes but spun away. Men and women trained by Arden began appearing. She gave instructions as she escorted them to Brandon's sanctuary where the children lay.

Ethan said, "Three are still missing. Let me talk to them, Jon."

Jon pursed his lips but made an open armed gesture and strode away. Ethan kissed Alex, then Jen and motioned her to leave. She took Dillion's hand and lead him down the road away from the dead men who were already attracting flies. She found a sunny spot out of sight of the carnage and sat with her back to a tree and let herself feel relief. Tears slipped down her cheeks as she rocked her son. Dillion patted her shoulder and rubbed

Alex's back. Ling and Sota joined them.

"Don't worry, Dillion," Sota said. "Jen is fine, it's just relief."

"I'm relieved too. Those men were really bad."

"That they were," Sota said and ruffled the short hair on Dillion's head. You kept a cool head though."

"You did," Ling agreed. "Jia will need friends like you. Someone to teach her but who doesn't feel anger when they cast. I worry contact with those men warped her, but if you'd be willing to come play with her…"

"Sure. Gwen lets me babysit Mason. He likes to knock stuff down."

Jen and Ling exchanged smiles as Dillion spoke happily of his foster brother. Both babies slept. Jen hoped Alex woke soon. She was worried he'd be frightened too, and she didn't like his snuffling snorts as if he cried in his sleep.

"They're so little they probably won't remember a thing," Sota said.

"Kidnappers are the worst," Dillion said.

Jen winced and Sota cleared his throat.

"Raising a child to use it and not caring if it hurts them is the worst," Ling said and handed Jia to Sota so she could hug Dillion.

"I can't wait until their old enough to

really play," Dillion said.

Ethan joined them before Jen could reply. It hurt her that Dillion was so lonely. Since Fredrick's murder, he avoided the human kids his age. And she couldn't blame him. It did hurt to lose people you loved, and it hurt more when you knew you could've saved them if they'd been Fae. She made a mental note to speak to Jon about finding new human playmates for Dillion.

She half rose, then resumed her seat when she saw her husband's expression. He said nothing, but she knew the three missing children had died.

"Warren and Cass are backtracking with Brandon and Trent. I got a list of names, most of them clergy, who were involved. Jon is questioning the captives now, but we'll be heading to Spain."

"Agila?"

"Yeah. He had grand plans and not just for us. He wanted to breed his own Fae. I think he sees himself as the new head of the church, the power behind it anyway."

"How did he plan to do that?"

"I'm not sure if he planned to kidnap or kill the pope or if Justinian promised his help."

Jen pulled Ethan down to sit beside her and handed him Alex. "You think Justinian is involved?"

"I'm rethinking that attack in Constantinople. I want to go back and spy a while. He's too powerful for us to ignore him. Someone paid for all this. The coins these men carried are mostly Italian, but some have Justinian's profile on them. Not proof but…." Ethan shrugged. "If he is secretly against us, we need to know."

"And Agila?"

"Will pay with his fu" —Ethan shot a glance at Dillion and winced— "freaking life."

Jen bent over head over son's fragile body. The Fae were at war and she would be called to fight. Her children needed her, but they needed a safe world to live in more.

"I'll do my very best," she said without glancing up from the child she held.

"I know. We all will but will that be enough?"

Jen said nothing, just clutched her child tighter.

Epilogue

Ultragotha peered from a window in her husband's study to examine the men gathering in the western field.

She estimated that over eight thousand men had already gathered and she thought them all fools.

Chrodesinde entered the room as Ultragotha strode to the eastern window to examine the busy streets. Women and men were headed to the castle in droves and she suddenly realized why Childebert insisted on using this hard to reach tower room as his personal office.

Everything in sight was hers and she was suddenly furious that he'd risked it all.

Daughter," she said briskly as she took the

seat behind the desk.

Her daring made her tremble. Childebert had never her allowed her into the room but Childebert was gone. He'd run from the Fea, leaving her behind to face their wrath.

That they'd done nothing except retrieve Chrodesinde who'd returned as soon as Childebert had fled still amazed Ultragotha.

This was her moment, she knew it.

She said, "Our people need our protection. Whether the Fea are demons or the children of the Earth is irrelevant. They have no right to rule men."

Chrodesinde said, "They don't really wish to rule. They're perfectly content on their isle. If we show Danu that we will care for the Earth, her Fea will leave us in peace."

"Can you convince them to remain on their isle? Will they let you take over the governorship of these lands?"

Chrodesinde nodded eagerly. "Yes. Jon has assured me he'll support me. Arden will willing teach our people how to make medicine. We can cure this plague and prevent others."

Ultragotha waved dismissively. She didn't care about the plague. She'd spent a fortune sending her personal guards to buy health potions and summon stones. Childebert had refused to cross the channel to see the Fea city for himself even though he knew it made them weaker to depend on others sharing the potions that their gold bought. She itched to own potions herself. It was one of the many decisions of her husband's that she disagreed with.

She said, "Perhaps you could have them come here so the ladies of the court can purchase the healing elixirs for themselves?"

"I'm sure they'd help us if we asked. We could open a clinic—"

"We have more important things to do."

"Mother, the people are dying of the plague. What could possibly be more important than stopping it?"

"Saving them from a war they can't win."

Chrodesinde mulish expression faded and she nodded thoughtfully.

Ultragotha said, "First we must unite the people, assert our rule— your rule."

A commotion in the hall drew Ultragotha to her feet. She was heading to the door when it burst open and Childebert strode inside. He glared as he snapped for his men to wait in the hall. Dante and Sir Ludwig bowed, and Dante closed the door.

"So, I'm gone a week and already you plot behind my back!"

Sweat sprang up on Ultragotha's brow. She hadn't thought he'd dare return. She'd assumed he go to his brother Theuderic and the two of them would kill their fool selves fighting the Fae.

Childebert strode past her to slap Chrodesinde's face.

"Traitorous whore!" He slapped her hard enough to bruise and smirked as he said, "And you're a stupid one, plotting in my own rooms! You urge our men to follow you while you spew lies about your brother. Do you think I don't see your intent?" He laughed a dark bark of laughter as he grabbed the neck of her gown and shook her hard. "The cursed demons potions make you arrogant, but you have none now!"

He hit her again with his closed fist, knocking her to the floor.

Ultragotha grabbed her husband's arm, pulling him away from their daughter who coward at the floor at his feet. Blood trickled from Chrodesinde split lip and she glared from blackening eyes.

Childebert backhanded Ultragotha, knocking her hand loose.

She sank to her knees and clasped her hands. "Please, husband, have mercy! She is our daughter!"

Childebert turned from Chrodesinde to glower at Ultragotha. "Do you encourage the traitorous lies that fall from her lips?"

"Mondred did kill them, Father!"

"Enough!" Ultragotha shouted at Chrodesinde. "You will keep a civil tongue in your head or I will cut it out myself!"

Chrodesinde blanched and lowered her head, rising her hands to cover her face.

Her daughter's submission pleased her, but she didn't trust her to remain meek. Living with the Fae had emboldened her. Patience and cunning were called for, not this brazen defiance. She glared heatedly at her daughter, willing her to shut up before she got them both killed and scrambled to her feet. "She will do as she's told. Confine her…" She trailed of as Childebert turned away, lifting his sword as if he intended to swing.

She hesitated to grab him again, instead blurting, "Kill the maid, but Chrodesinde has been promised to Agila. Will you be forsworn?"

Childebert hesitated and she continued eagerly, "No one will believe the Fae lies. Our men are gathering. Surely we can defeat them and then who would dare besmirch our son's honor?"

Chrodesinde said, "He has besmirched it

himself! They were just children! Do we not owe the nobles in our service our protection?"

"Shut up, fool!" Ultragotha snapped.

Childebert said, "You dare to lecture me?"

Ultragotha said, "She is a fool but not without worth. Perhaps we could trade her for our son?"

Childebert lowered his sword and turned to face Ultragotha. "The idea has merit although I'm loathed to allow her to spread her lies." His lips lifted in a sneer. "She thinks to make herself queen."

Sweat trickled across Ultragotha's brow and she avoided meeting Chrodesinde eyes.

"Mother..." Chrodesinde said.

Ultragotha lurched forward to slap her. "Silence!" She whirled and strode for the door. "Send her to her rooms. Let her think about what she owes this family! She is nothing without you, nothing!"

Ultragotha's heart pounded hard enough to muffle sound but neither Childebert nor Chrodesinde said anything when she yanked the door open and called for a guard.

She peered over her shoulder, hoping Chrodesinde would understand her warnings.

Chrodesinde was staring at her pleadingly but with the mulish expression that warned she might speak at any moment and

Childebert was in no mood to forgive. If he heard that she'd encouraged their daughter to seek the throne, he'd kill them both.

She said, "Have some sense, Daughter. If loyalty won't keep you silent than maybe practicality will. Your family is powerful. Will you make them all enemies?" She gave Childebert a meaningful glance and turned back to the guard at the door. "Take the princess to her rooms and see that no one enters, no one at all."

Dante said, "Yes, your majesty."

"Take her to the dungeons!" Childebert snapped.

"Your majesty?" Dante halted mid bow, staring with shocked eyes. His hand dropped to his pouch.

"You heard me!" Childebert's eyes narrowed.

Dante lifted his hands from his pouch, but he was pale and sweat beaded his brow. He glanced over his shoulder at the other men in the hallway. Ultragotha's personal guards were visible but they would do whatever Childebert ordered. She needed her husband dead if she ever hoped to rule.

"You cannot!" Chrodesinde said.

By her tone Ultragotha knew she'd keep arguing and Childebert was in no mood to hear it. She didn't trust that Dante would keep her quiet or even make her leave and she cursed herself now for speaking with her at all.

"Ludwig, disarm him!" Ultragotha said.

Dante gaped at her.

Ultragotha continued. "He's been possessed. Take his accruements and confine him with the princess!"

Before Dante could reach for a summon stone, she clasped his pouch. He reached for her hand but dropped his before touching her. He was clearly conflicted and offered no resistance as her guard confiscated his weapons.

Ultragotha said, "Go as you've been ordered by your king. All will be well, Daughter, *if* you remember your place. Pray and seek the Lord's guidance. It was our folly that sent you into that nest of vipers, but I have faith that God's grace will be stronger than their demonic influence. Ludwig, see that a priest is sent for. The princess will confess her sins and repent of these lies."

Childebert's lips tightened but he didn't contradict her. Ultragotha took a deep trembling breath, trying to still her pounding heart.

Chrodesinde scrambled to her feet. "I'm not lying!"

Ultragotha said, "Bind her and take her. Let no one see or hear her until she throws off this possession!"

Childebert snorted and hit Chrodesinde with the flat of his blade. She screamed and ducked away.

Dante yelled, "Stop! She is under the Fae's protection!"

Childebert spun from Chrodesinde, advancing on Dante.

Ludwig yanked Dante back, pushing him to his knees.

Sirs Chostin and Frant, two of Ultragotha's guards, ran forward and grabbed Chrodesinde by the arms and dragged her from the room. She continued to protest her innocence until Chostin clapped a hand over her mouth.

Ultragotha said, "Keep them in my sewing room until this evening. No one is to know!"

"Yes, your majesty." Ludwig bowed deeply

She forced a calm expression and took a seat beside the fire. Her hands shook so she folded them in her lap.

"All will be as you wish it, my lord husband," she said as meekly as she knew how.

Childebert gave her a scathing glance and

strode from the room.

Anger and fear left her breathless and she slumped to pat her wildly beating heart. She needed a Fae ally of her own.

"Damn him!" she snapped as she jumped to her feet and began to pace.

Mondred had made acquiring a Fae ally extremely unlikely. Chrodesinde was her best bet, but she was a fool to speak so brazenly to Childebert and it was clear her daughter wouldn't be led by her either. But she had another daughter and Chrodoberge was more malleable than her sister.

"I was a fool for stopping him."

She wouldn't make that mistake again, she vowed as she strode from the room, calling for her guard. It wouldn't take much to convince Childebert that Chrodesinde was beyond redemption.

She'd distance herself from him and when the Fae killed him, she'd put forth Chrodoberge as the queen. *Or maybe I can trade them Mondred and assume the throne myself.*

Despite the Fae's awesome power, they were human in their perceptions and could be manipulated. The future held both terror and possibilities. A smart man— or woman— could harness both and rule the world.

The End

Reach the Author

If you've enjoyed the book, please leave a review and follow me on <u>Amazon</u> and <u>Facebook</u>.
You can sign up for the newsletter at <u>Ace Lyon Books</u> for chances to win free books and to be notified on new releases.

The next book in this series, tentatively titled *Realm's Protector*, is due out sometime early next year.

I'd like to thank my ARC readers for their time and feedback. ARC (Advance Reader Copies) on the new book will be sent shortly and I look forward to hearing from you all,
S. M Savoy